Where No Shadows Fall

Helen Idris-Jones

To. Mary

Thank you for

your support

Helen Idris Jones,

March '25

ISBN: 978-1-0686071-3-4

Book Cover by Dan Smith, Aspect Designs, Malvern, UK

Printed in United Kingdom: 2025

For Mum

Your task is not to seek for love,
but merely to seek and find all the barriers
within yourself
that you have built against it.

Rumi

Chapter 1

Esther Morgan was responsible for three deaths. Now she was facing her own. Each passing moment increased her sense of hopelessness and inevitability. Was this it? Was this the end? The fading light of the cold November afternoon cast long shadows, amplifying her despair.

One minute she was rushing down the stony path as the rain drizzled down, the next her foot slipped. Time seemed to slow as she slid on the slippery mud and, with a startled cry, lost her balance. Before she could stop herself, she was tumbling downwards. Her heart raced as her flailing arms tried to grab onto something to break her fall. She landed hard on the cold, muddy earth. For a moment she lay disoriented, blinking into the darkness. Her heart pounded with the shock of the fall as she gasped for air. Panic filled her chest like a tidal wave as she realised she was trapped.

As tears rolled down her cheeks, she pulled strands of thick, black, wet hair out of her eyes. She couldn't shake the overwhelming sense of desperation as her heart filled with fear. No one would find her here. No one knew she was here.

Soaked to the skin and freezing, she lay at the bottom of the ditch, the damp earth clinging to her clothes as the cold seeped into her very bones. An uncontrollable shiver wracked her body. The sky was grey and heavy with clouds as a persistent drizzle soaked the leaves laying on the ground. The peaty soil and rotting vegetation filled her nostrils as she listened to the rain dampening any sounds in the forest.

Taking deep breaths to focus her thoughts, she needed to act. The first thing was to assess if she was hurt. She felt the back of her head and there didn't appear to be any bumps or wounds. Other than being drenched from head to toe, she experienced no pain as she pushed herself onto her elbow. But as she turned to pull her backpack from behind her, a searing pain shot through her left ankle and up her leg. Damn it, even if she got out of this godforsaken ditch, she wouldn't be able to walk. She flopped back down into the quagmire.

She tried to catch her breath as the pain eased to a throbbing ache. As the light faded, the futility of the situation filled her mind again. She tried to move into a more upright position, wedging herself vertically against the side of the ditch. Her feet were immersed in the thick tarry water which made her left ankle throb even more.

'Come on Esther, get a grip,' she told herself. As she tried to think of a way out of this situation, a thought flashed through her mind. She almost laughed at her own stupidity. Her phone, of course, she had her phone. Esther struggled to pull the backpack round to her front as she rummaged in the front pocket. Shaking off dirt with the sleeve of her waterproof, Esther let out a sigh of relief when the screen lit up. She pressed emergency services. Would they be able to find her in the middle of nowhere? They could track people from their phone signal, couldn't they?

Nothing happened. She tried again, but the phone failed to connect.

She looked at the top right corner. There was no signal. Shouldn't she be able to call emergency services? Maybe she needed to get further up the ditch.

Finding some Herculean strength that came from pure survival instinct, she clawed her way further up the gully towards the fading light. Gaining a few feet and hanging on to a tree root, Esther slid the sidebar across to make an emergency call. But still nothing happened. Raising her arm as high as she could, Esther looked desperately for the little 3G or 4G icon to appear. There was no signal at all. She let out a wail of despair.

Esther tried to haul herself further up the wet, slimy wall of the ditch and desperately waved her hand above her towards the gathering gloom. But still the previous saviour icon would not appear. Suddenly she lost her grip and fell with a thump, back down into the depths of the cold, damp ditch. As she crashed down, she landed on her ankle. An excruciating pain to shoot up her leg. She screamed in agony. 'Someone help me, please. For God's sake, someone help, I can't die here.'

Esther collapsed back, as if all her will had drained away. Why was she even here? As her breathing slowed, Esther tried to justify why she had lost her footing. Why had she climbed to find the source of the River Severn on a drizzly November day when it had proved a complete disappointment? Had it been worth it? To see that tiny marker in the middle of a peat bog on the top of a mountain in Wales? But she'd promised herself she would find it before she left for good. It was part of the process of closure.

Every winter she came to clear out the van to stop the damp permeating the bedding and clothes. With each passing year, she admonished herself for not making the most of the beautiful surroundings, but she was the only one who used the van now. Kate hadn't been for years with the boys. Why had she kept it? In the vague hope it might provide a bridge between her and Kate, that it might draw them back to each other.

Now the miserable old bugger who owned the site had put the price up again, it was time to admit defeat. By selling the van, she was finally acknowledging her relationship with Kate was irreparably damaged, especially after her breakdown.

Esther was selling it behind the back of the site owner. He was going to be furious. That was why she had been hurrying down the mountain before it got dark, to finish cleaning ready for the new owners. Then she planned to get out under the cover of the darkness of a winter's afternoon before he noticed. But finding the source of the Severn had seemed important, as if it offered some magical solution. This had been her last chance, but what a fiasco. Now here she was, soaking wet. Stranded in a ditch several feet below the path surrounded by thick pine forest? The van was inconsequential compared to her current predicament.

Was she dying here, in the middle of nowhere? This couldn't be the end. Was this retribution for the deaths of three people? Had the actions, or lack of them, resulting in those deaths brought her to this moment? Would she have been spared this ordeal if she had saved them? Was this her punishment? But she wasn't ready to die. There were wrongs to be righted, wounds to be healed, apologies to be made, forgiveness to be sought.

What had it all been for, this life? It had been a struggle, that was for sure, but there had been good times. A smile flickered across Esther's face as she remembered her mother setting out a tea party for her on the floor of their small dingy flat. The two of them against the world. Her heart ached with grat-itude to her mother, who had battled against the odds to give her a happy childhood. Her mother's face was then replaced by Ozzy's. Ozzy, her husband and saviour. Ozzy, who had been there to scoop her up after Frank cast her out. Ozzy with their little girl, Kate, on the beach building sandcastles. But it did not last. The dream turned into a nightmare as

Esther remembered having to save herself and Kate from Ozzy in the end. Another memory, happier this time. Her graduation, Kate waving, shouting out, 'Well done Mum,' at the top of her small voice. People turning to smile at the little girl's exuberance and pride. But her daughter despised her now, even hated her. All those wasted years of resentment that had torn them apart.

The faces of the patients, etched with worry and pain, flashed past like scenes in a blurry movie, each thanking her for staying with them as they slipped away. Their deaths were peaceful and pain-less. Hers would not be.

Her vision blurred as her mind floated. Esther wondered if there was anything afterwards - any-thing after death, or just oblivion. As her breathing slowed and her eyes flickered shut, a bright light shone down on her face as a voice called to her.

Chapter 2

Why were people so afraid of death Esther wondered as the pain from her damaged ankle and the bone chilling cold melted away. She was filled with a profound sense of peace. Tingling replaced the cold in her hands and feet as she experienced the sensation of rising upwards and away from her body. There was a strong sense of lightness and buoyancy as she was pulled towards a tunnel of light. Suddenly, a wave of energy sent her tumbling back towards her body. She had no desire to return to the place of pain and hopelessness. The peace vanished away like a beautiful dream replaced by a bright light penetrating her closed eyelids. Someone was calling her name.

Esther took a long, shuddering breath as the cold and distress returned. A soft voice calling her name.

'Can you hear me, Esther?'

As her eyelids fluttered, she couldn't help but shake her head as the vivid memory of the fall had returned. With it came a sense of loss. Why hadn't she gone to the light? How long had she been lying here? It could have been minutes. It could have been hours. Relief, panic, loss and pain surged through her. The most prominent was an enormous sense of relief. Someone had found her in this horrendous ditch.

But who? As she slowly opened her eyes, Esther couldn't see as a light was shining directly into them. Instinctively, she tried to raise her arm against the glare.

The light moved to one side, so she looked up once more, searching for the origin of the voice and light. She could just make out a face above her with eyes full of concern.

'I am so sorry Esther, I didn't mean to blind you,' said a man. He gazed down at her he said, as he adjusted his head torch. 'I am glad you're still here.' Esther thought this a strange thing to say. Where else would she be? The voice was soft but strong, gentle but confident, capable but kind. He looked tall, but it was hard to tell how tall as he was above her, which exaggerated everything. He wore a thick coat with a florescent strip across the chest.

'Sorry, who are you?' Esther whispered, completely taken aback by a stranger who knew her name.

'My name is Joseph,' he said. 'You called for help and here I am. Don't be concerned – I'll get you out.'

'How do you know my name?' Esther was confused. She had no memory of him, the voice or name.

'Here, reach up towards me,' he said, reaching down towards her. Uncertain of what to do and faced with no other alternatives, she placed her trust in the hands of this stranger. She had to get out of this ditch or stay here forever. Esther tried to reach up but had no strength. Before she knew what was happening, powerful arms grasped her upper arms without hurting her and lifted her out of the ditch. She was up out of the dank, dirty water, the smell of peat being replaced by clear cold air. Those arms laid her gently on the ground at the top of the ditch, using something soft as a pillow. 'How in the world did that just happen?' she muttered, a shiver of unease running down her spine.

'I thought I was going to die in that ditch,' she gasped, feeling light-headed and floaty with the sudden exertion. 'You're all right. Everything is going to be all right. Can you tell me if you're hurt?'

She tried to concentrate on what he'd asked her, but felt confused. The emergency services used the fluorescent yellow jacket he wore. As far as she was concerned, no one knew she was here, so how had they found her? His face was kind and open, framed by a mop of bright hair which poked out from behind a dark woollen hat. There was something familiar about him, but Esther had no recollection of ever meeting him before. He must be with mountain rescue or the ambulance service. Refocusing on his question, she answered in a voice that croaked, 'I've hurt my ankle.' Her throat was dry and sore from all the shouting earlier. Turning, Joseph produced a flask from a pack he must have been carrying and extended it towards her, saying.

'Here, drink this, it will help,' and waited for her to take a sip.

As she sipped from the flask, the liquid warmed her throat and chest.

'Thank you,' her voice clearer. 'How did you find me?'

'You called for help,' he said simply, which wasn't much of an explanation. Esther decided not to pursue it further until she was in a safe place.

'I'm going to get you down the hill so the emergency services can pick you up,' Joseph said.

'They don't know I'm here,' Esther replied. 'I couldn't get a signal on my phone.'

'It's all right when I can, I'll contact them,' Joseph seemed unconcerned. He must have a special radio, or something, Esther decided.

'Can you sit up?' She tried to push herself up to a sitting position as the dizziness subsided. He moved to sit behind her and helped her into a more upright position so that she could rest against him. His warmth seeped through her wet clothes. It was as if the heat permeated right inside her, warming her from within. Despite Esther feeling this should be awkward, they sat for several minutes. But, despite his warmth, Esther shivered again. The extended period of lying in the ditch had frozen her to the core. Even Joseph's warmth wasn't enough. Esther wondered if she really was to be saved or if this rescue attempt would fail. How was he to get her down the mountain on his own?

'How will we find the way? It's pitch black out here?' Esther queried as a flicker of concern took root. Joseph stood, having retrieved her backpack. 'Should we try my phone to see if there's a signal?' she asked, suddenly aware she was at the mercy of a stranger.

'Everything is going to be all right, don't worry. Let's get you down to safety. Are you able to stand now?' he asked, moving carefully from behind her. Getting to his feet, he wanted to make sure she could sit unaided. Coming to stand in front of her, he offered his hands. He pulled her to her feet. But as soon as she was upright, the pain shot through her left leg, causing her to gasp as the dizziness returned, threatening to engulf her.

'It's okay,' Joseph murmured, 'I've got you.'

He bent down and, swept Esther and her backpack into his arms as if she were as light as a feather.

'You can't carry me down the hill,' she protested. 'I'm no lightweight.'

'If I get tired, I'll put you down.'

His strength amazed Esther. She was a heavy middle-aged woman, but with the added weight of her sodden clothes and her backpack, she was even heavier. His footing was sure, and he seemed to know the path. He walked with confidence, as if it were full daylight. The only light came from his head torch. The light bounced off his fluorescent jacket, cocooning them in a circle of light. His strong arms carried her as if she were a child, light as a feather. Her mind drifted as the sway of his gait lulled her into an exhausted sleep supported by his powerful arms.

Before she knew where she was, Joseph was placing her gently on the ground. Not on wet ground, but on gravel. She could feel the sharp, small stones underneath her back and legs. Not uncomfortable, but hard, firm ground. She could hear the crunch of the stones as he moved around. She raised her head slightly and realised they were back in the car park at the beginning of the trail.

Esther couldn't believe they were down the hill so quickly. How long had she been asleep and how on earth had this man carried her all the way down? It had taken her over two hours to walk up the mountain. She was only a third of the way back down when she had fallen. He must have carried her for well over an hour without stopping. It was unbelievable, but at least she was here and safe. Relief flooded her as she let out a deep sigh. She was reassured knowing she was safe and back onto the solid ground where she'd started. Esther realised with relief that she would not die. Her prayers had been answered. She owed her life to this man. He had given her a second chance. But fear replaced the initial euphoria. What if the emergency services didn't come? The practicalities of life brought her back to the current situation after what seemed like a totally surreal experience. As Esther turned her head, she could see her own battered VW parked over to one side. Hers was the only one in the car park. Could she find her keys and get herself out of here if she needed to?

Joseph bent down beside her and, resting on one knee, he looked at her with clear blue eyes. He placed Esther's backpack beside her and handed her the mobile phone.

'There is an ambulance on the way. You are safe now.' As Esther strained to hear, she caught the sound of sirens approaching at speed. She looked into Joseph's eyes.

'I don't know how you've done this, but thank you so much for saving me.' He smiled down at her. 'Esther, we will meet again. I have saved you from immediate danger, but there is much more for us to do.'

She stared up at him, not fully understanding what he meant. He continued, 'We have work to do, you and I - to release the shadows that haunt you. The shadows of three deaths.' As the ambulance swept into the car park, Joseph continued, talking quickly,

'Have no fear, Esther Morgan.' The warm glow of his smile dispelled her misgivings as he gently touched her cheek. 'Go well Esther until we meet again.' Esther felt his departure deep within her and was filled with longing to be with him again.

Chapter 3

Esther lay motionless on the hard ground, each breath forming a cloud in the November air. The doors of the ambulance burst open with a metallic clang that echoed across the empty car park. Through half-closed eyes, Esther watched the paramedic snatch his response bag, his movements quick and urgent. The beam from his torch cut through the darkness, causing Esther to shield her eyes from the glare. The paramedic hurried to her side and knelt beside her.

'Hello, can you hear me?' As the paramedic dropped to his knees beside her, Esther tried to push herself up.

'Stay where you are for now.' His Welsh lilt made the command less frightening. 'I'm Josh. Can you tell me your name?'.

'Esther, Esther Morgan.' The words caught in her throat, barely more than a whisper. Something about his kindness almost brought tears to her eyes. She blinked them back, feeling the cold seeping deeper into her bones.

'Is it alright if I call you Esther?' Josh asked as she nodded. Josh worked with quick, precise movements, his torch light dancing across her face as he strapped a blood pressure cuff to her arm. As seconds ticked by, Esther didn't think he would get a reading over her coat. The cuff constricted tightly on her arm before deflating again. Josh seemed satisfied with the result. Esther shivered as a biting wind blew across the desolate car park. Where was Joseph? Where had he gone? Why didn't he wait to speak to the paramedics?

As Esther told Josh about her left ankle, a second set of footsteps crunched across the gravel. Another paramedic introduced herself as Sasha. Although she looked as if she should still be in school, her movements were practiced. Mechanically, she handed the equipment to Josh from the bag beside her. Sasha's black hair was tied back neatly in a bun as Esther realised what a mess she must look. As they worked methodically, Esther's own sense of helplessness heightened.

'I'm just going to check you over. Is it alright if I feel down your body, Esther?' Josh's professional tone didn't mask his concern. Guilt gnawed at her for the trouble she had caused, bringing these young people out in this godforsaken weather because of her foolishness. Another violent shiver coursed through her as she tugged her sodden woollen hat lower, knowing it was unlikely to offer any warmth. She missed the warmth of Joseph's body. She missed the sense of complete trust she'd had in him. Although Josh and Sasha were competent and kind, Esther longed for Joseph.

'Won't be long and we'll get you into the ambulance,' Sasha said, taking Esther's hand. The simple human contact broke something inside her, and tears spilled out, mixing with the moisture of the damp air on her cheeks. 'It's all right, it's the shock,' Sasha soothed, but Esther couldn't stop thinking about all the times she'd been the one offering comfort. Now here she was, broken, and dependent on the kindness of strangers.

The mention of the backboard sent a fresh wave of panic through her. Each movement was painful as they positioned her onto a stretcher, increasing her feeling of vulnerability. The click as it locked into place sounded unnaturally loud in the darkness. Esther was amazed that Josh and Sasha, two slim young people, effortlessly lifted her. But she also knew they'd done extensive training. This differed from the superhuman strength Joseph must have used to get her down the mountain. The metal board was hard and cold despite the blanket they wrapped around her like a mummy. The journey to the ambulance was excruciatingly painful, as the wind howled around them and the drizzle turned to sharp drops of rain.

Inside the ambulance, sheltered from the elements, Josh moved with urgency, connecting her to the monitor, which beeped and flashed. The strangeness of the situation struck Esther. Only this morning, she was planning her walk and worrying about Mr Evans. Now here she was being cared for by two youngsters with goodness knows what lying ahead. Fear clutched at her heart. What was going to happen to her now?

The pain in her ankle, which had been bearable, suddenly flared into life as Josh attempted to remove her shoe. A white-hot shaft of agony shot up her leg, making her cry out. Josh reached behind him and drew up a clear liquid before inspecting the back of her hand. The needle sliding in made her gasp but not with pain but the reality of what was happening. As the morphine rushed through her vein, its liquid comfort dispelled the physical pain. Esther relaxed with a sigh of relief.

Josh knelt beside her. 'Right Esther, I'm going to ask you a few more questions now if that's all right? Sasha is going to drive us to Bronglais hospital in Aberystwyth. It might be bumpy to start with. It will take about an hour from here. Let me know if you are uncomfortable at any point. Who is your next of kin please, Esther?'

The question hung in the air as Esther's throat tightened as she thought of Kate. Their last conversation had been tense. Something about Esther needing to get out more and move on with her life.

'My daughter Kate, but she doesn't live nearby.' Since moving to World's End, Esther hardly saw Kate. Their relationship was not just geographically distant. Kate had never forgiven Esther for the death of her father or for more recent events. 'You'll have to get her number from my phone.' Esther's fingers trembled as she reached for her backpack, and not just from the cold. The thought of Kate getting a call sent a fresh wave of anxiety through her. Her daughter would be furious. She could hear her voice now. 'What were you thinking, Mum? Going up there on your own.' When Josh handed her the phone, Esther's vision blurred. Was it the morphine or tears? She wasn't sure. The phone screen swam before her eyes.

'Go to contacts and look for Kate.' Esther handed the phone to Josh. He was so young, but he spoke with such confidence Esther trusted this lad with sandy hair, and a broad smile in his green uniform. After writing down Kate's number, he mercifully moved on with his questions. She had to concentrate hard so she couldn't think any more about Kate. 'Do you have any medical conditions I need to know about?'

'I take tablets for blood pressure,' Esther said, but did not to tell him about the anti-depressants. That wasn't relevant. Nothing to do with her broken ankle.

'Can you tell me what happened?' In a morphine induced haze, Esther told him about falling in the ditch and her rescue by a stranger. As she watched his expression, noting the slight raise of his eyebrows, she wished she hadn't told the truth. Why hadn't she just said that she got to the car park and the accident happened nearby? Her story sounded impossible even to her own ears, but she knew what had happened. Didn't she? The morphine was making everything soft around the edges, but Joseph's face remained sharp in her memory. More real than the ambulance around her, more solid than the hard stretcher where she now lay.

As she drifted into a drug induced sleep, the ambulance swayed beneath her. Esther couldn't shake the feeling that something fundamental had shifted in her world. Joseph's face floated before her with gentle concern. Would she ever know the truth of what had happened on the mountain? The last thing she heard was Sasha's voice, clinical and detached. She reported a possible compound fracture and hypothermia due to exposure. Esther thought how farcical it was that her entire experience could be reduced to two sentences of medical terminology. It couldn't capture what had really happened in the gathering darkness of this Welsh mountainside.

Chapter 4

A hand roused Esther by gently shaking her shoulder. 'We've arrived at the hospital,' said a male Welsh voice that she didn't recognise immediately. It took her a few moments to remember where she was. When she did, the pain in her ankle caused her to wince as Josh moved the blankets to tuck them in more firmly.

'Sorry Esther, we'll get you more for the pain when we get you inside. You've slept the whole way, which was good as the weather was terrible.' Esther wriggled uncomfortably. The cold damp of her mud-sodden clothes stuck to her back as they'd dried during the journey. Guilt rose like a bubble from the pit of her stomach. She was aware of the trouble she was causing. 'I am so sorry to have been such a nuisance,' she murmured.

Josh smiled. 'No worries, Esther. It's our job.'

A blast of freezing air hit Esther as he opened the back door of the ambulance. It was late. Sasha came round to help Josh manoeuvre the stretcher down and out of the vehicle. Again, Esther marvelled at how such a slight young woman had the strength to lift her out into the night air. A fine rain fell on her face as they moved towards the bright florescent lights of the Emergency Department. As they rushed in through the sliding doors of the A&E department, a waiting nurse greeted them.

'Is this Esther Morgan? Cubicle six please.' Josh wheeled Esther at speed through the department of curtained-off cubicles, hiding who knew what. The busy nurses' station was a hive of activity. Once in cubicle six, Josh and Sasha transferred her onto another more comfortable trolley. The actual process of moving her caused her to cry out in pain. Not only from her ankle, but from all the bumps and bruises she'd gained during her fall. Exhausted, she rested back on the pillow.

Stepping back, Sasha said, 'We'll leave you now,' patting her arm. 'All the best,' and they were gone back into the night.

As her saviours abandoned her, a terrible wave of isolation engulfed her. Esther knew the chaos outside the curtains. The doctors and nurses rushing about, focused on their tasks. She was just another case needing treatment, a name on a wristband. How she wished for someone familiar to be with her. As she assessed her situation, Esther realised she would be out of action for months. Who would help her? Kate would be angry if she caused more trouble. Esther didn't think she would be of much help. Was she going to depend on her neighbours' goodwill again? Esther wasn't sure how willing they would be to help her this time. She lay back on the pillows, feeling utterly alone in this sterile environment. As she lay waiting for something to happen, Esther realised she desperately needed the toilet. She was dirty, and dishevelled and was sure she smelt after spending all that time in the ditch. Pull yourself together, she told herself. It could be worse. You could be dead.

She was about to press the call bell when the curtains parted, and a nurse arrived. She was young as well. Was the NHS staffed by adolescents? This girl was plump, with a messy blond ponytail flopping over her shoulder as she bent over the notes in her hand. Thick eyebrows dominated her pretty face. Why do all girls feel they need to look like Kim Kardashian? It masked her natural beauty so. 'I would have her hair up and all that muck off her face,' Esther thought.

'Well, you've been in the wars by the look of it,' said the nurse with the same lilting Welsh accent as Josh. I'm Olwyn,' she said, pointing to her badge. 'Can I call you Esther?' She continued before Esther could reply. 'Let's have a look at you.' Nurse Olwyn helped Esther out of her dirty clothes and into a paper hospital gown. Removing the layers of sodden clothes made her shiver.

'Let's get you a blanket,' Nurse Olwyn said after checking Esther's temperature. She came back holding a sheet of tinfoil. Unwrapping and wrapping Esther made her feel like a Christmas turkey. She added a couple of cellular blankets, like the ones used in hospitals or for newborns. Nurse Olwyn connected Esther to a monitor which involved sticking things on her chest. She pressed buttons above Esther's head and turned down the constant bleep. She took a set of observations, then tapped the results into a tablet.

'Right, if you don't mind, I'm going to ask you a few questions to verify what the paramedics have told me. Is that all right with you, Esther?' Esther sighed, not wanting to explain again. She'd already told the ambulance staff.

Esther repeated her story of the trip up to the source of the Severn and her need to get down before it was dark, followed by how she had fallen as she was walking too fast on an uneven surface. She paused, considering what to say next, concerned how Nurse Olwyn would react to her rescue by Joseph, after Josh, the paramedic's response.

Nurse Olwyn prompted her.

'Tell how you got down the mountain to the car park. Josh said something about someone finding you?' She looked expectantly at Esther.

'Yes, that's right.' Esther confirmed.

'So how did you get to safety?' Nurse Olwyn pressed.

'A man who said his name was Joseph found me. I assumed he was with the mountain rescue or something. He was wearing one of those fluorescent jackets. He got me out of the ditch and carried me down to the car park.' Esther looked her firmly in the eye as she said this.

'Right,' said Nurse Olwyn, 'that's some feat, if you don't mind me saying. He must have been a very strong man.' Tact was obviously not one of her strong points. Feeling Nurse Olwyn's disapproval and annoyed by the suggestion of her difficult transport down the mountain, Esther replied, 'So it seems.'

'And you say this person went as the ambulance arrived? Is that correct?' It was Nurse Olwyn's turn to look at Esther directly.

'Yes, you're right,' Esther said, her neck reddening. What had this to do with anything? Why was this girl pressing her on this? It didn't make any difference how she got down. Her job was to get on and fix her ankle.

'Can I ask if you knocked your head or have had blackouts or any mental health problems?'

'Here it comes,' Esther thought.

'I have had anxiety in the past.' Esther replied as Nurse Olwyn tapped on her hand-held device. Why should she explain herself to this slip of a girl?

Her tone when she said, 'I see,' made Esther want to slap her.

'We haven't received your notes yet, but I'll have a look when they come through. Nurse Olwyn said, 'That's all for now, thank you for your patience,' the implication being that Esther wasn't completely with it. Why was she labelled a fantasist? Why did they find it so hard to believe her?

'Right. I've bleeped the on-call trauma and or-thopaedic consultant and you've an X-ray booked.

I'm just going to get you something to help with the pain. I'm sure you need something by now,' Olwyn was saying as she glancing at the monitor.

'Shall I call your daughter?' Olwyn asked, checking her notes. 'Kate, and let her know you are here?'

'Yes, I suppose you'd better.' Esther knew what Kate's response would be, but she needed to know.

'Is she local?'

'No, she lives in Surrey.'

'Right.'

Nurse Olwyn disappeared. Through the crack in the curtains, Esther saw her stop to talk to another nurse in dark blue at the nurses' station. Nurse Olwyn pointed to Esther's cubicle. They had an earnest conversation before the nurse moved away, and Esther couldn't see them anymore. Esther knew what they were discussing. They didn't believe her story about Joseph. But things would only get worse once her notes arrived, her secrets exposed. Some of her secrets, but not all. Others were so well hidden they would never be discovered; the shadows deep within, which forever haunted her. What had Joseph meant about helping her dispel those shadows? Esther shuddered. What could he possibly know about the three deaths she had caused? She had no intention of finding out. She had no intention of revisiting any of those experiences. Not if she wanted to maintain her sanity.

Chapter 5

Something disturbed Kate's sleep - a buzzing sound on her bedside table. She opened her eyes and saw the light from her vibrating phone. Instantly awake, she worried something had happened to Ben.

Grabbing the phone, she studied the message on the screen. There were several missed calls from a number she didn't recognise. Icy dread rose in the pit of her stomach as Kate pushed back the cover, her toes searching for slippers as her feet touched the cold floorboards. She shivered in the night air as she checked the time. It was 4.30 in the morning. Reaching for the bedside light so she could see her way out of the bedroom, she moved swiftly along the landing to check on the boys. As she did so, she dialled voicemail. Pushing open the door to Jack's room, the smell that hit her was of a ten-year-old's feet. The sight of his bulk sprawled across his bed and the sound of heavy breathing assured her he was safe and in a deep sleep. There was no need for her to check on Ben. She could hear the gaming chair squeaking and the urgent whispers into his headphones. As she turned on the light, he twisted round in his chair, a shocked looked on his face. Speaking rapidly into the mic, he turned off his laptop before shuffling back to bed. Grunting, he pulled the covers over his head. There was no need to say anything.

Kate resented his gaming addiction, but she found comfort knowing he was safe at home, rather than out on the streets. Reassured her children were safe, Kate turned her attention to the voice emanating from her phone.

'You have two new messages,' the phone told her. 'And six saved messages.'

'First message: Received at 00.11 am.'

'This is a message for Kate Cooper. This is Bronglais Hospital, Aberystwyth. Staff Nurse Williams speaking. Please call the Accident and Emergency department when convenient. Thank you.'

'Second new message: Received at 03.12 am.' 'This is Staff Nurse Olwyn Jones from Bronglais Hospital, Trauma and Orthopaedic Ward. I would be grateful if you could ring the ward. It is regarding your mother.'

Kate's heart dropped and, letting out a deep sigh. She sank onto the chair in the hallway by the top of the stairs. Why on earth was her mother in Aberystwyth? The news settled on her shoulders like a heavy blanket, weighing her down. What mess was she going to have to sort out now?

With a sinking heart, she headed downstairs to the kettle. Before facing this problem, whatever it might be, she needed tea. Settling herself at the kitchen counter, she poured hot water into her favourite big mug with a heart on it. As she re-listened to the second message, she wrote the number on a scrap of paper. The call rang out for ages before a voice answered.

'Staff Nurse Jones, Trauma & Orthopaedics.'

'Hello this is Kate Cooper. I'm ringing in connection with my mother, Esther Morgan.' There was a pause before Nurse Jones responded.

'Aw yes, thank you for ringing Mrs Cooper,'

'It's Ms,' said Kate tersely.

'Sorry, sorry Ms Cooper. I am calling to inform you, your mother's had an accident and broken her ankle.' Kate inhaled sharply. Why were they ringing her in the dead of night to tell her that? Couldn't this have waited for the morning?

'Right. Is it serious and why the hell is she in Aberystwyth?'

'According to the notes, she was walking in the Hafren Forest when she fell. As her next of kin, we are obliged to inform you,' Kate wasn't sure she liked Nurse Jones' tone. 'When she was found, she was suffering from dehydration and hypothermia but is resting comfortably now. We've had to contact you as she requires emergency surgery to save her foot.'

'I thought you said she had just broken her ankle?'

'Unfortunately, she has a complex fracture that is affecting the blood supply to her foot. She will need to have it pinned and will be on crutches for some months if the surgery is successful. Do you live far away? Will you be coming to see her? I only ask because she doesn't have any clothes or toiletries with her. Because of the surgery, she will be in the hospital for several weeks.'

'Oh, I see. It's serious then?' Kate paused. 'I live in Surrey, so I suppose I will have to come up. I'll have to make some arrangements.'

'She is scheduled for surgery immediately so we will have to ask her to consent to surgery.'

'So, what's the problem?'

'There are some concerns about her capacity. We are waiting for her notes, but I must ask, does she have any history of mental health issues?'

'Sorry, what's that got to do with her falling and breaking her ankle?' Embarrassed, the topic of her mother's mental health was coming up so quickly. Kate's neck flushed.

'I must ask you. Do you think she can sign the form?' Nurse Jones insisted.

'What makes you think she can't?' Kate's skin pricked at this insinuation.

'Your mother appears to be hallucinating and we must ensure she can consent to surgery rationally. It is our legal responsibility.' Kate sighed as her head pounded. Was it happening again?

'I am quite sure she is all right to sign a consent form.' She said emphatically.

'And the hallucinations?'

'It doesn't affect her ability to make rational decisions, I can assure you.' Kate said decisively. The last thing she needed was to have to go immediately. It wasn't possible. 'I'll try to get there in the next couple of days. If she is having an operation, there's no point in me coming today, is there?'

'No, I suppose not,' Nurse Jones replied tersely. She paused before continuing, 'Thank you for the information. If you would like to ring later this afternoon, we will give you an update on the success of her operation. Sorry for disturbing you.'

Kate sat back, irritated by the Nurse's tone but cross with herself for her reaction to her mother's accident. It sounded serious, the risk of her losing her foot. God forbid. The implications of that didn't bear thinking about.

What the hell was she doing in the Hafren Forest? They hadn't been there for years, not since the holidays in the van. Suddenly, her brain made the connection. It must be something to do with the caravan. Kate frowned, trying hard to remember her last conversation with her mother. Hadn't she said something about selling it? Kate didn't know why she'd kept it all these years. It wasn't as if anyone went anymore.

The tea was lukewarm, so she drifted back to the kettle to make a fresh one as her mind raced. If she had to go to Wales, she would have to get organised. The boys would be at school, which would mean trying to get a day off work and asking Shaun to pick up the boys. That meant having a conversation with him. Since she'd kicked him out for screwing that tart of a receptionist at his work, Kate had no desire to speak to him ever again. They got married too young, but it seemed perfectly logical when she needed stability in her life. He saved her from the years spent with her dysfunctional mother and that bastard Ray. She stared at the uneven tiles around the cooker. He was still the father of the boys and that relationship she could not ignore. If she had her way, he wouldn't see the boys at all. But he did - every other weekend and Wednesdays after school. He'd threatened not to pay the mortgage if she denied him access

Kate hated having to ask Shaun for a favour. Maybe if she swopped weekends, she could leave early on Sunday morning. It would be a lot of driving, but it was possible, and then she wouldn't need to take a day off. Kate was sure her mother would be all right for a couple of days. She'd be fuzzy and sleeping after the operation.

What about the stuff Esther needed? She could either go to the shops or stop at her mother's, as she would pass near there. No, she didn't want to do that. She should let Richard and Grace know. Why her mother had to move to the other side of the country when they'd always lived in Surrey was irritating. Kate assumed she wanted a fresh start after Ray. No, she didn't want to go to her mother's. She didn't want to stop at World's End and risk having to speak to Richard or Grace. Her mother's choice of location made her laugh at its irony. No, she'd get stuff in Tesco.

Wearily, she got to her feet and plodded dejectedly back upstairs. She'd better try to get back to sleep, otherwise she knew she'd be irritable all day. Why did she suddenly feel she had three children, two boys and her mother?

What was this talk of hallucinations again? I really hope she isn't heading down another slippery slope, she thought. Having to deal with that again was more than she could cope with right now. She'd never forgiven her mother for what she'd done, so why was she the one who had to deal with all this shit? Getting wearily back into bed, knowing she wouldn't sleep, a wave of hopelessness swept over her. Why did her mother have to be such a pain in the arse?

Chapter 6

Kate sat by her mother's bedside, watching her sleep. She arrived at around eleven on Sunday to find her trussed up like a chicken. A pulley mechanism elevated her leg, and there were metal pieces sticking out of her ankle. Why she couldn't she just have broken her ankle? She always went to extremes.

Kate noticed her mother's warm, cinnamon complexion was unusually pale and her thick, wavy hair was tangled as it splayed out on the pillow. Lying in the bed, she looked small and vulnerable. Her brown, deep-set eyes were misty. Kate did not possess the same exotic appearance as her mother. She took after her father. Smaller, fair, with an agile frame. She'd never met her grandfather, her mother's father, and as far as she knew, her mother never met him either. So, the mystery of her looks was a long-held family secret. Something to do with the Windrush scandal.

Kate had only met her grandmother twice when she was younger. She died when Kate was eight and she didn't remember her. Without thinking, Kate reached out and grabbed her mother's hand. The nurse said she was lucky, and the surgeons had saved her foot, but her recovery was going to be slow. This news filled Kate with dread.

What were the implications for Kate? Was she going to have to look after her mother? After what she'd been through with her before, that prospect was one she didn't want to consider.

What were the options? Looking into the middle distance, Kate considered asking Richard, although he would be reluctant after last time. He was far from pleased with her for dumping her mother on him last time. But she'd had no choice at the time, right in the middle of the COVID pandemic. As for Grace, Kate knew she would not help. Grace had made it clear she considered Kate a failure as a daughter. No. That would not be possible. She would have to go into a home or something.

Why was it so damn hot in these places? She took off her hoodie and left it on the chair. With a sigh, she got to her feet, leaving her mother to sleep, and went to find out someone who could tell her what was going on.

At the nurses' station, the phones rang constantly. There were people everywhere; doctors rummaging through notes, firing questions at the harassed-looking sister. Kate was about to give up when she caught the eye of a staff nurse.

'I'm Kate Cooper, Esther Morgan's daughter. Can you tell me how she's doing?'

The nurse's badge identified her as Staff Nurse Jones, who Kate realised was the one who had rung to tell her about her mother. Giving her a sideways glance, she said,

'Yes, come into the office for a minute.' Kate followed her into a pokey little room to the side of the nurses' station.

'Have a seat,' the nurse moved a pile of notes from a chair, plonking them onto the already crowded desk before she sat down.

'As I told you on the phone, your mother is making a good recovery from the operation but will be with us for several weeks.'

'I get that, but what's this about her hallucinating? Is she still having them?'

'We don't think so, no.'

Kate let out a breath. 'That's a relief.'

'Her notes stated she was on antidepressants, so we re-started those, as she didn't come in with any medication. We could refer her to the psychiatric team if you think that's necessary. The notes aren't clear about her previous episode. Not surprising as it was during COVID.'

'She worked on a dementia ward but got called to help on the COVID wards. Something happened, and she left work because of it. She's never told me what it was all about, but she started talking to some invisible person.'

'Is she a nurse, then?'

'Yes, yes, she trained when I was a child. After my father died. Could I speak to one of her doctors? I think, given the circumstances, it might be a good idea to have a psychiatrist see her whilst she is here.'

'I'll have a word with the consultant for you and let you know if he agrees once he has referred to her notes.'

'Aw, that's where the problem lies. As the last episode happened during COVID, her GP prescribed anti-depressants but didn't refer her. So that is all that will be in her notes. But you must believe me, it was serious. She had a breakdown. I had to look after her when she stopped eating or taking care of herself. Could you explain that to the consultant?' Kate asked hopefully.

'I'll pass on the information.' Nurse Jones said, but Kate doubted there would be any referral. From her own experience, despite the NHS claiming to look after the whole person, all they were interested in was getting patients fit to be discharged.

'I'll see if she's awake.' Kate left the nurse shuffling through the piles of paper on the desk.

Back at her mother's bedside, Kate squeezed her hand as she opened her eyes.

'Hi Mum, I've bought you some things. How are you feeling?' She seemed to have aged since Kate had seen her last. Giving her a tight smile, Kate pushed down the feelings of sympathy.

'Thanks for coming love. I appreciate it. I know how busy you are. Such a stupid thing to do.' her voice rasped. Kate offered her the glass of water from the bedside table.

'Mum, what on earth were you doing in the Hafren Forest?'

'I went to find the source of the Severn,' her voice wistful. 'Remember, we always said we would find the source of the Severn. Since I'm selling the van, I thought I wouldn't get another opportunity.' Esther was trying to sit up, so Kate instinctively got up to help, but she waved her away.

'It's all right, I get a numb bum sometimes,' Esther said, settling herself back on the pillows.

'I'd forgotten you said you were going to sell the van. I wish you'd told me you were going to shut it down.'

'Why? There didn't seem much point. You're always so busy.'

Kate ignored the pointed remark as Esther continued.

'It seems ridiculous to keep paying the exorbitant ground rent to Mr Evans. It was useful when I needed a bolt hole after, you know ...' Esther's voice trailed off as Kate realised she didn't know the first thing about her mother's life. She barely gave her a second thought, especially after her 'issues' had resolved, and she was well again. Or was she well?

'How long have you been here? Where are the boys?' Esther asked.

'I left the boys with Shaun. I've got to get back, so I'll have to leave at about three.'

'Well, I'm going to be here for a while to see if these pins work.' Esther said, looking down at her foot. There was some sort of metal brace surrounding her lower leg and ankle. It looked to Kate like a torture device.

'How did you fall and how did you get down to the ambulance? Kate asked as Esther settled herself again. 'It all seems a bit weird.'

Esther told her about hurrying to get down to clear the van and make a run for it before Mr Evans spotted her and how she'd fallen.

'I thought I was going to die.' She paused as tears filled her eyes. 'I remembered all the happy times. My mother before Frank, you and your father on the beach,' her voice trailed off. 'I'd all but given up hope.'

'Oh Mum, what would have happened if someone hadn't found you?' Kate felt a lump in her throat. She realised this could have been far worse. Guilt for not coming sooner made her stomach churn. How would she have felt if her mother had died?

'Well, someone did find me, and everything turned out alright,' Esther said pragmatically.

'The nurses are confused about how you got down the mountain. They said something about a man carrying you?' Kate queried. All this business about a saviour who carried out a superhuman feat? There was an awkward silence before Esther cleared her throat.

'Yes, that's right, that's what happened,' Esther's hands were busy folding the cover on her bed over and over.

'Mum, they think you might have imagined it. There was no-one there when they found you and for someone to you know ...' her voice trailed off. 'Are you sure you didn't fall by the car park?'

Esther was immediately defensive. 'I know what you're thinking. Those hallucinations are back, but it was real I tell you. It was real. The man was called Joseph.'

'But how did he carry you down the mountain, Mum? Was he superhuman?'

Esther's face hardened as she sat looking at her daughter, as if there was no point in trying to convince her.

'Mum, do you need to speak to someone? You didn't before, but now you're getting muddled again?'

Esther took a deep breath.

'No, no, I'm fine. The main thing is I'm all right and however it happened doesn't matter. I've got to concentrate on getting well again. You don't need to worry about me. I won't cause you any problems this time. Thanks for coming. You'd best get off, otherwise you might get stuck in the traffic.'

A surge of resentment ran through Kate. What an ungrateful cow. She'd come all this way to help her and now she wouldn't even let her have her say. 'But I've only just got here, Mum, and we need to discuss what's going to happen when you get out of here? You can't be at home on your own.'

'Why ever not?' Esther's voice made it clear that she wasn't open to other options. She smoothed the counterpane, signalling the end of that topic of conversation. Well, we'll see about that, thought Kate. How was she not going to be a problem? She was always a problem.

'Well, if you're staying, tell me about the boys. How are they getting on? I haven't seen them for a while. Is Jack still playing football with that dreadful coach?'

Kate knew not to push. There was no point in getting her mother to admit anything, but she wouldn't let it go. Following her conversation with the nurse, there may be a referral. The last thing she needed was another breakdown, but if she was on the mountain, how did she get down? What if this Joseph was real?

Chapter 7

World's End was quiet this morning as Richard gazed out of the window, but World's End was always quiet. Richard pulled the sleeve of his sweater over his hands. The air was very cool as the world began its winter sleep. He watched as the wind whipped dancing leaves into the air, blanketing the ground outside with a vibrant dying colour. Weak sunlight filtered through the trees, casting a dappled light. He loved this time of year, but his mind was elsewhere. He was unsettled and fidgeted at his desk. The downside of living in such a small community was everyone knew everyone's business. In a centuries-old rural community, Richard and Colin were outsiders, and they interested the local inhabitants of Wick and Coombe. Sometimes he felt he couldn't fart without everyone knowing.

But World's End was aptly named. This small hamlet halfway between Weir and Coombe seemed idyllic to Colin, who wanted to escape London. They certainly had achieved that, moving to this backwater. The house was fantastic and so cheap Colin couldn't resist it. But Richard wondered if Colin had properly thought through moving into the depths of Worcestershire. It was alright for him, going off every morning to his office in Birmingham, leaving Richard to work from home.

A surge of resentment welled up inside. Richard had to get up and move around the small office, waving his arms, to shake off the feelings. Where would he be without Colin? He breathed. The house was everything he could ever want. They'd had to do a complete renovation, of course. The kitchen was a triumph, and Richard could show case it on his website and social media.

Going into the kitchen, he made himself an espresso from the fancy Italian coffee machine. As he stood sipping his coffee, he tried to put a positive spin on his mood. Guests came nearly every weekend, or they went to London and regularly visited family.

Leaning against the marble counter, Richard gave himself a shake and turned his thoughts to their neighbours. It was incredible that his two closest neighbours, Esther and Grace, had led such traumatic lives. Who would have thought that, looking at them? Grace was through hers and out the other end. But Esther, well, she went from one disaster to another and now it looked like she'd done it again. How the hell had she fallen down a mountain in deepest, darkest Wales? If Kate had any expectations of him or Grace looking after Esther when she was discharged from the hospital, she could think again. He'd ring Grace - they needed to discuss strategy.

Going back to his office and retrieving his mobile, he tapped on Grace's number. It was ridiculous, really. He could see her house from his, but Grace was a private person, and it was best to ring or text before showing up.

'Good morning, Richard. What can I do for you?' Grace's elegant voice responded.

'I suppose you've heard the latest about Esther?' He blurted out.

'No, but I'm sure you're going to tell me. Do you want to pop round? I'm free until this afternoon's Move It or Lose It.' Richard chuckled.

'No need for sarcasm. It'll be your turn one day.' Grace retorted.

Grace had moved from Cheltenham and was the newest member of the World's end community. She lived in a 1970's detached at the end of a long drive, next to Richard's on the same side of the lane. Grace lived with her daughter Ella and granddaughter Hope, who was currently at university.

Esther, originally from Surrey, had lived at World's End for several years by the time Richard and Grace arrived. Old Mrs Braithwaite had lived in the semi-detached Victorian Villa, next to Esther, all her life. But she was good natured enough and tolerated the foreigners as she referred to them.

The Ring doorbell announced Richard's arrival. As Grace opened the door and nodded to him, he thought about how much better she looked. When she'd first moved in, she was a train wreck, stick thin and old. Now she seemed to have a new lease on life, and got on well with the local widows and spinsters in Weir. Her short hair shone, and she walked with a bounce in her step as she went into her large kitchen.

'What's going on with Esther, then?' Grace waved at the kettle.

'No thanks, just had one.' Richard didn't drink instant. Grace threw a spoonful of the dreaded coffee, into a cup. Richard waited as she poured boiling water on it before she turned to Richard with an expectant look on her face.

'She's being discharged in a couple of days and Kate, as usual, is nowhere to be seen.' He pulled a long face.

'So, are we expected to look after her again?'

'Looks that way.'

'I thought Kate said she was going to convalesce somewhere?'

'Apparently there isn't anywhere they can afford and Esther doesn't qualify for a community hospital bed.'

'I hope for your sake we don't have a repeat of last time.'

'So do I, but I think this time is different. This is a physical thing. Anyway, Kate wants me to get the spare bed downstairs and I offered to pick her up from the hospital.'

'Oh Richard. For God's sake, you're your own worst enemy. I'll get my handyman Vic to move the bed. I'm sure he won't mind.' She paused and looked out at her extensive but boring garden. Richard was dying to landscape it, but she'd refused his offer so far. 'Do we know how mobile she is?'

'I don't suppose they'd let her out if she wasn't able to look after herself.'

Grace scoffed. 'We are talking about the NHS here, Richard. Do we know how she is after this fall?'

Richard sat down at the pine kitchen table. The old furniture in this house wouldn't be what he'd have bought. His inner critic condemned his judgmental attitude. He didn't know the extent of Grace's finances.

'Kate was vague on that count. She said the hospital was happy for her to come home, and the OT would be helping with providing aids and stuff. But I got the distinct impression she wasn't telling me everything.' Richard sniffed.

'Do we know any more about what happened?' Grace sat down, cradling her coffee. It was cold in the kitchen. Richard suspected the heating wasn't on, as Grace was wearing a thick cardigan. He wished he'd put on his gilet.

'She fell into a ditch halfway down a mountain.' Grace nodded; she knew that bit. 'And an unidentified saviour found her. Kate thinks he is a figment of Esther's imagination.' Grace sat back in the farmhouse chair with her elbows on the armrests, looking down her nose.

'How else would she have got down the mountain?'

'Hard to say without talking to her.' Richard sighed. 'The trouble is I don't want a repeat of last time. I know we need to look out for each other, but that pushed the boundaries, Grace.'

'Well, Mr Too Keen to Help, you've lumbered yourself again, my friend.' Richard shot her a look, knowing she was right. He was always too quick to offer help, but then regretted it when he got sucked in to other people's problems. Should have kept his mouth shut when Kate called.

Grace was saying. 'I've learnt the hard way to set limits on what I'm prepared to do. I'll help, of course - cook food and make sure she's alright. And I'm sure Ella will give her a hand if she needs help with washing, dressing - that sort of thing,' she sighed. 'I suppose all we can do is wait and see.'

'What do we do if she's struggling again?' Richard had a bad feeling in the pit of his stomach. He always felt like this when he'd committed to something he didn't really want to do.

'We get Kate to come and take responsibility for her own mother instead of expecting neighbours to do her job for her. I can't work out what the problem is between those two. Kate actually seems to hate her own mother. Do you know why?'

'Not really. I know it's something to do with her father.'

'Didn't Esther get married again?'

'No. She divorced her first one and then took up with some lowlife, according to Kate, but I don't think she married him.'

'Well, whatever the reason, she's not getting away with dumping her mother and her problems onto us again.' Richard nodded, pulling his jacket round him and getting up to return to his warm house.

'When are you going to get her?'

'Wednesday. I'll go in the morning and hope she's ready, as I don't want to hang around. It's Wales, for God's sake. Funny lot, the Welsh. All those leeks and sheep.' Grace laughed as she showed him to the door. Richard knew she loved his indiscretion.

'I'll get some groceries when I go to Tesco tomorrow,' she offered. Richard nodded before turning to the door.

They were unlikely friends, but she accepted him without judgement, even if others in Weir were not so welcoming. Small-minded bigots could be cruel. 'I'll ring you when I'm on the way back. Let's hope she isn't seeing little green men again.'

'It was a child, wasn't it?'

'You know what I mean, Grace.'

Opening the door, he made his way back along the gravel drive. He would have to turn up the heating as soon as he got home. He was frozen.

Chapter 8

When Esther received the news, she could go home, one part of her was relieved to be getting out of the sterile isolation of the hospital room. But the news made her palms sweat. The constant noise outside would soon become silence. She would be on her own at home which made her nervous. How would she cope? She'd imagined being here for much longer, but they must be short of beds with the winter pressures. The physiotherapist had given her daily exercises to stop muscle wasting. The occupational therapist told her the local team in Worcester would provide aids to help her move around and shower. It was going to be about four months before she could have the metal frame removed.

Despite not visiting again, Kate had spoken to Esther on the phone. Kate told her in no uncertain terms she shouldn't go home, but offered no help. When Esther asked her what she thought she should do, Kate hadn't replied. They both knew there was no alternative.

Kate almost shouted down the phone, 'Don't be ridiculous Mum, you can't go straight home.' Esther stood her ground. Did she think Esther could stay in a hospital bed until she could walk again?

'I'll be perfectly all right. Everything has been or-ganised. The spare bed has been moved downstairs into the back room. I can get to the kitchen and downstairs shower room. Grace has organised help with food. I'll let you know when I'm settled.' She sensed Kate was grappling with a sense of duty, but was reluctant to help her mother. Before Kate could respond, Esther disconnected the call as a surge of disappointment made her eyes fill. She felt let down by her daughter, instead having to rely on the good heartedness of her neighbours.

Apparently, Richard, was coming to pick her up and take her safely home. Esther was concerned Kate had cajoled him into agreeing to come and get her. Esther knew he found it hard to say no.

Richard had struggled to help her. It was beyond the bounds of a neighbourly relationship. Kate con-veniently used the COVID restrictions to keep her distance so poor Richard had no choice. The last time Richard had to scoop her off the floor, literally. Embarrassment crept up her neck as she remembered how he had found her. 'I can get food for you and give you your tablets,' he'd said, but nothing else. But when Esther became overwhelmed and broke down, Richard broke down, too. She still felt shame about how she'd behaved, and their relationship never quite recovered.

It was better to shut herself away until she could face the world again. The isolation of lockdown was good for her. She appeared outwardly normal, although inwardly she was struggling. The time had allowed her to heal, leaving her feeling renewed and ready to move forward. Now she found herself in a position of dependency again and wondered how Richard and Grace felt about Kate's betrayal. She wouldn't be a burden this time. This was a physical injury. There would be no repeat of the last time.

Esther knew Kate was glad to be let off the hook, and she realised how lucky she was to have moved to the village. Grace's text said there were plenty of offers with shopping, cooking, cleaning, and more. The tone was supportive, but how did they really view her? Well, she'd soon find out when Richard came to collect her in the morning.

The following morning, Richard marched into her room saying 'Come on, young lady, let's get you home.' An enormous wave of gratitude swept over her. She loved Richard. He immediately had the nurses eating out of his hand with his Hugh Grant boyish smile and floppy hair. When she told him the only thing holding them up was her walking sticks to take home, he made his way to the nurses' station. Ten minutes later, the sticks miraculously arrived, even though Esther had been waiting half the morning.

As Richard's tall lanky frame manoeuvred the wheelchair out into the crisp winter sunshine, Esther breathed in the cold, fresh air, so glad to be free. He'd parked in a disabled spot even though she wasn't, which made her giggle. Richard supported her as she got into the car, ensuring her metal frame was properly positioned. He then wrapped her in a tartan rug before giving her a hot drink and snacks for the journey.

Setting the sat nav, Richard headed for the A44 out of Aberystwyth. The heated seats and spectacular road meant for a very pleasant and relaxing journey for Esther. Richard needed to concentrate until they reached Llangurig when the route became easier. Esther sensed he was eager to know all about her fall and rescue, but he shared the village gossip instead. His story about the Christmas Fayre running out of cake, had her crying with laughter. He made it as far as Oswestry before he began probing. Esther had mentally prepared herself, as she knew this was coming.

'So come on, out with it. How did you fall down a ten-foot ditch, for God's sake?' His tone was playful, but his interest was keen. He already knew why she was in Wales, but not the reason for the hike up a mountain. Esther explained about Mr Evans and keeping out of his way so she could leave under the cover of darkness and how she had always wanted to find the source of the Severn.

'But how did you get out of the ditch, Esther?' Taking his eyes off the winding country road, he gave her a hard stare. In that moment, she knew she had no way out of telling him the tale. 'Who was this bloke then, and why did he leave you in a car park?' Kate must have told him already.

'What can I tell you, Richard? I don't know who he was, why he was there, or what happened to him. It was weird, right? A stranger coming to my rescue and then disappearing, but I swear that's what happened. How else would I have got down the mountain on my own with a broken ankle?'

'It's so bizarre, Esther. What did he look like? Have the police found him?'

'He was tall, broad.'

'Hmm, sounds interesting.' His voice mischievous.

'Stop it, Richard,' Esther laughed. 'The darkness made it nearly impossible to see. It was pitch black, but he had a head torch. It was shining in my eyes.'

'But how did he get you down? No offence.'

'I don't know how he did it. I just know he did. To be honest, I don't think the police will look for him. After all, he did nothing wrong, so why would they?'

'I suppose not.' There was silence for a few minutes while Richard processed this information before he said what she'd dreaded.

'You don't think you banged your head or that it was some sort of dream or something?'

'No Richard, it was very real, I can assure you,' Esther changed her tone, trying to deflect his questions. 'Anyway, it doesn't matter now, as I'm alive. Just got to focus on getting better.'

He responded with a 'Yes, of course.'

Richard's reaction made her think he believed she was acting irrationally again. She also knew it would be round the village before she'd had time to put the kettle on. There was nothing to be done, so she would just have to hope it didn't stop people from helping her. She was going to need it. The heated car seat was so comfortable Esther's mind wandered to when she had moved to the village after Ray. How lucky she was when Richard and Grace moved in and their friendships had grown. For that, she was extremely grateful and was determined not to jeopardise their kindness. Staring out of the window, she made a pact with herself. Before she knew where she was, they were home. I won't give them any reason to question my sanity again. This won't become an issue. I'm recovering from a broken ankle. I doubt I'll ever see Joseph again, and if I do, I'll send him packing. I don't want anyone questioning my state of mind again or threatening my friendships.

Chapter 9

Richard helped get her leg out of the car door by swivelling her round in the seat before handing over the crutches. Esther breathed a sigh of relief as Richard unlocked her front door.

Balancing on her crutches, she looked at the door thinking it needed a coat of paint. Why they called her two up, two down with a galley kitchen, a villa she didn't know why they called it a villa.

She'd moved here after Ray. A new start, somewhere where no-one knew her. The job opening at Worcester Royal's frailty ward was just what she needed. This was her home, no one else's. As she moved toward the two steps up to the front door, she felt so glad to be home.

With a strong determination to prove her independence, she steeled herself, conquering the two steps, and then in through the front door. Standing for a moment, she breathed in the familiar scent of her home and felt the comfort of it. The trace of lavender. She touched the water mark where the rain seeped in around the front door. Then the battered banister where the old cat had scratched. This place was her sanctuary, a haven she loved dearly. The room was brimming with treasures she'd gathered over the years as well as a random selection of ornaments and photographs, each one a reminder of a special moment. As she moved into the back room she breathed again, recognising the smell of old incense sticks and something else - furniture polish.

'Has someone been in cleaning?' she asked Richard, as he moved past her to put the kettle on.

'You know Grace, she mobilised the troops. Hope that was all right?'

Esther smiled. 'Of course, I'm sure it's cleaner than when I left. Please tell her thank you.'

'You can tell her yourself. She'll be in later. Now you get yourself settled. Vic's bought the armchair through so you can sit by your bed. He's moved the settee around in the front room to make sure you have plenty of space to get in there. Grace left food in the fridge and there's a rota of meals planned. Just watch out for Sue's hotpot, is all I'll say. I'm doing

Coq au vin on Wednesday.' He smiled as he handed her a cup of tea, proud of his organisational skills.

She gazed around the back room. The table had been moved to the corner to make room for the bed. It was tight, but there was enough room to manoeuvre herself. She let out another deep sigh.

'It's so good to be home,' she smiled up at Richard, who was being very businesslike. He picked up a blanket from the bed and tucked it round her.

'We've got a raised toilet seat and a chair thing for the shower. Would you like me to make sure you're all right to use the loo before I go?'

Esther laughed, 'I'm sure I'll be fine. You know, I was a nurse for over twenty years.'

'You haven't been a patient,' he stopped, realising this wasn't strictly true. Esther saved him from further embarrassment.

'I'll be fine. I can ring if I get stuck and you can come and help me,' she giggled, knowing full well Richard would be mortified at the thought of helping Esther off the toilet.

'Right, I'm going to leave you to it. Grace will be here within the hour with lasagna.' his tone suddenly changed. 'Esther, I'm glad you're all right. You know what a special person you are, don't you? Oh, your post is on the table, just there,' he pointed to a small table squeezed in next to her chair.

Tears pricked the corner of Esther's eyes, overwhelmed by his kind words. When he had left, she picked up the envelopes. Everything was fine. She was home now.

Looking through the pile of mail, she could see the usual bills and a flyer invited her to view the new retirement village being built next to the crematorium. There were get-well cards from old work friends and people in the village, but there was also a manilla envelope. There was her name carefully in ink but no address. Carefully, she opened the envelope. Inside was a single piece of paper with a brief message.

Dear Esther,

I am glad you made it home and are recovering. If you ever need anything, just call me.

Joseph.

Esther went hot, then cold. He was real. This proved Joseph was real, but how on earth was she supposed to contact him? The letter confirmed Joseph's existence, yet a sense of unease was taking hold.

How did he know where she lived? How was she supposed to contact him? There was no email or phone number. Why would she contact him? She got up, suddenly nervous in her own home.

It was weird, bizarre? How did he know she was home? She had literally just walked through the door. The letter inferred he knew she was home before she had even got home. Was he spying on her? This felt strange, not right. Esther's emotions were a mix of confusion and unease. Was this history repeating itself? No. This was something different.

The problem was, she couldn't tell anyone. Esther suspected they already thought she was losing touch with reality again. Bringing up a stranger who was stalking her would only make things worse. She was just going to ignore it and get on with enjoying being home. She shut her eyes tight before shoving the note down the side of the chair where it was out of sight, for her and anyone else.

Grabbing her crutches, she tested how easy it was to get around. Leaning her weight forward, she navigated her way around. Going through to the front room, she dropped awkwardly down on the settee. Vic had placed a stool within reach, so she put a cushion on it before positioning her leg. She picked up the TV controls and began flicking through the channels, but her mind wouldn't stop thinking about the note. Esther remembered how

Joseph came to her aid. If he had any ill intent, why would he have saved her? But what did he want from her? His comments about the shadows of the three deaths returned to her, and she shivered. Turning up the volume on the TV, she concentrated on 'A Place in the Sun.'

She must have dozed off as a loud knock at the front door roused her and Grace swept into the room, full of concern and lasagna. Although Grace had been a recent addition to the World's End community, Esther knew as soon as she met her, they would be friends.

'That looks like an instrument of torture.' She said, looking at Esther's foot. How long have you got to have that on for?' Grace asked, coming back into the front room after depositing the food in the kitchen.

'Several weeks, I think, so the bones can knit together again. I made a mess of my ankle, that's for sure.'

'Do you have everything you need?' Grace asked. 'It's Pilates, but I can pop back in on my way home?' Businesslike as always. It was hard to image Grace as anything other, but Esther knew there were shadows in her past as well.

'Thanks, that's kind, but I shall be fine. I just want to eat and go to bed. To sleep in my own home is going to be a luxury. I don't think I've had a proper night's sleep since the accident.'

'Fair enough. Leave the heating on low, it's going to be a cold one. Just ring if you need anything. I'll be back in the morning. Richard doesn't want to come too early in case he finds you in the bathroom or something.' Grace winked, making Esther laugh. 'You can tell me all about it then.' Grace came gave her a peck on the cheek. 'Welcome home.'

A lump in her throat stopped her from replying, overwhelmed by Grace's kindness. As the front door shut, she also felt an immense surge of anger. Anger at Kate. Even when Esther most needed her, she'd refused to come and help. Did she hate her so much? Thank God for the forgiveness and kindness of friends. And as for this Joseph, well, best she ignored his note. It was far too risky to mention that to anyone. Now she breathed. Let's concentrate on the here and now, she said to herself. The joy of being home. Tomorrow was another day. Whatever will happen, I'm ready for it.

Chapter 10

Two weeks later, Esther pulled back the curtain a little and looked out at the garden. From her bed she could see it coated in a hard frost. The sun glinted off the covering of white, making the world shimmer. She'd had another good night's sleep with no nightmares. Even though the heating was on all the time, Esther shivered and pulled a jumper on over her pyjamas. It was cold when you didn't move around much.

Christmas was only days away. It had crept up on her. There were several cards on the mantlepiece from people in the village. A religious card arrived from Frank, her stepfather, causing a sharp surge of anger to pass through her. Esther instantly tore it up and chucked in the bin.

Esther sighed, sitting back against the mountain of pillows, looking out at the birds clustered on the feeder. Yes, he did a terrible thing, but his early life shaped him. He saw life differently. Giving her head a shake, she leant down and took the two torn pieces out of the bin. His writing was wobbly and spindly. Could she ever forgive him for what he'd done to her mother? No - the anger was back. Anger at Frank and her mother. There was no excuse for what he'd done.

Her poor mum. Getting out her phone, she scrolled down through the years and found a picture she'd found after her mum's death. It was the two of them sitting, smiling, on the beach. Esther must have been about four. Her thick black hair was scrapped back into a ponytail, to stop it from sticking out at all angles. She traced a finger over her mum's face. She looked so young. Well, she would have only been twenty or twenty-one. It must have been so hard for her being unmarried and pregnant with a mixed-race child in the early 1970s. Families were more concerned with reputation than supporting their own daughters.

After years of struggling to bring up Esther single-handedly, Frank had seemed like their saviour. A solid, upstanding Salvation Army man who took charge of their shamble of a life.

But Esther soon became sick of all his rules and regulations. It was a relief when he told her to leave. Said it was time she should make her way in the world. If Esther had truly known what he was, she would never have left her mother there. Tears sprung to her eyes at the memory. Giving herself a shake to dislodge those thoughts, she manoeuvred herself sideways so she could get up.

Grabbing her crutches, she headed for the kitchen to distract herself. Those thoughts needed to go back into their box. Her mother was one of her shadows. As she swung across the room towards the kitchen, Joseph came into her mind as she checked the kettle and flipped the switch. Mercifully, there had been nothing since the note. Thinking about her mother made her more determined than ever not to explore her past. There was enough to be done with Christmas round the corner. As she drank her tea, she decided cards and presents would be bought online.

Moonpig and Amazon helped with Kate and the boys. There weren't many other people to buy for, just some neighbours and old friends. People would receive their present wrapped in brown packaging with a smiley face, especially Richard and Grace. She must make a special effort with them after all their kindness.

Esther's conversations with Kate about Christmas had been interesting. She phoned asking Esther if she wanted to go to hers. Esther knew from the tone and the lack of anywhere for her to sleep that it was an empty offer.

Grace held the opposite view, insisting that Christmas should come to Esther. Esther had a hell of a job dissuading her. Grace always went away at Christmas to some posh hotel with her daughter and granddaughter. She was making an exception to accommodate Esther, but it felt uncomfortable. All she wanted was a box of Quality Street, a bottle of prosecco, Love Actually, Bridget Jones, and to be thoroughly miserable on her own.

Having successfully deflected Grace, she agreed to let Richard deliver a Christmas dinner. Grace organised a list of people who could be asked for help in her absence, but Esther knew she would call none of them. She asked for her keys back as there was a key safe down the side of the house. Esther found it disconcerting having Grace, Richard and even Mrs Braithwaite wandered in, saying, 'just popping in to check you're all right.'

There had been one embarrassing incident when Richard let himself in when she was on the loo, trying desperately to ease the constipation caused by the painkillers. He fled when he caught a whiff of what was going on. Esther laughed so hard it eased her constipation in no time.

After two weeks at home, the initial surge of goodwill tailed off. Ocado delivered the small amount she needed, and Esther was glad to have something other than Mrs Braithwaite's cottage pie for tea.

Her stupid mistake had caused a ripple effect, and she didn't want to feel guilty expecting people to help her anymore. As the holiday season kicked off, Esther sat with a glass of wine, feeling sorry for herself. The weight of her enforced isolation frustrated her. If only she could go for a walk and get some fresh air. But there was no alternative but to wait. She would start physio after the holidays. Hopefully, the hospital would provide transport. Asking Richard seemed too much.

There were no decorations up, save a rather pathetic wire tree on the coffee table which shed sparkly bits everywhere - a gift from two little girls in the village. Esther always gave them a big bag of kids' makeup, nail varnish and any other rubbish she could find in B&M, but not this year. This year would be like lockdown. That thought sent a shiver down her spine.

Not going there, she said to herself. There lay danger, but try as she might, by Christmas, Esther was heading down towards the bottom of a deep well of self-recrimination. While most of the residents of Weir were in the pub or busy wrapping presents, Esther's nightmares had returned. Despite the freezing temperature outside, she woke up drenched in sweat. Every night, she dreaded falling asleep because the dream was always the same. To quell the night terrors, she upped her dosage of anti-depressants, which left her constantly lethargic. She didn't know what to do. Richard delivered a Christmas dinner on Christmas Eve to fit in with his plans. He was off to visit relatives in Bath for the day. Her dinner waited in the fridge, but she had no appetite.

As Christmas Day dawned, the lack of proper sleep exhausted her. Last night, she'd heard the rowdy revellers stumbling home from the pub. As their laughter echoed down the lane, Esther couldn't help but feel a pang of envy. Normally, she would stumble home with them, her head spinning in mulled wine, gin, and minced pies.

Lying still in the frosty morning, she could hear the silence with the occasional gentle rustling of leaves and the distant chirping of birds. All that filled her mind was that child's face. Reaching up, her face was wet with tears as the overwhelming feelings of despair, guilt, and sadness took hold. She had no-one who cared.

Suddenly, the doorbell rang.

Oh my God, who the hell could that be? Esther panicked. She was in no state to receive visitors. They would be filled with good cheer, which she most definitely was not. Perhaps if she ignored the bell, whoever it was would go away. She held her breath, but after a few minutes, there was a gentle but persistent knock at the door. Slowly, she pushed herself into an upright position before swinging her legs over the edge of the bed. She grabbed her dressing gown and pulled it tight around her. Reaching for her crutches, she pulled herself up with the help of the side table. Lying in bed for so long had left her feeling stiff and achy.

Slowly and with a wince of pain, she hopped down the cold, tiled hallway towards the front door. Opening it, she peered around, expecting to see Richard, but the person on the doorstep made her gasp in surprise. It wasn't Richard. It was a tall, broad man with a mess of blond hair, which the brisk wind blew into his crystal blue eyes. She knew this person, but for a moment she couldn't quite place him.

'Hello Esther, it's Joseph. Do you remember me?' said the stranger.

Esther didn't know what to do or say. She stood transfixed with her dressing gown gaping as she tried to maintain her balance.

Chapter 11

Esther stood transfixed on the doorstep, unable to move. She wasn't sure if she was afraid or pleased or both.

'Hi' was all she could say. 'What are you doing here? How do you know where I live?' For a moment, panic surged in the pit of her stomach. No one was around to call for help.

'Please don't be concerned Esther, I am here to help you.' Joseph smiled broadly. She assessed him as if for the first time. It had been so dark before she hadn't really seen him. She had to tip her head back to meet his gaze, even though she stood on the step. The weak winter sunlight caught his golden hair, as it fell in waves around a face that seemed perpetually open and honest. He was dressed in casual but smart corduroy trousers and a plaid shirt under a thick padded navy-blue jacket.

'Help me with what?' she queried, feeling exposed and shivering.

'To recover,' he said, the words barely audible, before adding, 'I can come another time if this isn't convenient.' An icy wind whipped around her bare feet. 'I'm not sure.' Esther didn't feel she could simply shut the door on him. 'You can come in for a minute out of the weather.'

Esther needed to sit down, so letting him in seemed her only option. She stepped back, opening the door wider before turning to swing herself back down the hallway. Joseph came into the house, closing the door behind him.

As Esther made her way to sit down in the chair by the bed, her mobile rang. She couldn't manoeuvre herself and answer the phone so whoever it was would have to leave a message. She slumped down into the chair with a sigh. Why was everything so difficult today? She was grubby, tired and hungry. The house was a mess, with clothes strewn everywhere and dirty cups on the table. A wave of embarrassment washed over her as she ushered the imposing stranger into her home, but beneath that, an settling fear pulsed through her.

As she struggled to balance her crutches against the side of the chair, a hand reached out, offering her the phone that was buzzing relentlessly. Startled, she raised her eyes to meet his, and then silently mouthed 'thank you.' Esther answered without checking the number.

'Hello,' she said uncertainly.

'Mum, it's me. What took you so long to answer? I thought something was wrong.' Kate snapped.

Esther glanced at Joseph, who stood on the other side of the room watching her. She put her hand over the mouthpiece saying, 'it's my daughter.'

He gave the thumbs up and put an imaginary cup to his lips with a slight inclination of his head. She nodded gratefully, thinking she would have preferred something a little stronger, but coffee would do for now. He made the T sign or C sign. She whispered coffee as he disappeared into the untidy kitchen.

'Mum, mum are you there? What's going on?' demanded the voice at the other end of the phone.

'Nothing, I was just getting settled again.'

'Why, where have you been?'

'Just got up to ....,' Esther checked herself. Perhaps this wasn't the time to tell her daughter she had just let a stranger into the house, 'to go to the bathroom if you must know.'

'I rang to say Happy Christmas. Are you alright? You sound strange.'

'Fine. Richard bought me dinner. I'll have that soon. I'm having a lazy morning, then I thought I'd watch some films later. How are you?' Esther said, trying to deflect any more questions. She sensed Kate felt she had to check up on her out of a misplaced sense of duty. 'What are you doing?'

'Disaster. Shaun bought the wrong Xbox game for Ben, who is now having a full-on strop. Mum, are you listening to me?'

Esther's inability to focus was due to her preoccupation with what was happening in her kitchen. Had she flushed the downstairs toilet earlier this morning? Having someone she barely knew snooping around made her very uneasy. She pulled herself together.

'Oh dear, I'm sure he'll recover. I'm so sorry, love, can I ring you back? Someone's at the front door.'

'Yes, yes, that's fine,' Kate sounded relieved not to have a long conversation.

'Send my love to the boys and thank you for ringing and thinking of me,' Esther said quickly. She was about to say, 'love you,' but the phone went dead.

She put her mobile on the table, close to her, in case she needed to grab it to call for help. Joseph appeared in the doorway carrying two cups of coffee. Hers was in her favourite mug. A coincidence? He held it out for her, making sure she grasped it before retreating to the other side of the room. He swerved to miss the cheap chandelier that normally hung over the dining table. It was hard to determine his age. Esther reckoned he was probably mid-thirties.

Why on earth he would be interested in her? His enormous feet wore trainers. Blue to match his clothes. As he moved across the room, Esther noticed he wasn't as bulky as she'd first thought but lythe and subtle. She marvelled again at how he had carried her down the mountain, or had she imagined it? He placed his cup carefully on the utilitarian table before folding his long body into the metal chair, before turning to look at her with those intense blue eyes.

'Can I ask you something?' she began.

'Yes, I carried you down the mountain,' he smiled, his eyes glinting. Is he reading my thoughts? Esther didn't know what to say, so they sat in silence, which made her feel uneasy all over again.

'How did you know where I live?' she tried again.

'I visited the hospital in Aberystwyth to check on you. They told me you had been discharged, so I asked for your address.'

'But they wouldn't have given you my address just like that,' the disquiet was stirring in the pit of her stomach again. Why the hell had she let him in?

'No, you're right,' he replied. 'I saw it on the computer screen.'

'I'm sorry,' Esther's insides twisted. 'I'm sorry, but I must insist that you leave.'

Joseph sat back in this chair and took a sip of his drink.

'Esther, you do not need to fear me. I am here to help you.'

'Yes, as you've already said, but what does that mean?' She demanded.

'We have met before, many times, but you won't remember. I am here to help you make things better,' Joseph whispered.

Esther's eyes pricked as tears threatened. Why would anyone be interested in improving her life? Her life was shit and she couldn't imagine how this man was going to make things better. She sat looking at him. She had no memory of ever meeting him before. Surely she would have remembered. Was he a relative of a patient, perhaps? There was no logical reason for him being here, but he didn't feel threatening. Instead, there was an air of calm and peacefulness about him. As she sat looking at him she knew he could be trusted even though she had no memory of him.

'Okay,' she said, 'I have questions.'

'Ask away.'

'How did you know I was up the mountain in trouble?'

'Like I said before, I heard your call for help and came to you. Call it intuition if you like.' He leant forward, cradling his cup. Esther was none the wiser, so she tried a different tack.

'And how are you going to improve my life, may I ask?'

He smiled an innocent smile before putting his cup down and opening his arms.

'Tell me what you need?'

'I need a new ankle, a shower, a clean bed, and a nice fatty breakfast instead of that warmed-up Christmas dinner in the fridge.'

'Unfortunately, I can't do anything about your ankle, but you have a shower, and I'll start tackling the rest.'

She sat looking at him.

'You're serious, aren't you?' she checked, and he nodded.

'Do you need help to get up?' he asked, but she waved him away as she finished her drink and retrieved her crutches. She would feel so much better after a shower. He kept his distance as she made her way to the downstairs bathroom. Once inside, she locked the door before moving to turn the shower on. This shower room was small as it doubled as a laundry room, but it worked to her advantage in the current situation. She could swivel round from the sink to the loo to the shower. Undressing, she perched on the seat Richard had bought her, the warm water cascading over her in the shower.

When she emerged, she was clean, fresh, and rejuvenated. She'd showered, brushed her teeth, put on clean clothes from the pile she'd kept downstairs and combed her hair. As she looked in the mirror, she looked almost human again. As she hobbled into the back room, she was astonished to see the bed made with fresh linen; the room tidied and a plate of what looked like bacon and eggs with toast, butter, and marmalade on the small table in the corner.

Joseph stood by the door, out into the hallway.

'Hope that's made you feel better, Esther,'

'Whoa, thank you so much. That's wonderful.'

'I am going now as I don't want to overstay my welcome, but I am here anytime you need me. I have left my phone number by your bed. If you need anything, please call me. Not just for practical help, I want to help you heal all of you.' He tapped the side of his head. 'Go well Esther Morgan, I hope we meet again,' he moved out into the hall. 'I'll lock the door and post the key back through the letterbox,' he called before Esther had time to react. She heard the front door opening and close, then the clink of the key landing on the tiled floor. Esther stood rooted to the spot. Her mind didn't know how to process what had just happened, but the smell of the bacon made her realise how hungry she was.

Chapter 12

Esther sat outside her kitchen door on a garden chair she'd forgotten to put away in the shed last autumn. Her ankle was propped up on an upturned bucket, which she used to mop the quarry tile floors. It was one of those rare, mild January mornings when the sun hit the back of the house, spreading an unexpected warmth. She turned her face to the sun and breathed deeply. It had been two weeks since Joseph's visit. She couldn't stop thinking about him. Part of her was scared. She knew nothing about him and his appearances were uncanny and unworldly, which made her nervous. Was he a product of her imagination, or did he truly exist? No-one else had seen him. A chilling wave of doubt washed over her; the thought of him potentially being a figment of her imagination causing her to shiver. But that was ridiculous. She knew he'd visited on Christmas Day.

Another problem was his offer of help. She knew he meant more than just physical help. She could feel the dark parts of her beginning to stir. Esther thought about her mother, and the nightmares returning, all related to memories long buried. Joseph potentially threatened to expose those shadows if she allowed him too close. Whilst they were locked securely behind the closed doors in her mind, she could pretend to ignore them. Could she feel free of them? Could she ever be happy? But the thought of having to revisit those dark shadows made her heart race and filled her with dread.

Taking another deep breath, Esther focused on the birds clustered on the bird table, pecking mournfully at the remnants of crumbs.

Making her mind concentrate on the present, she needed to solve the problem of how to get to her physio appointments. The holiday season was over. The festive bustle had been replaced by the quiet hum of everyday life. She was alone, forgotten about, yesterday's news. But that didn't bother her. She'd been grateful for Richard and Grace's help, but she also appreciated the peace she now had. She found their unexpected visits invaded her privacy and made her feel on edge. It was time to get back on track, to find her way out of the rut. It was time to sort her life out.

Her first appointment with the physiotherapist was next week. Putting her foot to the floor, her ankle felt more stable. She was fed up with having bits of metal sticking out of her. For one thing, it was hard to keep it warm. The bed sock on her toes helped, and she created a tent over the metal frame using a fleecy blanket. She couldn't wait to have it removed, but the consultant said it wouldn't happen for several weeks yet.

I hate asking for help, especially after last time, Esther thought. I don't want to be a burden again. So, who could help? Richard and Grace were the obvious choice, but they'd already done more than enough and she didn't want to impose further. Esther knew Grace hated driving. Her eyesight wasn't so good anymore. Richard had told her he had a big new contract, so she didn't want to bother him. Funny how the people who offered were always the ones who were already busy. Ask a busy person if you want something done, her mother used to say. The image of her mother brought dread with it.

Quickly Esther re-centred her thoughts. She needed to arrange a lift to the physio at the local general hospital. When she'd rung for patient transport, it was fully booked. That was a relief. She re-membered the poor patients waiting for ages in the draughty entrance hall waiting for the ambulance to take them home. She didn't want to be one of those, thank you. Especially as it would increase the likelihood of someone recognising her.

As she wrestled with the problem, the piece of paper with Joseph's phone number niggled in the back of her mind. She'd hidden it in the journal she started writing after the accident. It was in one of many exercise books filled with her scribbled hand, secreted away in the bottom drawer of her bureau.

After her previous illness, Kate made it clear she needed to see a therapist. Esther wrote things down after watching a documentary about the power of self-help. It was hard at first, but now she could let the words flow. It didn't matter that they made no sense. No-one was going to read them. The thought of Kate reading them almost made her stop. But not if she disposed of them when the time was right. She shifted in her seat. The warmth of the sun was masked by a thin veil of cloud. She hoisted herself up and went back into the house. As she did so, her thoughts returned to Joseph.

Should she call him? Did he even have a car? Yes, he must otherwise how would he have come on Christmas Day. What should she do? It would prove beyond a doubt he was real. After struggling to open the bureau drawer and rummaging through her notebooks, she found the scrap of paper. The number was a mobile. Esther sent a text before she could change her mind. She text rather than ring to avoid putting him on the spot, doubt creeping back in.

The reply came almost immediately.

'What are the dates, please?'

Esther felt completely stupid. Why hadn't she included them in her original text? She sent a reply listing the dates and times of the weekly visits for the next four weeks.

'I will be there to take and bring you back,' came the reply.

Perfunctory, thought Esther, like she was putting him out. She sent another text.

'If you're not able to make it, that's fine. I don't want to put you out.'

As soon as she sent it, she felt foolish, like a teenager who kept changing her mind.

'No trouble at all. I am happy to help,' Joseph replied.

She would now see him again and indeed, regularly for the next four weeks. That was the impression he had given. He would be there to take her, otherwise he wouldn't have asked for all the dates, would he? She sat down on the sofa, considering how she felt. The whole relationship was bizarre. There was that word again. Never in her long career as a nurse had she come across anything so bizarre; it gave her goosebumps. She thought about the selflessness of friends and family, volunteers who ferried people backwards and forwards, but this was different. Although Esther had no long-term memory of ever meeting Joseph, she felt connected to him. He was familiar to her, as if she had known him for a long time. His presence was comforting, somehow.

She sighed. She'd found a solution to the problem, and that was all she needed to worry about. Esther relaxed. Next Tuesday was days away. She stiffened, sitting upright. But somewhere in the pit of her stomach, she knew there would be consequences. She regretted her decision when she realised he wouldn't let the opportunity go to persuade her to talk about the past. His words as he left her in the car park came flooding back. 'I am here to help you dispel the shadows that haunt you.' What would be the price of asking for Joseph's help? While Esther desperately wanted to keep her painful past buried, a deep-seated feeling told her Joseph was planning something that threatened to unearth it.

Chapter 13

The following Tuesday, there was a knock at the door shortly before ten in the morning. Her appointment was at ten thirty, so they would be there early. It was only ten minutes away. Esther had taken care of her appearance after her last encounter with Joseph, making sure she was presentable. This was hard when all you could wear was tracksuit bottoms and layers to keep out the cold.

'You look better,' he said as she opened the front door. 'You'll need a coat. It's cold.' He was wearing a big puffer jacket and a woollen hat. Somehow, he looked younger. He waited patiently, as Esther managed the steps without incident. She turned to move onto the street, looking for his car. He pointed to a brand-new Range Rover parked next to her battered VW. It was still in the same spot the AA had left it when they bought it back from Wales. It looked shabby and dirty next to the gleaming white of the Range Rover.

He opened the door and waited as she used her good leg to step up and, grabbing the door handle, positioned herself on the seat before moving her damaged leg into the footwell. There was plenty of room, and the plush leather seats were so comfortable and heated. It was wonderfully warm, after the icy blast of the north wind whipping down the road.

'All in?'

'Yes, thank you,' Esther said as Joseph carefully closed the door. Esther was sorry Richard was away and not witnessing her luxury ride. She knew he would want to meet Joseph. Such a handsome man wouldn't be missed by his eagle eye. He would see for himself, Joseph was real. If anything happened, he would have been a witness. Was she mad to trust a man she barely knew? Her stomach bubbled with unease. She knew Joseph had another agenda. As Joseph manoeuvred the car out into the road, he asked how she was feeling.

'Much better thank you. I'll be glad to get these bits of metal out of my leg, though.' Her response was guarded. He removed his hat as he glanced over and gave her a nod.

'Yes, it must be frustrating not being able to get around.' Esther was struck once more by his empathetic manner. She relaxed and decided to find out more about him. Perhaps that would help allay the unease she felt.

'This is a posh car. Thanks for coming to get me. Have you come far?'

'No, not far. I'm staying nearby.'

'Where do you live, if you don't mind me asking?'

He glanced across at her with that slight smile he had. He really was the most enigmatic man she had ever met.

'I live in Wales, near Aberystwyth.'

'Oh, of course, that makes sense,' she said, but wondered why he was here in middle England. Esther looked at him. He had the sculpted beauty of Michelangelo's David, especially in profile. His features were so striking, he seemed unreal. He reached up, his fingers brushing through his hair, pulling it away from his eyes. Despite Joseph being the most beautiful man, she had ever seen, Esther had no sexual feelings towards him at all. When she met a handsome man, she would normally get silly and blush. Why any man would find a menopausal overweight fifty something attractive was ludicrous.

'So, you're staying nearby?'

'I am here to help you deal with those experiences you have locked behind that steel door in your mind. Until you deal with them, you will continue to feel as you do. Is this where we're supposed to be turning?' he asked, distracting her from what he had just said.

Oh God, she knew there would be a price to pay for this favour. A red warning light went off in her head. There was no way she wanted to deal with 'those' experiences. There was no mistaking what he was talking about. Once she was safely back home, she resolved to have no further contact with him. The sooner this encounter was over, the better.

Joseph parked right outside the entrance. He helped Esther out of the car and to the reception desk. A porter came with a wheelchair to take her to the physio department. Joseph stood in the corridor, the porter's cheerful whistling echoing in the air as he wheeled her away. Esther's face flushed with embarrassment as she protested, but a wave of relief washed over her when she realised how far the physio department was from the entrance.

The throbbing in Esther's foot, her pale face, and her frail body all screamed her invalid status as she sat there, her foot dangling over the end of the footrest. She fidgeted as she waited. Her mind was in overdrive. Who the hell was Joseph? Esther didn't like him, but deep down, she knew he spoke the truth. The deaths she'd caused. Why was he so intent on trying to force her to revisit those demons? The physio called her through just as she was trying to hatch a plan to get out of the hospital and home without Joseph's help.

After the appointment, Joseph was waiting outside the entrance as the porter wheeled her out, the Range Rover parked in the disabled bay to the right of the doorway.

'I'm not disabled,' Esther protested.

'Aren't you,' Joseph replied, raising his eyebrow? Esther's colour rose as a flush of irritation swept over her. She was on the verge of saying something when she momentarily missed her footing, causing her to cry out. Joseph was by her side immediately.

'Are you all right?' he said with such tenderness, tears sprung in her eyes.

'Just jarred my leg. It's sore after all the manipulation from that torturer who said she was a physiotherapist,' she grumbled.

'Here, let me help you.' Joseph practically lifted her into the passenger seat. How does he do that? He doesn't look like he has that kind of strength.

Esther sank back against the smooth leather.

'Do you need any painkillers?' he offered her a bottle of water and two tablets. 'It's just paracetamol.' Reluctantly, Esther took them from him, the pain overcoming her mistrust of him. She closed her eyes, feeling exhausted. They drove back to her house in silence. She came back to herself as the car pulled up and the engine died. Richard's car was parked on his drive. That's odd. I thought he was away, Esther thought.

Once again, Joseph was at the door to help her out and into the house. He seemed to gauge her mood completely, allowing her to take her time. Once inside, he went to the kitchen and made her a cup of tea before turning to leave.

'I'll be here for your next appointment unless I hear any differently.' He knows what I've been thinking Esther squirmed. Did he realise he's pushing me somewhere I don't want to go? But he hadn't finished. The next sentence made her spine tingle.

'The other help I can offer will be something you can't do alone. It will take you to places you never thought existed and give you the peace you seek.' He paused, fixing her with his penetrating gaze before saying. 'Take care, Esther.' As he took her hand, her mind momentarily lost focus, as if she was moving out of herself. Detaching from her surroundings. It was the same feeling as she'd had in the ditch, right before Joseph found her.

As he let go, Esther found herself back in her chair as the front door closed. What the hell was that? Esther was left to grapple with the whirlwind of emotions swirling inside her about this enigmatic man and a past which was inevitably drawing her back.

The doorbell startled her. Why had he come back? I won't answer, she thought, but then heard a voice calling to her through the letterbox. It was Richard. 'For God's sake, let me in. It's freezing out here.'

'Where have you been?' He said coming in and plonking himself down at the small table.

'Physiotherapy appointment.'

'How did you get to the hospital? Please tell me you didn't go on transport with all the incontinent elderly.'

'Richard, you can't say things like that,' to which he gave her a look which said, 'Oh yes I can.'

'I had a lift. I'm surprised you didn't notice.'

'What are you inferring, Esther Morgan? I'm no busybody,' Richard feigned shock before saying, 'Who is it then? Who's giving you a lift? I noticed the brand-new Range Rover.'

'You don't know him' she smiled, but Richard was not letting it go.

'He,' Richard leaned in with interest as Esther leaned back.

'Richard, for God's sake, look at me. I'm not exactly a sex goddess. He's a friend, that's all, and he's helping me out.'

'What's his name?'

Should she be honest with Richard? He didn't know who Joseph was. She hadn't told him the name of the man who rescued her, so he wouldn't make the connection, she was sure.

'Joseph.'

Richard sighed and leant back, frustrated he couldn't gleam anymore.

'When's your next appointment?' he asked casually.

'It's Thursday, but I was wondering if you were free.'

'Why? Can't your knight in shining armour make it?'

Esther leaned forward. 'To be honest, Richard, I would rather he didn't take me again.' Richard's eyes lit up, and he clapped his hands.

'Intrigue and mystery, Esther Morgan. I love it. Tell.'

'I just don't feel comfortable asking a stranger to help.'

'I thought you said he was a friend. Did he say something to upset you?' Richard leaned closer.

'Could you take me next week, please?' Esther put on her most pathetic smile.

'Alright. I suppose so.'

Esther nodded, patting Richard on the hand as relief washed over her. She could avoid Joseph's probing. 'Oh, Kate texted to say she's popping in on her way to a meeting in Birmingham.'

'That'll be nice,' Richard's smile was tight. Then as an afterthought. 'Tell her to pop round to mine if she has time.' But before Esther could ask why. 'He was moving to the door, 'Ciao Bella.'

Chapter 14

Kate thought her mother looked well ... considering. The exception being the prominent metal frame and protruding bolts on her lower leg.

When the meeting request in Birmingham came through, she felt duty bound to call in and see her mother. She was practically passing the door. As she'd hadn't seen her since the sterile environment of the hospital, guilt drove her to visit.

Her mother had looked so fragile and vulnerable in the hospital, but back in her own home, her stoicism had returned. Kate asked a few polite questions about the physio sessions and how she'd been managing, but her mind was elsewhere. Her mother was just one problem in her shit life. Shaun was an absolute tool, and she couldn't understand why in God's name she'd married him, let alone had children with him.

Her jaw clenched. It was her mother's fault, of course. If only she hadn't met bloody Ray, Kate wouldn't have been forced to leave with Shaun. Her tightly crossed arms couldn't contain the rising anger and disgust she felt. The air was heavy with untold grievances on both sides. Esther coughed awkwardly, trying to break the tension.

'How are the boys?' She asked. Kate couldn't contain herself.

'If you really want to know, Shaun stopped paying the maintenance again. Something about changing jobs and a shortfall. I checked on Instagram and he's at some match in Paris with his mates. I could scream. How the hell am I supposed to manage? I can't do any more hours, and even if I could, the extra would go on after-school club. God Mum, it's a fucking mess.' Kate spat, releasing her pent-up frustration. The silence stretched between them.

'I could probably lend you a bit if it would help,' Esther leant towards her daughter as if to take her hand. Esther's early retirement meant she made ends meet with her meagre NHS pension, and Kate knew she had little to spare.

'Thanks, Mum, I'm sure I'll work it out,' she sighed, feeling a twinge of remorse for dumping this on her mother. She needed to go before she said all the things she longed to say. As she was getting ready to leave, her mother said,

'You're not going already, are you? You've only just got here. Can you sit down for a minute? I need to talk to you about something.' Kate sat back down, clutching her bag, wondering what the hell was going on now.

'I've updated my will. You are the sole benefi-ciary. Because of my health problems, I decided it was wise to take out a power of attorney. As you are my daughter, it is logical to ask if you would act as the executor. Would that be some-thing you'd consider? It would be for financial and health which are two separate things.' Esther spoke quickly, trying to get the all the information out before Kate reacted.

Kate's initial thought was no. She had enough to deal with, but then she thought about the inheritance. The financial one would be fine but the health one. Did she want to decide about her mother's health?

'What do I have to do?' Her voice was abrupt.

Taking a large white envelope from the table, Esther handed it to Kate.

'You need to sign these forms and provide proof of identity and post them back.'

'I don't know, Mum. I'll have to think about. I know about the financial one, but what does the health one mean?'

'If I can't decide about my health because of incapacity, you would decide for me.' Esther said bluntly. Kate was surprised by her frankness.

'That's quite a responsibility, Mum. How do I know what you would want?'

'Well, I don't want to be kept alive if I'm not able to be independent,' she paused, 'if I couldn't manage.'

'Right.' Kate took the envelope and stuffed it into her bag.

'Just so you know, I have put all my personal documents in a green folder in the bottom drawer of the bureau.' Esther pointed to a battered upcycled desk in the lounge.' Kate nodded, getting up to leave.

'Oh, I nearly forgot. Richard wants to have a word before you go. Could you pop round to his whilst you're here?'

Kate breathed, 'I don't really have time, Mum. Tell him to ring me, will you? What does he want?' Esther shrugged. Kate picked up her bag and coat and headed for the hallway as the doorbell rang.

'Kate, darling, lovely to see you. You look smart and businesslike,' Richard said as she opened the door.

'Just stopped on my way to a meeting in Birmingham,' she returned his two air kisses, cursing under her breath.

'If you have five, I could do with a quick chat.'

'I'm running on a tight schedule,' Kate said. 'Bye Mum,' she called, moving past Richard.

Richard followed her as she moved down the lane towards her parked car. She'd spotted her mother's old VW and wondered why she didn't park it somewhere else to give other people room.

'I'm worried about Esther.' Richard was right behind her. Kate stopped and turned. It was no use. She'd have to hear him out.

'She seems to have a "friend",' Richard made speech marks with his fingers, who took her to her physio appointments. Someone said they saw the same car here on Christmas Day.' he paused for dramatic effect, 'the only problem is I've never seen him.'

Kate let out a breath. Is that all this was about? What a relief. She thought he was going to give her a lecture about not coming to see her mother.

'Are you sure you haven't just missed him?' Kate asked the obvious question. 'Are you sure she's even going?' Kate persisted.

'Yes, I rang the hospital to check, and she went for her appointment.' Kate was surprised by Richard's diligence. He was presenting evidence she could not refute.

'Has she said who this man is?

'He's a mysterious friend, apparently.'

'Called?'

'Joseph?' Kate's gut clenched. Wasn't that the name of the man who rescued her from the mountain?

'Why are you so concerned, Richard?' Kate asked.

'Listen, Kate, if there's something going on here, I don't know what Esther's getting herself involved in. She asked me to take her this week as she didn't want to ask this Joseph again. There's an undercurrent of something going on. I'm telling you, I don't want to deal with your mother. This is your responsibility. You are going to have to sort this out.' Kate's face flushed despite the cold. There it was - the recrimination. Taking a deep breath to stop herself from biting back, she reconsidered the power of attorney for health. If she agreed, would she have some control over her mother if she started behaving strangely again? An uneasy feeling made her turn back towards the house.

'I thought you were on a schedule?' Richard called at her retreating figure.

Kate's reappearance surprised Esther.

'Have you forgotten something?' She asked.

'Mum,' Kate sat straight down at the small table. 'Who is this man taking you to your appointments?'

'Just a friend helping me out.' Esther's back straightened, flustered by the directness of the question.

'Mum, who is he?' Kate demanded.

'It's the man who rescued me, if you must know.'

'What the hell?' Kate muttered, her brows furrowed in confusion.

'This isn't like before. This has nothing to do with you, Kate. I am managing perfectly well, thank you. If I need help, I'll ask. I suggest you go now before you're late for your meeting.'

'Now you listen to me. If you're getting yourself involved with someone, I need to know. I can't keep traipsing up here to sort you out and Richard's had enough.' Kate glared at her mother before marching out of the house and slamming the front door.

Relieved Richard had gone back across the lane to his house, Kate got into the car. Revving the engine, she sped down the lane, nearly running over a large ginger cat sauntering across her path. Cursing under her breath, she concentrated on putting as much distance as she could between her and her mother.

Chapter 15

As she joined the M5, her breathing slowed. Why was her mother such a pain the in arse? Who the hell was this, Joseph?'

Her thoughts went back to when Esther quit her job mid-pandemic. Something had happened, but Kate never found out what it was. She despised her mother and her inability to deal with life. When the NHS needed her the most, she was the nurse who let them down. She knew why Richard was so reluctant to get involved. The sequence of events came flooding back, sending her memory down a rabbit hole of unease.

When her mother didn't answer the phone after she'd called several times, Kate had rung Richard.

'Richard, can you check on Mum? I've had a message saying she's sick. I've been trying to ring, but she's not answering.'

He'd rung her back, saying he hadn't got a reply either, but she was home as the car was outside. Kate told him to use his spare key to let himself in.

'I can't. What if she's got the virus,' he'd said?

'Put a mask and gloves on. Just find out if she's okay,' she'd insisted, suddenly worried he would find her dead in her bed. Richard had found her mother. She wasn't dead but curled up in a ball.

Kate told Richard to call the doctor, but they weren't making house calls. Next, she told him to take her mother to the hospital, but he flatly refused. Kate had to travel up to deal with her, even though she wasn't in her bubble.

Even though it was prohibited, she'd had no choice but to make the journey. Kate remembered walking into the bedroom and finding her mother, just as Richard had described. She hadn't washed for days and the whole place stank. Kate threw open the windows and curtains even though it was cold.

'Mum, for God's sake, what's happened to you?' Kate was furious. Her boys were at home, with Shaun keeping an eye. She wasn't in a bubble with Shaun, so she silently prayed he would keep his distance. Her mother had caused all this stress, and she felt a deep resentment towards her. She kept asking 'What's the matter with you, Mum?' but her mother remained silent. Kate called to Evergreen, the ward where her mother was Ward Sister, to find out what happened, but the automated voice informed her that Evergreen had closed, and all the staff were redeployed.

Kate roused Esther and got her into the shower. She cleaned the house, headed to Tesco where she'd shopped for supplies. Then she'd rung the doctors and waited two hours for a reply.

'You can have a telephone consultation tomorrow morning,' the harassed girl at the other end had informed her.

'But I need help now,' Kate almost wailed at her.

'Do you want the appointment or not?' came the reply.

The doctor prescribed anti-depressants for Esther, which Kate had collected before packing her bag and leaving for home. She'd asked Richard to make sure she took her tablets. Reluctantly, he promised to monitor her, but that was only the start.

Richard rang to say the lights were on all night, but he couldn't rouse Esther during the day. He said he'd seen Esther in her garden at three in the morning pacing up and down. Still, Kate did nothing.

Eventually Grace, who didn't mince her words, rang Kate and told her to do something.

After two weeks of hoping the situation would improve, she went back and found her mother curled in a ball again. The empty fridge and empty gin bottles confirmed her worse fears. She'd stayed for a few days and got her mother cleaned up and eating again before leaving. Within two weeks, Grace was back on the phone.

'She's screaming in the night. The entire lane can hear her. She's scaring poor Mrs Braithwaite. When Richard went round, she was mumbling about someone called George, but there's no-one there.'

'Can't you increase the dose of her pills?'

'Can I do that without consulting the doctor?' Grace's voice was incredulous, as if she couldn't believe Kate's disinterest.

'Listen, I'm stuck here with the boys. I'll ring the doctor and ask.'

So once again, Kate rang the doctor, waited two hours to be told to leave her number. Eventually, new drugs were prescribed. Richard called to say they seemed to be working, thank God. Her mother was calm, but moribund, which was better than the wandering, screaming and sobbing.

'Just monitor her until lockdown eases. That shouldn't be more than a couple of weeks, then I'll come.' But the weeks turned into months and Esther slowly recovered all by herself. Kate's relationship with Grace and Richard was never the same. Kate knew Grace held her responsible for abandoning her mother. Grace remained oblivious to the painful reality of why Kate couldn't give a shit about her mother.

When lockdown lifted, Esther refused to go back to work and then retired on the grounds of ill health. Kate never had the luxury of being so pathetic. She had to be strong …there to mop up her mother's mess.

Refocussing, she sighed as she navigated her way up the motorway. Now here they were again. What the hell was going on? Kate really didn't have the energy to deal with any more drama. Her attention moved to the satnav which navigated her through Birmingham city centre. She hated driving in cities. There was so much traffic, and people never gave way; never gave credence to the fact you might not know where you were going. She found the hotel on the Hagley Road, a converted double-fronted Edwardian house with a modern two-story concrete block on the side.

Kate pulled into a parking space at the front. She had made good time, even though she couldn't remember the drive. Kate sat back and closed her eyes. God, she was so tired, and sick of being responsible. Was the shit hitting the fan again? Was this Joseph real and if he was, what was he doing with her mother? Getting out of the car, she was determined to take her mind off her mother with a large gin and tonic.

Chapter 16

Esther sat looking out at the weak winter sun on the back of the house, her journal on her lap. When she returned from Wales, she found solace and comfort in the familiar routine of writing every day. She'd started after her 'breakdown' and there were several filled notebooks hidden in the bottom draw of the bureau.

As she wrote, she untangled the threads of her experiences. The journals contained her innermost thoughts. About her mother, Ray and George, but also her guilt about Ozzy and Lily. If anything happened to her, would she want Kate to read these? What if Joseph was offering her some way to deal with the inner pain which was always there? A constant reminder of her life choices. Could he help rewrite the stories written within these journals? But that would put herself at risk. Was she strong enough to survive? For now, the journals helped her write her own version of the events that had shaped her life. As she looked at her frantic scribbling, that had nearly filled another exercise book, she wondered if she could rewrite her future. Putting the book aside, she listened to the silence.

One advantage of living in World's End was the quiet. Hardly any traffic came down the lane and it was one reason she bought her Victorian semi. Her previous life had been full of noise. Unanswered call bells pierced through the cacophony of the ward. The endless bleep from the drip counters and air beds; the constant hum of conversations, ringing telephones, squeaking trolleys and the sharp orders of hospital life. She never realised how the noise, commotion, and constant activity had drained her. But the noise that ended her career was when that noise meant the difference between life or death.

Esther sighed. Part of her missed being useful, but after what happened with George, she was no use to anyone. Instead, she was a burden. She knew she wasn't alone in having her life irrevocably altered by what she'd witnessed, but while others had moved forward, she couldn't.

It was over two weeks since Kate visited. There had been no further discussion about the power of attorney. A thick grey blanket descended on her. Here she sat, a shell of the person she had once been. But it was more than that. As she reached into late middle age, she realised she was anonymous. No one gave her a second glance unless she bumped into someone from the village. She was a burden to her child and invisible to the rest of the world.

Her physiotherapy appointments had been cancelled, so Richard had a reprieve and she had a legitimate reason to stop Joseph coming round. Apparently, there was a staff shortage.

As the doorbell rang, Esther carefully put down her foot and reached for her crutches. Sighing, she made her way down the hallway. I don't want to talk to anyone today. She hoped it was just Nick, the postman. Glancing at her reflection in the hall mirror, she realised what a mess she looked.

She ran a hand through her tangled mop of unruly, thick black hair. It desperately needed a cut. Her usually bright skin was the colour of weak coffee, with dark circles under her eyes. When she opened the door, she gasped in surprise for on the step stood Joseph, holding a bouquet of vibrant wildflowers.

'What on earth are you doing here?' she said, pulling her old Primark cardigan tighter. 'My physio appointments have been cancelled.'

'I've come to see how you are,' he said.

Esther stood thinking for a moment before glancing across the road to Richard's. Before the blinds twitched, she'd better let Joseph in. She moved to the side, giving him enough room to squeeze past.

Her rumpled sweatpants and lack of a shower made her feel uncomfortable and self-conscious. The sound of their footsteps echoed in the silent passageway as she followed him down the black and white tiled corridor to the back room.

'Not feeling too good today?' Joseph asked, sitting at the small table as Esther settled into her chair, wondering how he knew.

'No, not especially.'

'Are you in pain?'

'No, it's not that, just feeling down, you know. Everyone has their off days.'

He nodded.

'Shall I make a drink?' he offered. Esther didn't want him here.

'No thanks.'

Joseph sat quietly, looking at her. Why was he sitting down? She wanted him to leave. She felt awkward, not knowing what to say. After a minute, she felt compelled to say something.

'With all this time on my hands, I don't know what to do. I don't have a job anymore. I can't get around. If you must know, I feel like I'm stuck in a cage and can't do anything to help myself.' Why was she saying all this to someone she hardly knew?

'You are restricted now, but could you see this as an opportunity? Maybe you might get an idea of what you would like to do in the future if you consider where you've been.'

Esther found this question strange. 'What do you mean?' she asked.

'Esther, I know what worries you.' he paused. 'You know, I know about the deaths.'

'What the hell? I don't know what you are talking about. Who sent you?' Esther's heart was racing. Was he the police or investigator?

'No Esther, I am not the police.' As a cold sweat trickled down her back, Esther's panic grew when she realised he could read her thoughts.

'Get out!' she shouted. If I scream, will Richard hear me?

Joseph slowly stood and came towards her. She shrank back into the seat, putting her arms up to protect herself as he knelt beside her chair. Slowly, he took her hand and as he did so, something extraordinary happened. All the fear vanished in an instant.

'It's alright Esther. What if I told you that you could have a new life free from fear and regret? It would take a great deal of courage and trust from you.'

'What do you mean, what are you talking about?'

'We arrive in this world to learn, Esther. Through learning, we grow. Experiences may be positive or negative, depending on our reaction to them. Some lessons are hard and our ability to see the reason behind them is difficult. It also depends on how we see ourselves. The experiences you have had, Esther, have had a profound effect on you because you are a caring person. You absorb other people's pain. My purpose is to support you in making sense of the experiences. Help you understand.'

The world seemed to stop as Esther considered his words. Joseph let go of her hands and sat back on his heels, giving her time and space.

'What would I have to do?'

'There is a place we can go which is yours. In that place, you can go back and revisit parts of your life. Through this process, you'll discover a different way of looking at things, and you'll come to accept that you have no power over how others behave.'

'If I don't want to?'

Joseph looked her directly in the eye. 'Then nothing will ever change, and you will continue to be as you are,' he said sadly.

'If I agree, what happens?'

'You place your trust in me and take my hand.'

Esther sat frozen on the spot. What should she do? Should she trust this man or tell him to go? Did she want to spend the rest of her life feeling like a failure, or was Joseph offering a way out? Esther took a deep breath, closed her eyes and slowly reached out to take his hand.

Immediately, the room lost focus as familiar objects blurred and faded. Esther felt herself float. A calmness settled over her, and she wasn't afraid. The peace was profound, a stillness that permeated her being, like the effect of a strong sedative. She was moving fast. The feeling was like riding a log flume, but faster, with a rainbow of lights flashing behind her closed eyes as she descended rapidly before just as suddenly coming to a halt.

When she opened her eyes, she was standing in a wide-open space with Joseph beside her, still holding her hand. The light was translucent, with soft pastel shades. The air smelt fresh, as if there had just been an April shower. Esther was lightheaded and her heart raced again as she shivered, hot and cold all at once. But she wasn't afraid, merely curious.

'Where are we? What have you done? Is this an illusion, some sort of hypnosis?' she asked, her voice trembling. There was a wooden bench in the middle of the space and Joseph slowly led her there and indicated she should sit.

'This is a garden,' he said, simply.

'How did we get here? I was just sitting in my chair at home.' she sat carefully on the bench expecting pain from its hard wooden surface but there was none. She glanced down at her leg. There was no metal frame. Why was her leg better?

'Joseph, what's going on? I want to go back.' She cried, suddenly afraid.

'Just sit for a moment and let me explain. This is *your* garden.'

'This isn't a garden. It's a space floating in nothingness.' Her panic began slowly, but was gaining momentum as she glanced around. As she looked around her, she noticed a series of doors that hadn't been there before. 'What are those doors? Why didn't I see them before?'

'Behind each door is a memory, an uncomfortable memory. Each memory represents a trigger point in your life.'

Esther sat back against the bench, her stomach churning. Why was he making her think about things she didn't want to remember?

'I hope you have realised I want to help you. You are stuck in a mire of self-recrimination, regret and self-loathing. But that is not who you are, Esther. There is another you, a better version of yourself, where you will find peace. But before you can, you need to face what is behind those doors. With a sweeping hand, Joseph pointed to the three doors, his expression unreadable. They were distinct from one another. The shapes, woods, and designs were unique, each piece reflecting the past. The ivy, thick and green, clung to them, partially obscuring their features.

Joseph sat at an angle, looking at her with those fathomless blue eyes. 'Take your time Esther and if you feel able to go through a door, you will feel so much better afterward, but if you feel this is too much, we can go back.'

Esther sat wringing her hands, trying to decide what to do. Part of her knew what was behind the doors, but she was terrified and wanted to get the hell out of here.

'What happens if I decide not to go through the door?'

'We will return to your home, and I will leave you to your life.'

Esther's mind raced. She wondered if she was having another breakdown or if Joseph had drugged her. Was this some sort of weird trip? If she was tripping, then what had she got to lose? She got to her feet and moved toward a door. Just as she reached for the door handle and pushed, Joseph appeared by her side, intertwining his fingers with hers. Together, they pushed against the heavy wood and crossed the threshold.

Chapter 17

Joseph still held her hand as Esther looked around her and shuddered. She knew exactly where they were. She immediately turned to leave, but Joseph was standing between her and the door.

'I don't want to be here. Get out of my way.' She tried to push him aside, but he was solid and immovable.

'Esther, you have come this far. Try to stay.' His voice pleading. 'There is no way forward if you do not face this.' Esther stood for several minutes, pushing against Joseph until the voices of the people in the room behind her made her turn. A younger version of herself stood beside the doctor as they stared with horror at the bed.

Dr Graham's face was ashen. 'Frank, there is nothing to be done. You must let her go. This is torture. Can't you see what state she's in?'

The scene was visceral. As if it was yesterday. Esther remembered every moment with pinpoint clarity. The bed, the smell, the horror.

Her gaze moved to her stepfather. He had always seemed big, strong, but he had become a shadow of that man.

Esther remembered the phone call from Dr Graham, asking her to come. She'd left Kate with Ozzy and returned to a house she hadn't been back to for sixteen years. When she'd arrived, she faced horror beyond her comprehension. Esther watched herself approach the bedside as the scent of death filled Esther's senses. Her mother's flesh rotting as she lay unconscious in the bed.

'I will not kill her. Not my darling Marge. What you are suggesting is murder,' Frank screeched, before turning, slamming the door behind him.

Esther recalled the exact sequence of events as the doctor turned to her.

'Please give the word and I will do this.' Dr Graham's face was grey. 'I had no idea, Esther. I had no idea.'

'Nor did I,' Esther heard herself whispered reply.

As she watched standing by Joseph, who had taken her hand again, Esther heard the doctor's voice echoing down through the years.

'Esther, how did it come to this?' Dr Graham's voice filled with disgust and dread as he asked, 'How did this happen? I know Frank. We play golf, for God's sake.'

'I didn't know either. I haven't seen Mum for a long time, at least six years. You know about me and Frank.' Esther remembered, feeling the need to justify the reason for her lack of contact with her mother.

There was a small moan from the mound on the bed.

'Esther, there is only one thing to be done, but I need you to agree to this. I have never seen a case as bad as this. He must have been feeding her for years. She's got to be well over 36 stone. He can't have been able to move her. Now poor Marge, she's rotting in the bed.' His hand flew to his mouth, unable to carry on.

Esther watched herself take her mother's swollen hand in hers.

'I don't know if you can hear me. It's Esther, Mum.' There was no response from the wall of flesh on the bed. Her mother's bloated features made it difficult for Esther to recognise her.

'Mum, the doctor and I think it would be best if we helped you on your way.' The stench emanating from her mother's body was so overpowering that it made her want to gag. 'Mum, we want to help you go. Do you understand?' The minutes ticked by until suddenly Esther felt mother's fingers press into her hand.

'Oh God, I think she can hear us, Dr Graham?'

His hand was still to his mouth as he shook his head, tears in his eyes.

Esther looked back at her mother and a wave of pity swept over her as she gasped. 'Mum, I'm so sorry. I didn't know. I've let you down?' A sob rose in her throat. After another long silence, Esther whispered.

'Do you want us to help you, Mum?' She waited as Dr Graham stood beside her. There was no sign from her mother and Esther was about to remove her hand when Esther felt that slight pressure as her mother tried to grip her hand.

Esther leant forward and spoke directly into her mother's ear.

'Are you sure, Mum? You know what we mean, don't you? We'll give you an injection and you will go to sleep and not wake again.' Again, the pressure, more urgent this time.

Esther watched Dr Graham, his expression serious, as he reached for his bag. The glint of metal catching her eye as he pulled out a syringe and an ampule of morphine. Together they turned her mother's head, searching for a vein.

Esther couldn't take any more. Her eyes, wide and glistening with unshed tears, were fixed on Joseph in a silent plea.

'Please, can we go?' He nodded silently as they turned away from the scene and back through the door into the endless space.

Esther clutched her chest, wanting to vomit. She looked for the bench, but it was replaced by a table and chairs. Closing her eyes, she didn't want to see or speak to anyone. She didn't want to think about what she'd just seen again. At that moment, she hated Joseph with such intensity she wanted to hurt him, really hurt him.

'Esther,' a voice spoke her name. A voice so familiar it reached down deep within her. She opened her eyes and saw someone was sitting at the table. Someone she recognised immediately. She was young again. There was no hideous wall of flesh. She looked like Esther remembered her before she married Frank. When it was just the two of them.

As Esther approached, Margery stood and held out her arms to her daughter. Esther sobbed as she went willingly to her mother.

'Esther, you had to relive that so that I could tell you it was not your fault. Any of it.' Esther went to speak, but her mother held up her hand.

'Let me finish. I know I shouldn't have let Frank send you away. I have always felt guilty about that, but he had a hold on me, Esther. A hold I couldn't escape. He started the feeding slowly, but overtime I became so addicted to food I couldn't control what he was putting in my mouth. I wanted it, but as the years passed, the amount increased until I couldn't move.'

'But Mum, you were only forty-seven.' Esther wailed.

'Esther,' her mother whispered, 'I know you have spent years blaming yourself for not coming to see me. For feeling responsible for killing me. But listen to me. I was so relieved when you found me. I couldn't wait to leave. To die. I was in so much pain. Even though I was disgusted with myself, I couldn't do anything to stop Frank. You must let go of the guilt you feel.' Margery held tightly onto Esther as if she never wanted to let her go. 'Know that I love you Esther and I am so proud of the woman you have become. The memory of my beautiful daughter was my strength through the darkest times. Though I can't undo the past and relive our lives without Frank, I have found peace now. Maybe I had to go through that experience to realise that every one of us is a beautiful person inside, regardless of what we look like on the outside.'

'You never told me why we were on the streets when Frank found us. Why your parents threw you out? It was because of my dad, wasn't it?'

Margery looks Esther directly in the eye, her voice sad. 'Yes, my love.'

'It's because I'm mixed race, isn't it?'

Margery nodded. 'Your grandfather just couldn't accept it. I was so young. He wanted to go to the police. I tried to stop him, but he got George, your father deported. The last time I saw him, he was being led up the gangplank in handcuffs. But know this, I loved him with all my heart and treasured the gift he left me. When we were rejected by my father, I vowed to keep you safe with every breath in my body. If it hadn't been for the Salvation Army, we would have stayed on the streets. I regret marrying Frank, even though he appeared to solve our problems. A beacon of hope that turned out to be false.'

Margery released Esther and together they sat at the table.

'Remember when you were little? Frank piled our plates high.' Esther nodded as she clung to her mother's hands. 'You know, I think it was something to do with his childhood. They never had enough to eat, you see. Still, that's no excuse, is it? But know this Esther I forgive him, and I forgive you. You didn't kill me, I killed myself. You just released me from my living hell, which was the greatest gift you could have given me. Thank you so much for releasing me, my darling girl.' Her mother turned to look up at Joseph.

'Joseph, I appreciate this opportunity to speak to Esther. Before I leave, remember this, my child. My love for you has been a constant, unwavering presence throughout my life, and it continues. A love as deep as the ocean and as warm as the summer sun. Now go back and live your life.' As Esther wept with relief, her head cast down; she didn't see her mother leave. When she looked up moments later, she was gone. A great weight lifted from Esther's shoulders, but there was a deep yearning for her mother. Joseph came over and rested his hand gently on her shoulder.

As Esther looked around, the door to her mother's room had become a stunning rose-covered arch. A breathtaking cascade of her mother's beloved crimson roses, their sweet fragrance filling the air. Great banks of flowers were growing and spreading around the arch, filling the space with vibrant colours and the beauty of it took her breath away.

'See Esther, your garden is growing. Joseph was smiling down at her. 'How do you feel? Do you see what opening doors you have so firmly shut can do?'

As Esther turned to Joseph, the air began to shimmer and vibrate.

Chapter 18

Esther tried not to think about her encounter with her mother. A weight had lifted and she no longer blamed herself for her mother's death. The problem was the circumstances of that revelation. Esther had awoken sitting back in her chair, but Joseph was nowhere to be seen, even when she called for him. Was it a dream or had it really happened? Her mind was a jumble of uncertainty. Before the entire episode faded, she wrote it down in her journal. Just as she finished, the doorbell rang. It was Richard. Unable to contain herself, she had told him the whole story. Richard had little to say, and she immediately regretted telling him. Richard decided he needed help. Things were not going well again.

Grace received a summons from Richard to come and discuss the ongoing concerns he had about over the road, as his text put it.

'There's something funny going on.' Richard leant his back against the expensive marble countertop in his expensive teal kitchen as Grace balanced precariously on a too-high stool at the island.

'Could I have a cup of coffee please Richard before you start?' Grace swivelled backwards and forwards on her stool, her petite frame reminding Richard of a child.

'I'm just saying, that's all,' Richard busied himself with his Nespresso.

'Look, I know Esther has her issues and since her accident, she's been more reclusive, but what is it really to do with us?'

Richard tutted,

'That daughter of hers is useless. After what she told me when I popped in yesterday, I think we need to act swiftly to avert another crisis.'

'So, what is it that's worrying you exactly?'

'Well,' Richard placed a tiny cup of ridiculously strong coffee in front of Grace, who interrupted his train of thought.

'Can I have a bigger cup, please? I'll be high as a kite if I drink that.' Grace pushed the cup back across the island, causing Richard to tut.

Once he'd decanted her coffee into a mug and added hot water and milk, he suggested they move onto the sofa. Grace carefully negotiated her descent from the stool and joined him in the breakfast room next to the kitchen. His settee was built for its looks and not for comfort, Grace thought as she lowered herself down onto its hard base. The fabric was velvet and a cornucopia of colour. It must have cost a fortune.

'Now, Richard, do you think we should interfere?' she asked as she removed some cushions so she could sit back.

'Grace, we must. Otherwise, this will spiral out of control.' He waved his arm dramatically, as if to make his point.

'What makes you say that?' Grace asked

'She was talking bollocks, pardon my French.'

'What do you mean?'

'She was going on about her mother.'

'And that's significant. Why?' Grace leaned forward and took a sip from her mug before putting it carefully back on the small occasional table beside her. It was too hot.

'She said she'd realised she'd got it all wrong. That her mother loved her.' He paused for more dramatic effect. 'She's had some sort of experience. I know her mother died years ago. Esther left home at sixteen and hadn't spoken to her mother in years before she died. Something about an evil stepfather. Now she'd had some sort of experience,' he waved his hand and rolled his eyes, 'her mother has forgiven her. For what, I do not know.'

'What was this experience?' Grace tried her coffee again.

'She wouldn't elaborate, but she was all twitchy about it.'

'And this is significant. Why?' Grace repeated herself.

'It's all to do with that Joseph fella she keeps banging on about,' he whispered conspiratorially.

Grace looked at Richard with more interest.

'This is the man she insists carried her down the mountain and gave her a lift to the hospital, right?'

'The very same,' Richard said.

'So, what's his involvement with the mother business?' Grace needed details.

'Esther said she has Joseph to thank. Couldn't get any more out of her than that.'

Grace sat back, thinking. She'd became friendly with Esther not long after they moved to the village. She knew Esther had been through a hard time, as had she, and that somehow bonded them.

Grace was through the other side of her trauma, mostly. She had come to terms with the past with the help of Ella, Hope and the therapist, but Esther was still struggling. Grace did not know the specifics, but thought Esther carried some heavy burdens around with her. What Richard was saying was interesting. Was she unlocking her past like Grace had compelled herself to do?

'Do you think she needs sectioning?' Richard asked energetically.

'Oh, for God's sake, Richard. Don't be so dramatic,'

'She could have schizophrenia. They see people, don't they? Colin had a cousin who was schiz, and they had a mare with him.'

'Honestly, Richard, I think we need to explore this a bit more before spot diagnosing Esther.'

'Just saying,' Richard said, turning slightly away and retrieving his coffee, 'I'm showing concern, that's all.'

'Now don't get huffy,' Grace patted his arm. 'Have you heard anything from Kate?'

'No, and not likely to. She's as much use as a chocolate teapot.'

'True. Maybe I'll call round and have a chat with Esther. We can compare notes and decide if we need to ring Kate. What do you think?'

'Sounds like a plan. Would you like a Florentine? I'm trying a new recipe.' Richard said, getting up and moving back towards the kitchen.

The next morning, Grace knocked on the door and waited patiently for Esther to answer. She hadn't texted to say she would call round, as she wanted to see how Esther was. If she pre-warned her, she felt she wouldn't get a true picture of what was going on. She waited, but nothing happened, so she knocked louder in case Esther hadn't heard her. Grace was about to give up when she heard the key in the door and as it swung open, Grace was pleased to see Esther looking well. Her cheeks were flushed, and she looked freshly showered and dressed.

'Sorry to call on the off chance. Just thought I'd swing by and see how you are.' Grace offered her some flowers from Tesco.

'Whoa thanks, Grace,' Esther went to take the flowers, but showed no signs of inviting Grace in.

'How are you doing, Esther?'

'Good, thanks.'

Esther was glancing behind her as if there was someone else there.

'Have you got visitors?' Grace asked.

'Umm, now isn't a good time,' Esther said.

'That's fine. Could I just pop in and get that casserole dish of mine? I need it tonight.' She moved up the step, taking Esther by surprise. She instinctively moved to the side to let Grace in.

'Is it in the kitchen?' Grace moved with purpose down the hallway, with Esther as hot on her heels, as fast as she could manage. As Grace entered the back room, she noticed there were two cups on the small table in the corner and before Esther came in, she quickly touched one. It was still hot. She glanced round the room, but there was no sign of anyone there. As she looked out of the window, and she thought she glimpsed someone by the greenhouse. Esther appeared in the doorway, glancing anxiously around as if expecting someone to be there. She seemed relieved when there wasn't. They both looked out into the garden. Was that someone by the back gate? Grace wished she'd worn her glasses. Although she hated wearing them, she had to admit her eyesight was getting worse.

'Esther, did you have someone here?'

'No, no. Why would you think that?' Her tone was defensive.

'Well, there are two cups on the table, and I thought I saw someone in the garden.'

'Grace, if I had a visitor I would tell you and anyway, it's none of your business, really.' Grace moved quickly into the kitchen, found her dish on the drainer. She picked it up and turned to leave.

'I'll leave you to it, shall I?' Grace said, her smile not reaching her eyes.

Esther was distracted as she stood looking up the garden.

'Don't worry, I'll see myself out.' Grace needed to update Richard. She didn't care if Esther saw her as she crossed the road straight to his house, rather than her own.

She quickly explained as she made her way upstairs. Two cups of coffee. The possibility of someone being in the garden. In Richard's spare room, whose side window gave a view of the top of Esther's garden, they peered out to see Esther was hopping up the path on her crutches, calling someone. They craned to look, but could see no one. Richard and Grace quickly went to the front landing and were just in time to see a white Range Rover, disappearing down the lane.

'There's something funny going on. I need to ring Kate,' Grace said, and Richard nodded.

Chapter 19

Stuck on the M25, Kate hit the steering wheel in frustration. She would never get back in time to take Jack to Scouts. Maybe she could call Claire and ask if she could take him with Oscar. Was a half hour meeting in North London worth three hours of driving. It was questionable whether she would get an order, anyway. She hated working for the company which pressurised her to sell as many overpriced blinds and curtains as she could to make enough money to survive. As there was an offer on, there were a ton of visit requests. The offer promised twenty per cent off, but the customer ended paying the same price as the blinds were originally.

It was pathetic how gullible people were, but Kate was good at her job. She could chat and build up a rapport before going in for the kill. It was a quality she had inherited from her dad, who could hold the attention of a room as soon as he walked in.

Even if he wasn't a good-looking man, his easy manner and charm won people over. A lump formed in her throat as the unwanted memory of his death caught her by surprise. Her stupid fucking mother. She shook her head vigorously, hoping to break free from the repetitive cycle of her thoughts, but they turned to Ray instead.

Kate couldn't believe her pathetic mother, who stayed with Ray until his death. How many times she'd tried to make her see that Ray was a manipulative bastard, but she'd done nothing to get them out of there. Her mother was scared, scared of Ray. The New Year's Eve fiasco, at least, got her out.

Shaun saved her from her miserable life with Ray. But Shaun proved to be an utter disappointment when it came to supporting his family. Shaun married her when she got pregnant, but it was a mistake. After a couple of years of watching his mates having fun, he decided to be part of it again. He spent money they didn't have down the pub instead of paying the mortgage. Her job at least gave her the opportunity to be someone other than Jack or Ben's mum. But it came at the cost of trying to juggle family life and a full-time job with no help. Now she'd got rid of Shaun. It was doubly difficult. Her musing was interrupted by her phone.

'This is Kate.' She said in her professional voice.

'It's Grace, do you have a minute to talk?' Kate's inwardly groaned. What the fuck did she want? The last time Grace rang Kate was to tell her to come and sort her mother out. She'd didn't need this, she really didn't.

'Grace, what can I do for you?'

'Do you know about the man visiting your mother?' Direct and to the point, as always.

'Yes. What's this got to do with me?'

'Richard says it's the same man who rescued her from the mountain. I'm telling you, Kate, as both Richard and I are worried he may try to scam her.'

'Why would he want to scam her?'

'Well, you hear of these horror stories of woman meeting men who seduce them, then empty their bank accounts.' Kate knew of Grace's past concerning abusive men. She's overacting, Kate thought.

'I'll ring Mum and ask her what's going on.' I'm in no mood to get into this now.

'Thank you, Kate. You know Richard and I are here to help, but there are limits, and you are her family.' There was a long pause before Grace asked Kate something she had not expected.

'Kate, why do you hate your mother?'

Letting out a long breath, Kate said,

'It's a long story.'

'Well, I think both Richard and I would like some sort of explanation.'

There was another long pause before Kate spoke in clipped, short sentences.

'She's responsible for killing my father.' That silenced Grace for a moment before she continued.

'That's quite an accusation, if you don't mind me saying. How did she kill your father?'

'Why don't you ask her?' Kate spat. Grace held her breath, shocked by the venom in Kate's voice. Kate was speaking again.

'Then she got together with that bastard Ray.'

'The second husband?'

'They never got married. He was a manipulative little narcissist who wormed his way into our lives. He met Mum at the hospital, and he prayed on her pathetic gullible nature and made our lives hell, if you must know.'

'I'm sorry, Kate. I know how that feels.'

'Do you, do you really? He moved himself in and wouldn't let anyone come to the house. Mum was completely taken in by him. Do you know he made me clean the house from top to bottom every weekend so I could go out on Saturday for a couple of hours with my friends? He'd wait for my favourite weekly TV show to come on and turn it over. She never stood up to him. Took his side when he accused me of stealing food or money.'

'So, your mother's relationship with Ray worsened your relationship?'

'Yes.' She coughed, suddenly embarrassed, and changed the subject quickly before Grace could respond.

'Listen, I'll ring and ask her about this Joseph. Grace, I must go. I have a work call.' Kate pressed the 'end call' button on her display, and then let out a frustrated scream. Her face flushed with anger, as the man in the car beside her, stuck in the same traffic queue, raised an eyebrow. A wave of uncertainty wash over her as she considered the implications of her choice to confide in Grace. The thought of Grace and Richard scrutinising her private life made her cringe, and she recoiled in disgust. She leaned back in her seat, her gaze fixed on the dusty roof of the car in front. The quiet hum of the engine was a constant background noise. The cold air made her breath visible.

Perhaps there was a silver lining to the situation. Maybe they'd understand her a bit more now. Kate was sure her mother had never told either of them the mess she'd made of their lives by getting involved with Ray or what she'd done to Dad. A lump formed in her throat, as the ache of betrayal brought tears to her eyes as she thought about her poor father again. She would never forgive her mother for leaving him, leaving him when he most needed them. But would Grace take her words literally? Neither of them would want to help if they thought there was some truth in her accusations. How would they view Esther now? Had she just incriminated her mother?

Chapter 20

A few weeks later, when Kate got home from a night away for work, she found Shaun asleep on the couch and the boys playing in Ben's room. She asked, what they had eaten, and they'd got themselves a pizza. Dad had been busy on his phone and told them to get on with it and not to bother him. Recognising that tone, they left him alone. Kate wanted to kill him. Lazy bastard.

Kate shook him awake.

'WTF, Shaun. Couldn't you even bother to get your own sons some food?' She spat.

'Sorry babe, feeling a bit out of sorts. Didn't want to pass it on.'

'For one, don't call me babe and for another, tell me where my maintenance is?'

'Bit short this month. Work's slow.' He sat up and scratched his bald head.

'Oh, so it's got nothing to do with that gig you went to at the weekend, then?'

He looked up at her, his tone accusing, 'How'd you know about that?'

'It was on Beefy's insta.'

'Well, that not why. Like I said, work's slow.' Shaun looked down, shuffling his feet.

'Why is work slow? I thought you were working on that big estate?'

'They had to lay a few off. Money's run out.' Shaun mumbled.

'You got fired, didn't you?' she shouted. 'You use-less lump of shit. What happened? Too many sick days?'

'I don't have to listen to this. I'll try to get you some cash by the end of the week,' he said, getting up abruptly, retrieving his coat and heading for the door. Kate sighed and helped herself to a large glass of wine from the bottle she'd hid in the laundry cupboard where he wouldn't find it. Anything that was left out, he had.

After an awful night's sleep, she lay in her bed as the alarm roused her at seven, unable to motivate herself to get up. As she hauled herself out of bed, she exhaled. Kate's routine was to get as much done before she attempted to get the boys up. The stress of the last-minute dash out of the door was drain-ing, a daily challenge that had to be endured. That's when she missed having someone around to help corral the boys, but had Shaun ever helped?

The coffee was running low. This was the last coffee pod. Kate wrote it on the whiteboard on the fridge. She felt remarkably tired. Wasn't she supposed to feel rejuvenated after a night's sleep? Instead her body had emptied. She stared out of the window that needed cleaning at the lawn which needed mowing. It was all too much. But her bloody mother was prodding her for atten-tion. What should she do? Kate sank into the chair and put her head in her hands. As if reading her thoughts, her phone pinged. It was her mother.

The text message told Kate she was having the metal frame from her leg removed. Kate bit her bottom lip, trying to decide how guilty she felt. She hadn't rung as Grace had suggested. Kate didn't want to get drawn into her mother's issues again, not this time. The whole situation was one to be avoided. I have enough to contend with; she told herself. Shaun playing silly buggers with the main-tenance was causing her so much stress.

Her inner voice said her mother would be fine. She was only having the frame removed. Sitting back in the chair, Kate wondered if she could use this opportunity to her advantage? Would a few days away give her a break? If Shaun came to look after the boys, Jack could work on him about the football kit. He'd have to pay for food and anything the boys wanted, leaving her wages safe in the bank. He obviously wasn't working, so he'd have no excuse. She picked up her phone and messaged him.

'I need you to look after the boys again for a few days next week. Mum's got to go to hospital for an operation and I need to look after her when she comes out. Be here by eight on Thursday morning. You'll have to get the food. I'm broke.'

'Can't you get someone else?' came the reply.

'You're their dad, and it's about time you acted like one.' Nothing came back, so she knew he'd come.

Getting up, she popped two pieces of bread in the toaster before opening the dishwasher to unload its contents. Then she messaged her mother. The thought of a few days away lifted her mood, and she went upstairs to get the boys up with a spring in her step. She could also find out who this elusive Joseph was and see him off.

Esther looked at the letter from the hospital again, confirming her operation to have the frame removed. It was a week tomorrow. She stood leaning against the sink looking out at the fence, which desperately needed painting again. The daffodils turned their golden heads to the weak February sunshine. Despite their strained relationship, she had let Kate know she was going back into the hospital. Kate was now officially Esther's next of kin. She had agreed to the power of attorney, bringing a sense of relief. Esther suspected Kate's motivation was more to do with her inheritance than any genuine concern.

She raised an eyebrow when she got the message from Kate, saying she would come to look after her. Did she want her in the house? The operation was straightforward, and Esther could be home the same day. Why was Kate coming? She must have an ulterior motive. She couldn't risk Kate knowing she was having strange experiences again. Esther had genuine concern about how her daughter might view this. Was giving her power of attorney over her health a good idea? Would Kate use this to wreak revenge? Shaking her head, Esther tried to dispel such gloomy thoughts. No, she thought, just let her come and play it by ear.

Esther needed to avoid Joseph at all costs. She'd had no contact with him since her strange experience in the garden. An enormous sense of unease pervaded her thoughts. Had he put something in her tea? A psychedelic drug which had caused the whole weird encounter. Esther had an unnerving feeling that the reconciliation with her mum was just the start of Joseph's plans. There had been other doors in that garden.

She felt free from the dark memory of her mother's death. No, she didn't want to see Joseph again for a while to give her mind time to process and recover from what had happened. This was not the time to allow Joseph to come anywhere near her. She needed to concentrate on getting her physical health better. Better Kate didn't meet him either.

Now, how was she going to get to the hospital?

What about Richard? She hadn't seen either Richard or Grace for a while. Not since Grace stormed in and Joseph vanished. He must have left through the side gate. Why would he not want to meet her friends? This was getting ridiculous. She'd message Richard on WhatsApp, hoping he'd agree to take her. If something was up, she'd know. Turning around, she found her phone and sent the message.

As she waited for a reply, she made a cup of coffee. Carefully navigating to avoid spilling her drink, she made her way into the back room and settled into her chair. The birds were pecking hopefully at the bird table. Although she hadn't put out any food for them in weeks, she hoped that the warmer weather would tempt some juicy worms out of their hiding places.

Her phone pinged. 'Sorry Esther, I cannot take you this time,' came the reply. The feeling of uneasiness was warranted then. What had she done to upset him? It must be something to do with Grace coming to the house. She couldn't ask Grace as Ella used the car on Thursdays to see her clients in Worcester. What was she going to do now? She'd get a taxi. But she wouldn't get away with it that easily.

Her phone pinged with a message from Joseph offering to take her. How the hell did he know? The message from Joseph made her realise he hadn't gone away. Part of her didn't want to speak to him for fear of raking up more of the past. This wasn't a time for facing more terrible memories. What to do. After several moments of indecision she replied.

'I don't want to visit the garden again, Joseph, but I need a lift to the hospital.'

She would make sure the conversation did not stray into unwanted territory. He couldn't do anything if she was going to the hospital for an operation and she needed a lift.

On Thursday, Joseph stood on the doorstep. He looked different, as if he had aged somehow. There were lines on his face that she hadn't noticed before. He looked thinner, and had lost the glow that she always thought emanated from him.

'Joseph, are you okay? You look different today.' He smiled a sad smile before picking up the bag, which was ready by the door. If anyone asked Esther to describe Joseph, she would have difficulty determining his age, his physical appearance, but the way he calmed and cared for her was real. The journey was mercifully quiet, but as they neared the hospital, Esther's tensed.

As Joseph pulled up outside, Esther's stomach churned. Joseph gently placed his hand over hers before getting out of the car in search of a wheelchair. Esther shuddered as a ripple of fear took hold. Going back to a hospital where she had once worked bought a variety of feelings. Joseph made her jump as he tapped on the window and pointed to the chair. He had a knack of appearing without a sound.

She opened the door and allowed him to help her settle in the chair. He got her bag from the boot, and she held it on her lap. Would anyone recognise her? Would anyone ask her about why she'd left? Questions she didn't want to answer.

'All will be well, Esther,' Joseph whispered in her ear. She breathed deeply, allowing the anxiety to move out of her body. As they arrived at the trauma and orthopaedic ward, Esther said a brief goodbye to Joseph as a healthcare assistant whisked away her to undergo her pre-operative checks.

Esther sat in her hospital gown on the uncomfortable plastic mattress, which made the sheets slip and slide. She fiddled with the hem as she waited anxiously to go to the theatre. She wasn't worried about the operation more about the experience of being in the hospital. So far there was no-one she recognised. But the porter who came to take her down to theatre gave her a second glance, as if he knew her from somewhere. He made no comment. The theatre nurse and anaesthetist were too busy to notice her. The same calm, practiced reassurance was given to every person who entered the anaesthetic room. A long-forgotten face materialised vividly just as she drifted into unconsciousness, counting down from ten. With it came a memory she had buried deep within her subconscious.

Chapter 21

As the anaesthetic clouded Esther's consciousness, she felt herself falling, as a myriad of soft lights swirled around her. As the sensation slowed, she found herself back in the place Joseph called her garden. And there was Joseph. Joseph, whose skin seemed to shine. The weariness she had seen early had completely disappeared. Her throat tightened as she realised there was no escape.

'Why am I here? I don't want to be here.' Her voice was only a whisper, which echoed in the vastness of the surrounding space. 'I told you I didn't want to come here again.' She almost shouted at him. 'How dare you take advantage of my weakened state to bring me here?'

'I did not bring you here, Esther. Your subconscious has. Deep down, you must want to be here.'

'You're saying I came back of my own volition? Well, I can assure you I didn't.' She sat down abruptly on the wooden bench.

'Whilst I facilitated your first visit, to show you the garden and the doors. You have brought yourself this time.' She didn't believe him for a second. Why would she put herself through more pain?

As she looked, the archway around her mother's door had all but disappeared amongst the profusion of flowers. The garden extended outwards but stopped abruptly as it butted against the next door, a door she knew Joseph was hoping she might go through.

Joseph went to the bench, which once more stood in the centre of the semicircle created by the doors. As Esther looked around her, she noticed two more doors had appeared on the opposite side, but they were different. They weren't solid as the others were. Those heavy solid wooden doors had weight and size. No, these were barely visible, merely a shape merging with the surroundings. Joseph followed her gaze.

'Do not concern yourself with those doors for now, Esther. I am unsure what they represent.'

Turning towards the middle wooden door on the other side with its ornate carving visible through the strands of ivy which surrounded it, Esther saw it was not as old as her mother's door. The memory Joseph wanted her to revisit was more recent.

'You remembered something as you were going to sleep, Esther. Would you like to talk about it?' Esther couldn't speak. The memory came flooding in unbidden. Tears filled her eyes as the image of that little body brought a surge of anguish, which was almost too much to bear.

'I can't, Joseph. Please don't make me.'

Joseph nodded. 'You have buried this memory deep, but it has profoundly affected how you treat yourself. But if this is too much, then we will wait.'

Esther's legs were weak as if they would give way, so she moved towards the bench, sinking down next to Joseph, her head in her hands.

'Esther, you have made it this far.' Some part of her knew he was right. Consumed by a feeling of inevitability, she dragged herself to her feet and moved towards the door.

'If I want to leave, you must let me,' Esther said. Joseph nodded.

Taking a deep breath, she pushed open the heavy door and was immediately met with a cacophony of sound. The Unit was filled with a constant hum of medical equipment, alarms, and the beeping of monitors. Shuffling feet were interspersed with the muffled, anxious voices of healthcare workers speaking through layers of PPE. As Esther watched her colleagues navigate a sea of complex tasks and urgent decisions, the feeling of her own uselessness rose like a wave from the pit of her stomach. She had been drafted here from the frailty ward.

Extra beds and ventilators made it difficult to move around the bed spaces and Esther could see herself wedged between the wall and a bed. It held the body of a small boy, George.

During her early career, she had worked on acute surgical wards, but that was years ago. But she'd found herself faced with the almost impossible task of trying to dredge up long forgotten knowledge when COVID hit. She had been terrified.

On this day, there was one critical care nurse to every three patients. Esther had been assigned to look after George, a seven-year-old who had been placed in the adult ICU because there was no room on the paediatric acute ward for him. His condition was stable, and he was coping well with the tight mask, forcing oxygen into his small body. But Esther was hypervigilant, not able to relax for one moment.

As she stood trembling with Joseph, she saw Sally, the critical care nurse, check his chart. 'Esther, he needs his Dex. Can you get it, and I'll check it for you?' An icy dread passed through her as she watched herself, lost in layers of PPE, move towards the drug cupboards.

Esther watched herself hold the prescription chart and open the fridge where the dexamethasone syrup was kept. She watched herself measure the dose into a small plastic administration cup. Replacing the bottle back into the fridge, she turned back to the bedside, looking for the critical care nurse to check the drug.

'Esther, where's the bottle?' Sally queried, 'Oh never mind give it to him, anyway. Watch his stats when you take off his mask and give him a drink, will you?'

Esther watched as she approached the small boy on the bed. He was propped up high with several pillows. His face was red with a sheen of sweat and his breath laboured. Carefully removing the mask, talking to him all the while, Esther took the syringe of medicine and squeezed it into the corner of his mouth. Then she gave him some sips of water, but he coughed, and the monitor bleeped. Esther quickly replaced the mask and said she would give him more to drink in a few moments. As she gently wiped his forehead, she watched his eyes close once again.

Her heart ached for this poor child, unable to be comforted by his family. His only help came from an unrecognisable person clothed in masks, face shields, gowns and gloves. She sat holding his small hand for a while until suddenly his monitor alarmed. Esther watched herself jump to her feet. The feeling of pure panic radiated from her, right into the core of her being. The sensations transferred to her as she stood shaking next to Joseph.

Doctors and nurses appeared from nowhere and Esther was moved aside so they could get to the small figure fighting for breath.

'His stats are crashing. We're going to have to intubate. Cricoid pressure nurse, get some sedation into him. It's on his chart.' A consultant anaesthetist barked at the critical care nurse. Nurses rushed past her, so she moved further away. Esther watched as the child had a tube inserted into his windpipe and was hooked up to a ventilator. Her feeling of helplessness was profound.

'Right, let's get him stabilised. Sally, stay with him, please.' The consultant instructed the critical care nurse.

'Esther, see to Mr Cornwell, please. Do his obs for me and check his saline. He's due another bag.' There was no recrimination in her voice, but Esther watched as she dragged herself to the bed next to where George lay. 'Esther, when you've done that, we'll need to contact George's parents. Can you find the contact details and get the iPad?' Sally called over to her.

Esther was numb as she went to see to Mr Cornwell and retrieve the iPad from the office. The PPE shielded her reactions from the rest of the staff, but she was devastated. What had she done wrong? Esther watched herself crumple, as any confidence she had drained away, but she knew this was not the end.

Joseph touched her arm, showing they should leave. Esther was confused and felt she needed to stay to support herself through the next part of the journey.

Chapter 22

Back in the garden, Esther went and sat on the bench. She doubled over and rocked from side to side.

'You needed a break, Esther. Let's talk about what happened next before we go back.'

Esther was quiet, so Joseph sat patiently by her side until the words formed.

'Sally, the critical care nurse, was swamped with work, so she asked me to get in touch with George's mum.' Esther stopped, the weight of her fear pressing down on her, making it impossible to go on.

'That was very difficult for you, wasn't it, Esther?' Joseph sat next to her, close enough for her to feel his warmth but a respectful distance to allow her space.

Esther nodded bleakly. 'I had many chats with his mum over the next few days, trying to stay in touch and keep them updated. She told me about George and his mischievous nature. She kept talking about when he got better, all the things they would do. It was hard. He wasn't doing well. She kept asking to come in. I had to keep telling her about the strict restrictions. She got angry and shouted at me.' Again, Esther was silent. Moments passed until Joseph got to his feet.

'We need to go back and watch this play out, Esther. Only then will you realise the truth.' Esther turned to him, suddenly angry. 'I know the truth. I killed him.'

Joseph stood and held out his hand. Esther stayed sitting on the bench. Why would he want to make her relive this? It was agony. It was the one thing above all else that haunted her dreams and occupied every waking moment.

'No Joseph. I can't.' Joseph sat back down, and silence descended once more. They didn't speak for a long time. Esther wanted to leave and never have to look at Joseph again. It was overwhelming. This was pushing the boundaries beyond what was acceptable. This was cruel, harsh, unnecessary. What was he hoping to gain from making her go back?

Another thought pushed its way into her mind. She sat up suddenly. But had she got it wrong? Was there another explanation? What was Joseph trying to show her? She stood and walked purposely towards the door. Joseph was taken by surprise, and jumping to his feet, chased after her.

In the dimly lit critical care unit, the soft hum of machines continued to punctuate the heavy silence. George lay, frail and pale, motionless in a bed surrounded by the tangle of tubes and wires. The ventilator hissed rhythmically, struggling to maintain the breath that George's weakened lungs could no longer manage on their own. The monitor's display showed fluctuating numbers, a silent testament to the battle raging within his body.

In a nearby chair sat his mother, Dawn. Pain edged into every fibre of her being, holding onto her child's tiny hand, as if this touch alone could anchor him to life. Only Dawn had been allowed in. George's dad sat in the waiting room. He couldn't face seeing his son anyway, not like this. The burden of watching her son lose his fight for life rested solely on Dawn. The tiny woman with thin hair would not leave George's side and she'd been there for hours.

'Do something, Esther. You said he was getting better. Why did you say that?' She rocked backward and forwards. 'You've only let me in because you've given up, haven't you? You're not even trying to save him!' Her anguish was palpable. Esther stood near, feeling completely and utterly helpless.

She watched herself lean over and speak through the mask, 'Dawn, you need to take a break. Get a drink. You're no good to him like this. You need to be strong.'

'Don't you tell me what I need to be? How would you know how it feels?' Suddenly the alarms rang out on the ventilator as the consultant and Sally ran over.

'Esther, his pressures look at his pressures. For God's sake, what have you been doing? Get her out of here' pointing at Dawn. Esther tried to drag Dawn away, but she would not move. In the end, the consultant shouted at her.

'You need to leave, you are in the way, or we won't be able to help your son.' His voice of authority moved Dawn from her seat as he pushed her chair aside, and went to George.

Esther let Dawn into the decontamination room and told her to wait there. She couldn't decide if she should stay or go back to help. But what help was she? Why hadn't she noticed his pressures dropping? What happened to the alarm?' As she looked through the glass window into the unit, the registrar indicated they should flip him over onto his stomach. The consultant straightened up after listening to George's chest and shook his head. He moved to the ventilator and changed the settings, his face a mix of determination and sorrow, knowing that his efforts would not be enough. 'Get the mother back in.'

Dawn returned to the bedside, visibly shaking. George's small chest rose and fell irregularly, each breath a painful reminder of the cruel grip of COVID. His once bright eyes were half closed, fluttering weakly, barely conscious of the world around him. The room was thick with unspoken fears and a weight of helplessness. Despite the best efforts of the medical team, the disease has progressed, leaving little room for hope.

As the minutes passed, the child's breathing became more laboured, the intervals between each breath growing longer. The doctors and nurses gathered around the bed with the shared understanding that the end was near. Esther watched herself as Sally held her hand - that tiny gesture of kindness, the most heartbreaking of all. The heart monitor beeped sporadically, signalling the final moments of a life too short.

There was nothing different. The scene she was witnessing was as she remembered it. What was the point of putting her through this agony again? Did he want to send her back into the mire she had only recently crawled out of?

In the end, a profound stillness filled the room as the machines fell silent. Everyone was still as if cast in stone. The child's suffering was over, but the pain of those left behind had only just begun. Esther watched herself crumble before her eyes as she stumbled back through the door, back to the garden.

Chapter 23

Esther collapsed back onto the bench, completely overwhelmed by what she had just been forced to witness again. The death of that little boy had haunted her ever since it happened. The guilt had ended her nursing career. Her complete inability to look after him caused his death. She knew it. Why had she been in that situation? Surely they must have realised that she didn't have the skill set to look after patients who were so sick.

And why had Joseph made her go through that again? Was he mad? She'd made a big mistake trusting him. She should have never allowed him into her life. Now she was back where she started, filled with self-loathing and recrimination. She was a mess, a failure of a human being.

Joseph sat gently beside her, his presence a weight that she couldn't shake off, as if it lingered in the very air around them. She stood quickly. She needed to distance herself from him. That need grew stronger with each passing second. Her body tensed with a mixture of disbelief and disgust. What kind of sick bastard was he? She could feel the bile rise in her throat as the scene they had just witnessed played over and over in her mind. Without a second glance, she walked briskly away, as far from him as she could manage. The door which had led to George's death had moved. It was in front of her, but it was no longer a door.

As she neared the threshold, her focus shifted. The doorway was gone, and in its place stood a graceful archway, open to the world beyond. Through it, she saw a valley stretching out before her, bathed in sunlight. Tall, majestic trees dotted the landscape, their leaves a mix of deep green and gold, whispering softly in the breeze. The grass beneath her feet was lush and vibrant, the green that only seemed possible in dreams. A small stream wound its way through the valley, its waters sparkling as it danced over smooth stones, creating a gentle, melodic tinkling sound that filled the air.

Esther stepped forward, her senses drinking in the surrounding beauty. She closed her eyes for a moment and breathed deeply, allowing the crisp air to fill her lungs. The tension in her chest slowly eased, the tranquillity of the scene washing over her - an escape from the turmoil that had raged inside her. After a long pause, she turned back toward Joseph, her gaze steady. The storm within her hadn't completely calmed. 'Would you like to explain yourself? What the hell were you thinking putting me back there again?'

He pointed to the archway.

'Esther, look through the archway.'

She turned to where he pointed. The wide expanse of velvet green grass, gently undulating, was filled with children. All ages, race and colour. They were squealing with laughter as they played with enormous bubbles, which they patted to each another. Their exuberance was infectious, and Esther laughed along with them. As she looked, she spotted a small boy who was looking at her. She stiffened as he made his way over to her.

'Hello Esther. What are you doing here? Are you dead?'

'No, I don't think so?' He put his head to one side, a puzzled look on his face. 'I'm not sure why you're here.' He smiled up at her and took her hand. 'Don't be sad Esther.' He turned and waved towards the children, who had stopped to watch.

'This lady tried to save my life,' he called before turning back to Esther. 'We all died of COVID. There was nothing anyone could have done to save us. I was sad for Mum, but she has a new baby now and is happy again.' Esther was dumbstruck. He moved towards her and reached up to take her other hand, holding them tight to his little chest. In a voice that belied his years, he said 'Thank you for trying so hard to save me. You didn't kill me, the virus did. Same as all the other kids here. Stop punishing yourself, Esther. Please stop.' He paused and looked up at her with such wisdom. 'There was nothing you could have done to change what happened. It had already been decided. Esther, you know our lives are mapped out before we are born. I had a brief life. Forgive yourself. You have given too much to too many people. Be kind to yourself.' He bent and kissed her hands. She felt his warm breath as a great wave of emotion rose inside her.

George looked up and smiled before turning to run back to his friends. They all smiled and waved to Esther before going back to their game. Esther couldn't move. She was rooted to the spot. How could a child be so wise? Why had she carried such guilt over his death when she could never have saved him? As she watched him move away with his friends, she sobbed. Every fibre of her being was releasing the tension she had held within her since George had died.

She felt a hand on her elbow and turned to Joseph. He gently led her back to the bench where they sat in silent companionship. After a long time Joseph cleared his throat but it was Esther who spoke first.

'Thank you for helping me see the truth, Joseph.' Her simple words couldn't express the relief she felt inside.

'I did not Esther. You are healing yourself.' He paused and then continued, 'There's something I need to tell you.' Esther roused herself, bringing her attention back to the moment. She turned to Joseph, waiting to hear what he had to say.

'When you are back, you need to know Kate's concerns have led her to ask for you to be referred to a psychiatrist. If this happens, Kate will continue to imply that your state of mind is such that you should receive inpatient treatment. Now she has power of attorney, she may get her wish.'

Esther stared at him as a fresh fear gripped her. Why would Kate do that?

'So, what should I do?' she frowned as a new wave of fear gripped her.

'I am offering you an option. Instead of heading home after you are discharged, consider staying with me in Wales. You can recuperate with no worries. Esther, I assure you. There's no hidden agenda here. I'm just trying to protect you from Kate, whose understanding of the situation is completely wrong. There is no pressure for you to do so. Just know that the offer is there.' As his words echoed through her mind, the garden began to vibrate as the scene dissolved into a blaze of colour.

Chapter 24

As Esther blinked open her eyes, the lingering effects of the anaesthetic left her feeling disoriented and groggy. A slight shift in her position made her realise she was lying in a hospital bed. The entire episode in the garden and her release from the burden of killing George seemed a distant dream. A sound made her turn to see someone sitting beside her. It looked like Kate, but she seemed out of place in this unfamiliar setting.

'Hello Mum, how are you feeling?' Esther looked at her face. Although Kate's words were kind, her eyes betrayed a lack of genuine concern behind her forced smile.

Esther tried to sit up. 'No, don't move Mum. You need to rest. The operation was a success, and the metal cage is gone. There's a bandage and they'll keep you in tonight.'

Looking down, Esther saw the blankets lifted off her leg by a cradle under the blankets. She couldn't feel anything, but knew from the weight of her leg on the mattress that the metal frame was gone. She turned back to Kate.

'What are you doing here?' Esther mumbled her mouth like cotton wool.

'Do you want a drink? They said you can have sips.' Kate reached for a plastic glass with a straw and offered it to her mother, who propped herself on her elbow to drink. She knew anaesthetic could make you have vivid dreams. Was that all it was? Esther tried to concentrate.

'Kate, why are you here? What's happened?' Her mind cleared.

'I told you I would come to look after you for a few days.' Again, the half-smile. Esther shifted uncomfortably in the bed. 'Do you want to sit up more? Here, let me adjust the pillows.' Kate offered.

The idea of Kate being in the house while she was trying to recover made her feel uncomfortable and anxious. Esther knew she shouldn't feel such animosity towards her own daughter, but Kate's piercing words, laced with accusation and judgment had cut deep. Esther wasn't sure she had the strength to withstand an onslaught from Kate about her father or the state of her mental health.'

'I text to say I was coming. Don't you remember?'

'How long are you staying?' Esther asked, searching Kate's face. Kate tucked a strand of her short hair behind her ear. 'A few days, maybe a week. Depends on how you're doing.' Joseph's words flashed through her mind. What was Kate up to? Esther's brow furrowed. 'What about work?'

'I'm taking some time off.' Kate sounded irritated. 'We need to talk, Mum.'

A chill ran through Esther despite the warmth of the hospital room. 'About what?'

Kate leaned forward, her facade of cheerfulness cracking. 'About Joseph.'

Esther's heart quickened. 'How do you know about Joseph?'

'Richard and Grace have both spoken to me.' Kate's eyes hardened. 'They're worried about you, saying that you've been acting strangely again.'

Esther closed her eyes briefly. 'It's not what you think.'

'Then what is it?' Kate's voice rose slightly. 'Because from where I'm sitting, it looks like you're being taken advantage of by some con artist.'

'He's not a con artist, Kate. He's helping me.'

'Helping you with what? Losing touch with reality again?' The bitterness in Kate's voice was palpable.

Esther stiffened. 'You don't understand. The things I've seen and learnt. He's shown me that not everything is my fault.'

'What? What are you talking about? I suppose he's told you weren't responsible for Dad!' Kate interrupted, her face flushed with anger, her composure finally giving way. The words hung in the air between them, heavy and sharp. Esther's face paled.

'Kate, please. That's not fair. This really isn't the time to be talking about that.'

'Fair?' Kate laughed, a harsh, hollow sound. 'Was it fair to let Dad die?

Esther reached out, her hand trembling. 'Your father's death was not my fault, but you'll never accept the truth.'

'Dad was getting better, Mum. He was trying.' Kate snapped.

'He was just out of rehab. You know as well as I do, that wasn't the first time and unlikely to be the last.' Esther couldn't help the bitterness creeping into her voice.

'It would have been different if you'd stayed to find out.' Kate's fists clenched at her sides.

'Kate, if you knew the truth of why we left…' Esther's voice trailed off. Kate stood abruptly, pacing the small room. 'The truth? Mum, listen to yourself. You sound like you did before. It was all his fault, not mine. And then there was Ray. The icing on the cake.'

'I made a mistake with Ray.' Esther was only a whisper.

'A mistake?' Kate's voice rose. 'He terrorised us, Mum! He beat Shaun half to death.'

Esther bent over as the silence stretched between them. Esther said eventually.

'No words could alter the reality of what happened. He was an evil man. A man I couldn't escape from. I want you to know it wasn't a matter of choosing him over you Kate. I was scared and didn't know what to do. I didn't know how to get away from him.'

'Stop it. Just stop.' Kate shouted, then immediately lowered her voice, glancing nervously at the door. 'I can't listen to this anymore. You're still guilty, Mum. Guilty of ruining my life.' She paused, gathering her thoughts. 'And as for this Joseph, bloody hell, Mum. I don't know what happened to you last time and I don't want to know, but I can't watch you spiral downwards into another fantasy to escape your guilt. Not again. I'm going to do something about it this time.' Kate moved towards the door.

'Kate. If I could explain.' Kate turned and glared at her mother. 'The time for explaining is over.' The door slammed behind her as Esther slumped back against the pillow as tears streamed down her face, grateful she was in a side room, so others would not witness her shame.

Kate headed straight for the nurses' station. She was shaking with anger. Why had she let her mother get to her again? Bringing up the past had killed any sympathy she'd had. This wasn't how it was supposed to be. This was supposed to be a break away from her shit life. It had taken only minutes for her to realise she could not be in the same room as her mother. She hated the way she looked, all small and pathetic. The smell of hospitals made her stomach churn, all that antiseptic masking other unpleasant smells. How anyone could do this job, especially her mother, astounded her. The sooner she could get out of here, the better.

A nurse glanced up as she approached.

The nurse surprised Kate by recognising her, 'Mrs Morgan's daughter isn't it?' Kate leant over the top of the counter. 'Can I speak to you privately, please?'

Nurse Singh pushed herself out of the chair, sensing that this was not a conversation to be had in public. She showed Kate into the office off to the side. As Kate followed her, she couldn't help but marvel at how this young and delicate girl possessed the strength to move the bodies she had seen in the beds on the ward. Nurse Singh sat at a desk, which groaned under the weight of files and stacks of paper. She pointed to a plastic chair opposite and nodded for Kate to begin.

'I imagine you have my mother's medical records now?' The nurse nodded her head. 'So, you know she takes anti-depressants?' Again, an incline of the head.

'Mum worked on the frailty ward here. When COVID hit, they redeployed her to help on the COVID wards and critical care. Something happened, and she had some sort of breakdown. We couldn't get help.' Kate glanced at the nurse to gauge her reaction. The nurse nodded for her to continue. 'Eventually, the doctors prescribed antidepressants for her. I couldn't come because of the restrictions, but her neighbours reported bizarre behaviour, including hallucinations. By the time the travel restrictions lifted, she seemed to have recovered.'

'I see. And you never found out what happened?' Nurse Singh's tone made Kate shift in her seat. There was a subtle insinuation that Kate could have done more, or was she imagining it? She went on quickly, 'Now there seems to be something going on again. It's to do with the man who found her when she fell when she was in Wales. I wondered if he'd been to see her?'

Nurse Singh shrugged. 'No, no-one has visited.'

'I am not sure he exists.' Kate let out a sigh, knowing how ridiculous that sounded. 'My worse fear is that she's hallucinating again. Last time she talked about an hallucination called George. This time Mum is talking to Joseph, but no-one has seen him. I'm wondering if he's real. And if he does exist, I think he may manipulate my mother.'

'And what is it you want us to do?' The nurse asked abruptly. Kate gave her a hard stare.

'I want you to refer her to a psychiatrist as a matter of urgency and get her assessed before she's allowed home.'

'She's due to be discharged tomorrow. I'll make sure it's on her discharge notes so her GP can refer her, but that's the best I can do.' Nurse Singh said, looking at her watch.

'Well, that isn't good enough. I have power of attorney. My mother is a vulnerable adult and cannot go home until she's had her mental health assessed. There's no-one at home to look after her and if she's heading for another breakdown anything could happen.'

'I will contact the on-call psychiatrist and ask for her to be seen before her discharge tomorrow. Hopefully, they'll fit her in before she leaves. If they can't, I'll ask her surgical team to ask for a psych referral on her discharge letter.' Her voice was flat.

Kate got up to leave. She turned at the door, and with a flash of anger, said.

'I hope she is seen before she is discharged. If she leaves and something happens, I hope your notes will show I raised concerns about her mental health.'

Chapter 25

Esther did not see a psychiatrist and was unaware Kate had asked for her to be referred to one until Nurse Singh told her. Shaken by Kate's outburst, it took several hours for her to recover.

Nurse Singh came to see her as she was going off duty to say she would be discharged the following day. As Nurse Singh straightened her pillows, she offered Esther a hairbrush to tame her unruly hair that was sticking out at all angles. The coarse, dark hair, a constant reminder of a father she never knew, felt rough under the brush as she tried to decide what to do. She needed a good shower and hair wash to feel human again and couldn't wait to leave the hospital. Now Kate had gone off in a huff, she realised she was back to relying on the kindness of her neighbours again. Then Joseph's words about Kate came back to her.

'Did my daughter say anything to you when she was here?' Esther asked the nurse, who was checking her charts. Nurse Singh looked up, a slight frown on her face. 'She asked me to refer you to the psychiatrist.'

Esther gave a high laugh. 'I see.'

'Unfortunately, the on call wasn't able to come,' Nurse Singh said, looking her directly in the eye. Esther realised at that moment the nurse was on her side. 'I have asked the consultant to refer you to your GP for postoperative follow up,' she continued.

'Thank you,' Esther said simply, grateful for the nurse's silent support.

'Do you have someone to help you at home for the first few days?'

'Yes, I do.' Esther said quickly, sensing it would be unwise to stay in the hospital any longer than she had to. When the nurse had gone, Esther sat for a long time. Was her distrust of her own daughter warranted? Could she trust Joseph and his comments that Kate thought her unstable? Was she insane?

She was under the influence of an anaesthetic the last time she visited the garden, which was different, but the result was so worth it. The guilt, which had been a constant companion, was finally gone, leaving her feeling a newfound peace. The visit to the garden released her, and she felt a million times better about George. She was going to have to trust Joseph. He had been right until now. Esther rang his number, and he picked up immediately. She told him she was to be discharged and about her conversation with the nurse about the psychiatrist.

'You can come and stay in Wales. There you will have time and space to consider your options, Esther,' he said simply.

Esther said she would ring him back. She needed to think. Would she be safe with him, or would he continue to force her to confront her past? From what he'd said, she initiated the visit to the garden. Was she sub-consciously driving this change?

Could she take herself off somewhere? Somewhere where no-one would know where she was. She clearly couldn't trust her own daughter. If she went with Joseph and finished 'the work' would she then be free? Would he leave her alone to get on with her life? She was deep in thought as a nurse wheeled the drug trolley into her room.

'Would you like anything for the pain, Mrs Morgan?' Esther nodded. Her ankle was throbbing. It wasn't just her ankle; her head was throbbing too.

As the nurse handed her two tablets in a little plastic pot, she said,

'I have your drugs to take home, so you're free to go when you can arrange for someone to collect you in the morning.'

Esther collapsed back against the pillow. She didn't know what to do. Did she trust Joseph? Did Kate really think she was insane? She was going to have to decide, and quickly. The clock was ticking.

It took two days for Kate to calm down after visiting her mother. She headed straight home to Raynes Park to rescue her boys from their father. Suddenly, the idea of a break didn't appeal anymore, and she wanted to be back home. The boys were pleased to see her. Both gave her an enormous hug, making her eyes fill with tears. Why had she wanted to leave them?

Shaun left immediately, without asking her why she was home early or how her mother was. She had to hold her anger in check as she inwardly seethed. She couldn't stand his selfish, self-centred attitude. Every time she needed him, a bitter taste of resentment filled her mouth.

The house was warm, the air thick with the familiar scent of sweat-soaked trainers and testosterone. She sank gratefully into the battered armchair. It might not have been the perfect home she dreamed of, but it was her home.

When she finally felt calm again, she rang the hospital to ask if the psychiatrist had seen her mother.

'Mrs Morgan was discharged yesterday morning,' the ward clerk said after Kate had waited several minutes for her to find out.

'Why wasn't I informed?' She sat up straight.

'One moment,' the line was quiet until the clerk said, 'there was no record of a request to call you.'

'Who came to collect her?' Kate demanded.

'I'm sorry I don't have that information.' Kate disconnected the call and immediately rang her mother. There was no reply. She tutted as a surge of irritation ran through her. Obviously, her mother didn't want to speak to her. The problem with her mother was she couldn't face the reality of the consequences of her actions. It was too uncomfortable for her to face the truth. Now all this business with Joseph added another level of concern. Despite the fight, Kate still needed to know her mother was home, so she dialled the number again. Still no reply, so she tried Richard.

'Kate, how's your mother?' Richard said unenthusiastically.

'I was about to ask you the same question. Haven't you been round since she got home yesterday? Who's looking after her?'

'What are you talking about?'

'She was discharged from the hospital yesterday morning. I only just found out.'

'Well, she isn't home. I can tell you that,' he snapped.

'What do you mean, she isn't home?'

'Kate, there has been no-one at the house since she went in for her operation.'

'Then where the hell is she?' Kate's raised voice was too much for Richard.

'Look Kate, I don't know where your mother is, and you must stop using me as her support worker. She is your mother; you deal with her.' The line went dead.

Richard's sudden vocal outburst startled Kate. It was so unlike him, but she had to find her mother. She took a deep breath and dialled Grace's number. Her fingernails tapped on the kitchen counter as she waited for a reply.

'Kate,' the terse voice was not encouraging.

'I'm sorry to bother Grace, but I was wondering if you know where my mother is. She has been discharged from the hospital, but she didn't come home and I'm worried.'

'Are you indeed?' Grace's tone was icy. 'Look Kate, I have problems of my own to deal with, so I would be grateful if you could sort this out yourself.' Grace's voice was shaky.

'Grace, are you alright?' Kate asked without thinking, sensing something was wrong.

'It's personal, Kate. Nothing to do with you or your mother. I really can't help you.' There was a pause. 'I'm sorry.'

What the hell was going on? Both Grace and Richard showed no interest in helping her. She relied on them, but that support was no longer available. What was she to do now?

She rang the ward back. This time, Nurse Singh answered it.

'I'm sorry to bother you,' Kate mumbled. She knew Nurse Singh had not formed a good opinion of her, but she was desperate. 'Could you tell me if you were on the ward when my mother was discharged?'

'Yes.'

'Do you know who picked her up? Please?' Nurse Singh paused as if sensing trouble.

'I wheeled her down to the entrance and there was a Range Rover waiting to take her. She told me she was fine. I left as someone got out of the car, but I didn't see who it was. I had to get back. There was an emergency on the ward,' she added, as if trying to justify why she had not made sure Esther was safely handed over to whoever collected her.

Kate took a deep breath, trying to decide if it was worth challenging the nurse. Deciding against it, her mind was whirred. Then she remembered that Richard had seen a brand-new white Range Rover speeding away from Esther's. Was it Joseph? Was he real? Had Joseph taken her mother? A wave of panic shot through her. Where the hell was her mother and what the hell was going on?

Chapter 26

The car stopped in the drive of a small stone cottage at the end of a dirt road.

'Let's get you inside, Esther, and make you comfortable.' Joseph handed her the crutches and walked beside her to make sure she negotiated the uneven paving slabs to the front door. As she breathed in, the air felt briny on her tongue, making her realise they were close to the sea.

Making her way to the sofa in the lounge area, Esther realised she was exhausted, so she flopped down into the warm hug of the sofa. The windows were small, which only allowed in the diffused light of late afternoon.

'I'll get your things from the car, then I'll make us some tea,' Joseph disappeared out of the door as Esther surveyed the room. The fragrant smell that filled the air immediately overwhelmed her senses. It was like the garden. It must have one of those plugin things. She had slept for most of the journey, comforted by the heated seat and smooth ride. She wished she had paid more attention to the route they'd taken, but reassured herself she could look it up on Google maps.

As she surveyed the open plan space, she noticed original beams divided the areas. It must have been three rooms at one time. There were two armchairs with billowing cushions, as well as the sofa, which led into the small dining area. Recycled wood had been used to make the kitchen, giving the whole place a feeling of comfort. She exhaled. Had she made the right decision coming here? It had all been so sudden. Was the news about Kate wanting to have her committed true? She would never get over that. Betrayed by her own daughter. But Esther wasn't ill. Joseph's assertions that Kate wanted her committed, well, that was just far-fetched. What was his motive in all this?

Esther suspected he wanted her to go back to the garden to face the last door, but then what? What else did she have to confront?

'Esther, do not worry. You can leave at any time.' His voice startled her. 'Just say the word and I will take you home.' He handed her a mug of tea before sitting in the armchair opposite.

'Is this your house?' Esther changed the subject.

'No, it is rented. Do you like it?'

'Yes, it's cosy and right by the sea, isn't it? I've always wanted to live by the sea. How long have you lived here?'

'Not long.' Was the non-committal reply. Why was he always so evasive?

'You know, Joseph, one of the main reasons I have trouble trusting you is I know nothing about you. I don't know how you transport us to the garden. The only way I can think of is by drugging my tea or ensuring I'm under anaesthetic.' She quickly put the mug on a small coffee table by the side of the sofa.

Joseph laughed. 'Esther, I am not drugging you. Who I am is not important. It is the work we do together that is important. As I said before, this entire experience is driven by you. There is one more major challenge to face, then you will be free of the burdens you have carried for so long. You can be who you want to be. You will have the strength to deal with the other issues in your life, on your own. That is why I am here, Esther.'

'What other issues? I thought the three deaths were enough?'

'There is still Ozzy, Kate and Lily to think about, but those issues are part of your future. I am here to help you with the deaths.' Esther stiffened. Could she ever get Kate to understand about her father? What of Lily, her child? Would she have the courage to reclaim her? How did he know about Lily? Releasing herself from feeling responsible for the deaths of her mother and George lightened her. It made her feel like she could face the world, deal with Kate and find Lily. But she still had to face Ray. A dark cloud descended as she thought about Ray and his death.

'Yes, Esther, there is still Ray.' Joseph's words startled her.

'Can you read my mind? Are you real, Joseph?' Joseph stood and smiled down at her. His beautiful face was open and full of care.

'I am real to you, Esther, and that is all that matters. Now I am going to cook some food for us. Once we have eaten, I think you should have an early night. It has been a long day. Tomorrow you can decide whether to continue or whether to go home.'

As she heard Joseph in the kitchen, Esther wanted to trust him. She thought he was somehow an extension of herself; a guide to help her make sense of her life rather than be consumed by self-pity. Would she wake from her sleep, the warmth of the sun on her face, to discover these adventures had been nothing more than a figment of her imagination?

She couldn't decide if this was an illusion. Was she going mad? Had she engineered this whole thing herself? Was Kate right? Was she living in an alternative reality? But were the visits to the garden helping? Yes, she felt better, lighter somehow. Was it worth resolving the last issue, Ray?

He had said she would not see him after that. How did she feel about that? In Joseph, she had found a champion. Someone who was on her side. He was kind, generous and treated her with respect and understanding. Could she be the person she wanted to be? Positive, happy, alive, confident, enthusiastic, motivated. How good it would be, to feel free. How good to start again without all the burdens that had plagued her life. Whatever this was, it was helping her. Deep down she knew that whether it was illusion or reality, it was freeing her from her shadows.

Chapter 27

Kate sat at her desk in the cubicle, the oppressive heat making her sweat, and stared at the phone. Why was she having to deal with this? Why was no-one else prepared to step up and deal with her bloody mother? Resentment gnawed at her, but she had to push through it and figure out how to find her. The question lingered in her mind. Did she really want to find her? If her mother had gone off with this Joseph, why should she care? It was almost a relief to be rid of her. To be rid of the feeling of obligation she had even though she hated her mother. But what would other people think? No, it was no good, she would have to do something. Even though Richard and Grace no longer wanted to help, they would still judge her if something happened. The whispers would turn to murmurs, and then to outright questions, all directed at her, 'Why didn't you do anything, Kate?'

Then it came to her. A different option existed. She could go to the police and let them handle the situation. She would call and say her mother was missing, that she suspected she had gone with a strange man known to no-one, and that she was a vulnerable adult with mental health issues.

Typing in Google, she found the number of the local police station in Worcester, the nearest sizable station to the village. After navigating a series of questions asking if this was an emergency. Then press one to report a crime, press two for advice, press three for anything else. She pressed three and waited.

'Worcester Police Station, how can I help you?'

'I would like to report a missing person who is a vulnerable adult.' Kate said.

'Please, can you tell me your name, the name of the person you suspect is missing, and your relationship with that person?' The voice on the other end sounded younger than Ben.

Kate relayed this information, giving her mother's name, address and date of birth.

'And you are?'

Again, Kate gave her details.

'And what makes you think your mother is missing?'

Kate explained her mother's disappearance following her discharge from hospital, the fact that she hadn't returned home and that no-one seemed to know where she was.

'I see. Does the hospital have details of who collected her?'

'No. But she seemed to have been involved with a man called Joseph. She was picked up by someone in a brand-new white Range Rover. This car has recently been seen at her house and it's assumed by the neighbours that it belongs to this Joseph.'

'Can you tell me anymore about this individual?'

'I'm extremely concerned about this person's motives towards my mother. I consider her to be at risk as he appears to influence my mother. If he is real.'

'I'm sorry. What do you mean?' The police officer sounded confused.

'My mother's had psychotic episodes in the past where she's suffered from hallucinations. I'm unsure if this is another episode or if this Joseph is real and manipulating my vulnerable mother.'

'And no-one else has met this gentleman?'

'No.'

'Right, I see,' said the police officer, sounding more interested. 'I am going to pass this onto missing persons, and they will be in touch after some preliminary enquiries. In the meantime, could you check with her neighbours to see if they know anything?'

'I have already done that. They haven't seen her since she went into the hospital. Please find her.' Kate's voice strained with feigned worry as she expressed her concerns, though deep down she felt anything but worried.

'Do not distress yourself, Mrs Cooper. We will be in touch as soon as we know anything.'

Good, thought Kate. The last thing she needed was to be held responsible for her mother's demise. What she needed was proof. Something to spur the police on. Sitting back in her chair, she chewed on her pencil. Could she stimulate Richard's interest and ask him to look for evidence? It was worth a try. The sooner her mother was found, the sooner she could get on with her own life. Picking up her mobile, she rang Richard's number.

Richard was at the kitchen island gathering the ingredients for seafood linguine to cook as soon as Colin arrived home when his phone rang. When he saw who was calling, he hesitated. What if something had happened? This thought made him press the green button.

'Sorry to trouble you, Richard.' Kate swept on before he could answer, 'First, I want to apologise for the way I spoke to you and second, I want to ask for your help.'

'Right,' Richard said slowly, wondering what the hell she was going to ask him to do.

'Could you go round to Mum's and see if you can find anything that might give us a clue where she is?' There was a pause.

'I suppose I could.' Richard said cautiously. Secretly, a surge of excitement ran through him as he thought of searching through Esther's stuff. What might he find? 'What exactly am I looking for?' he asked.

'I don't know. Evidence of this Joseph, I suppose.'

'Okay, I'll go round after supper, and if I find anything, I'll call you back.'

'Thanks, I appreciate it.' Kate said, ending the call. As he went back to chopping garlic, Richard mused about Kate's change of heart. Maybe she was worried about her mother for once.

When Colin got home, Richard was stirring a pan on the stove. Colin slammed his briefcase down on the kitchen counter. This was not a good sign. He'd had a bad day. Richard poured him a glass of wine and knew he'd have to wait to talk to him. When they were sitting eating their seafood linguine, Colin calmed down enough to ask Richard about his day.

'Well,' Richard paused mid-mouthful for dramatic effect, 'I think something has happened to Esther.'

'What do you mean?' Colin didn't sound at all interested. His view was that Richard should never have got involved with Esther. Richard had to pick up the pieces when her useless daughter did nothing last time. Colin made it quite clear he didn't want Richard getting involved again. But now it looked like he was becoming embroiled in her problems all over again.

'I've told you not to get involved,' he said, giving Richard a hard stare.

'I know, but Kate's rung and asked me to go round to the house.' Colin let out an exasperated sigh. 'Just wait and hear me out. What if this mystery man has done something to Esther? I would never forgive myself.'

'Did it ever seem like he might do something to her ... if he even exists?'

'No.'

'Then why do you think he might?'

'Well, she's disappeared. With him.'

'You don't know that for sure.'

'I have to do something.' Refilling Richard's glass from half empty bottle on the table, Colin said, 'have a drink. It'll stop you from worrying.' But Colin knew from experience there was no use saying any more, so he went back to his dinner. 'I'll have dessert when I get back,' Richard mumbled.

'Why? Where are you going?'

Richard looked confused. Colin raised his eyebrows at Richard. 'Darling, do you think you need to get your memory tested? I told you. It's the parish council tonight.

After dinner, when Colin had left for his meeting, Richard let himself into Esther's with the key from the key safe. The house smelt musty. As he made his way to the kitchen, he realised there was a strong smell coming from the bin. After he'd put the rubbish out, he focused on her bureau in the front room. As he moved through, the hair on the back of his neck stood on end causing him to turn round, sensing someone was watching him. Shaking his head, he focused on his task. He pulled open the top drawer and began working his way methodically through.

All four were crammed with papers, and carefully leafing through them took a while. Mostly old bills and bank statements. Why did people keep these things? He found nothing until he came to the bottom drawer where he discovered a folder tied with a ribbon which said 'important documents' on the cover. He leant back on his heels, his legs cramping from kneeling too long, and tapped the folder on his hand. No, it wouldn't be right to look at her private papers. Just as he was going to put it back, he noticed a small purple exercise book underneath, like the ones he'd had at school. Pulling it out, he flicked through the pages. A small slip of paper slipped out. On it was a phone number and the name Joseph. He'd struck gold. Excitedly, he got to his feet. At the same time he scanned the notebook. The scribbling described the death of a child. A child called George. Richard stopped. That was the name Esther had cried out in the night when she was ill. Did she have something to do with the death of a child? Quickly, he closed the drawer and reached for his phone to ring Kate.

But the uneasy feeling was back. Stuffing the notebook inside his jacket to protect it from the light rain that was falling, he locked the front door and headed for home. Maybe he'd better give some thought regarding his next steps. He was unsure how Kate would react, but at least there was a contact number for this Joseph ... he must be real.

Chapter 28

Richard retrieved the purple notebook from his coat and went into the kitchen, where the light was bright. Colin was out at the Parish Council Meeting and wouldn't be back till late as they went to the pub afterwards to revive themselves. Richard settled himself on the kitchen peninsula. He'd poured himself a glass of whiskey and opened the notebook. Sprawling writing filled the pages, and it was difficult to decipher, but as he persevered, it became easier. He shifted uncomfortably, knowing this was an invasion of Esther's privacy, but he felt it was his duty to do as Kate had asked. The reason he had taken the notebook in the first place was because of a name he spotted. Joseph.

What he read made him reach for his phone.

'Grace, I need to pop round.'

'What now?'

'Yes.'

'But we're just having dinner. Can you leave it an hour?'

In that hour, Richard paced. What the hell was going on? Colin told him not to get involved, but it was all so strange, he had to understand it. He knew Esther was eccentric, even before her fall, but her recent actions were alarming. Something needed to be done.

Sitting on the velvet couch, resting his elbows on his knees, he tried to get his thoughts in order. Did he really want to get caught up in Esther's life again? Could he ignore what he had read? Richard wanted to speak to Grace before he contacted Kate to make sure his interpretation was correct. The clock ticked by too slowly and after forty-five minutes; he went to get his jacket before locking the front door and hurrying up the road, pulling up his hood against the keen wind and drizzle of the damp February night.

Grace's large 1940s double fronted property had a long gravel drive. Ella's treatment room was one of the four bedrooms and now Hope was at university, Richard wondered if she would work from home more. Ella had a natural infinity with people and her practice was successful, attracting clients from miles around.

Richard's friendship with Grace began after she moved in. He'd sensed something in her. She had led a less than usual life, like himself. It was a strange twist of fate. Both washing up in the outskirts of a near picture-perfect English village. Its outward charm masked the toxic reality of old versa new, as Colin found out as he battled bravely each month at the Parish Council meetings.

Richard invited Grace, the beautiful Ella, and Hope to their annual Christmas party. They'd drunk too much, and at one point Grace ended up telling him why they'd moved to the village. Ella had gone missing when she was fourteen, returning home fifteen years later after her abusive uncle died, and bringing a daughter with her. Her daughter, Hope, was the result of that abusive relationship. Moving from Cheltenham was their new start. Grace came round the next day filled with remorse for telling Richard her story. She swore him to secrecy, and he had been good at not telling, except for Colin, of course.

Richard rang the Ring doorbell and huddled against the gathering gloom in the doorway. What was taking her so long? Richard was impatient to talk. Despite her horrific past, Grace was strong and wise. Richard trusted her opinion and often sought her out.

Ella opened the door, wafting jasmine out into the evening air. Her long black hair scooped into a messy bun, and her pale eyes smiled. She held the door open wide as Richard stepped forward to kiss both cheeks lightly.

'Beautiful as always, my darling,' he smooched. Ella stepped aside to let him in.

'Mother's in her study. Go through, I'll make some coffee.'

'Black and strong for me, darling.'

Richard crossed the hall to the study and, tapping lightly, before through the door. Grace was sitting in her comfortable leather chair behind a large wooden desk filled with papers.

'My, you look busy,' Richard said, slouching into the ultra-modern wooden chair designed to help your back but which was in fact acutely uncomfortable.

'You're supposed to sit upright to get the benefit,' Grace said, peering over the top of her reading glasses. 'Now what's so urgent you must disturb me on a Tuesday night? I have my own problems to deal with Richard and I don't need any more drama.'

'What's happened?' Richard leaned forward.

Grace glanced towards the door as Ella arrived with the coffee.

'Thank you, my darling,' her tone, full of love.

'I can leave it, if this isn't a good time?' Richard tensed, feeling guilty for having disturbed her.

'No, go on. It'll give me something else to think about.'

'If you're sure?'

Grace nodded and waved her hand to show she was listening.

'Kate asked me to go to Esther's looking for clues.' Grace sighed, leaning back in her chair. 'Oh Richard, what are you like.'

'I found this.' He pulled the purple notebook from inside his coat and passed it across the desk to Grace. She raised an eyebrow as she reached across to take it. 'I'm not sure that's terribly legal,' Grace said, taking the journal from him.

As Grace's attention was absorbed in the pages, Richard picked up his cup and, cradling it in his hands, waited for her pronouncement.

'Well,' she said, letting out a breath, 'That is worrying.'

'Kate needs to contact the police again. This proves she is with this Joseph somewhere in Wales. God knows what's going on.'

'It certainly gives cause for concern, I grant you that. This Joseph is real to her, and she has gone with him, to save herself, whatever that means,' said Grace reading from the book.

'I mean, what the hell, the garden at the end of time? Do you think he's drugging her?'

'It's possible, but you remember last time when she was hallucinating, calling out for George. More worrying is this passage about George. Esther seems to say she can free herself from the guilt of his death. Does that mean she thought she'd killed him? This is explosive stuff, Richard. I'm not sure I want to be any part of it. And as for this Joseph ... is he real or a figment of her imagination?'

'Joseph appears to be a real person. I mean, we've seen his car even if we haven't seen him.'

'We saw a car, Richard. We cannot be sure it was his.'

'I'm sure it was his. Remember, I've seen it there before.' Richard sounded like a spoilt child. Grace sighed.

'Let's think,' Grace sat back and spoke almost to herself. 'Esther had an accident. She was miraculously rescued and since then she claimed to have a relationship with someone called Joseph. No-one has seen Joseph except for Esther, but wait a minute? Wouldn't they have seen him at the cottage hospital when he took her for her appointments? I think Kate needs to contact the police again. There must be someone there that could give a description.'

'You're right, but I'm concerned about what Kate will do with this information.' Richard's voice was quiet.

'What do you mean?'

'We both know her relationship with Esther is bad. I'm worried she might exaggerate Esther's mental state.'

Grace waited for him to continue.

'I think she might try to get her mother sectioned. If she does, then she's off the hook.'

'That's brutal, Richard, even for you,' Grace replied. 'We know Kate hates her mother. She told me it's because Esther killed her father.'

'What.' Richard sat up straighter. 'When did you find that out?'

'I rang Kate to tell her to speak to Esther about Joseph. I felt we were getting too involved again, and it was time she stepped up.'

'Why didn't you tell me?' Richard bristled, cross that Grace failed to tell him this bit of news. 'So, Esther could have killed two people?' he gasped.

'I don't think this is anything we want to get involved with.' Grace's tone was firm. 'Sorry, Richard, but I have so much going on. It must have slipped my mind. You were busy with your project and by the time we caught up, I was embroiled in my own problems.'

Richard sighed. 'I'm sorry to come and dump this on you when there's clearly something going on.'

'I think once you've spoken to Kate and handed over the notebook to the police, I'm afraid it will be time for me to duck out of this entire business.'

'Why what's happened, Grace?'

'My ex-husband Robert has been arrested in Thailand. He's facing a string of charges over there, but my fear is the British police will want to extradite him for crimes he's committed here.'

'I suppose it depends on what the charges are in Thailand. With any luck, they'll lock him up over there.' Richard said, trying to sound supportive.

'I agree, but this news has opened up old wounds for me and Ella. It's hard to concentrate when your past rises to meet you. I'm waiting to hear more from the British police. Let's hope they find enough to keep him locked away in Thailand. As far as Esther is concerned, the police just need to find her. This information gives them a lead. I'll ring Kate.

The police should follow up on the physio appointments. Let's hope they find Esther fit and well. My fear is she's having another breakdown. If that's true, God knows what has become of her.'

Chapter 29

Esther had the best night's sleep in weeks in the comfortable little bedroom at the top of the steep stairs. The room was quaint, with its floral wallpaper and small windows which looked out across the beach. The sea was calm this morning, and the waves lapped gently onto the shore. It was hard to make out much as a thick sea fog blanketed everything. Esther wrapped herself in a thick jumper from the suitcase she found in her room. Joseph must have collected these belongings from her house. When had he gone there? Her journals had been brought to her, all except the latest one with the purple cover. Why was that one missing? She heard Joseph calling to her. Making her way carefully down the narrow stairs clinging to the bannisters on each side, she realised her foot, though sore, felt solid in the support boot the hospital had given her.

Joseph came to the foot of the stairs. 'Can you manage?' concern in his voice.

'I'm alright, thank you,' she smiled at him as she navigated the last step. He handed her the crutches so she could make her way to the table before heading back to the stove where he was frying bacon. The room was filled with its delicious smell, making Esther wonder why anyone would want to be vegetarian.

The table was set with cutlery, napkins, and mats, together with condiments. Sitting at the table, as Joseph served her bacon, eggs and grilled tomatoes, she felt embarrassed.

'Don't worry, I'm not doing all the work,' he said, sitting down and sliding the tomato sauce in her direction. This morning his face was flushed with a healthy glow, and his eyes sparkled with newfound energy. A strange thought crossed Esther's mind. Was his health linked to hers? Redirecting her attention, she tucked into her food, realising she was ravenous. When they'd finished eating, Joseph cleared the plates and refilled their coffee mugs from the cafetiere.

As Joseph settled himself back at the table, Esther said 'Thank you for bringing my stuff, Joseph, including the journals. They are so important to me. The latest one doesn't seem to be there though. The one with the purple cover. Have you seen it?'

'Are you sure?' Joseph looked momentarily floored. 'I can go back and have a look.'

Why is he so worried? Esther wondered, but was distracted as Joseph changed the subject.

'Esther, why is your relationship with Kate so poor?' Why was he bringing this up? Surely, he already knew the answer.

'She blames me for her father's death,' her tranquillity dissipating as she wondered where this conversation was going.

'That's interesting. You don't seem to agree with her.'

'No. Ozzy brought about his own death. I was trying to protect Kate, not ruin her life. But that's not how she sees it.' He nodded. 'Have you ever thought of writing a letter to Kate?' Esther shook her head, but wondered whether that might be a good thing to do. Maybe it was time to tell Kate her side of the story.'

'Tell me about Ray.' Why was he changing the subject? Didn't he want to know what happened to Ozzy?

'Kate hated him, and I didn't do enough to protect her from him. I was caught in a delicate dance, attempting to appease him while also trying to protect Kate. I lost my independence and felt powerless to make my own choices under the weight of Ray's dominance.'

Esther stared at Joseph.

'This is to do with the last door, isn't it?' Her voice was barely above a whisper. He nodded as he leant across the table and held out his hands. 'Do you want to understand? This is the final hurdle be-tween you and freedom. There are other issues, but you can resolve them yourself without my help. Do you want to do this, Esther? What is your intuition telling you?'

Esther sat back in her chair. If she allowed this last episode to play out, she would be free. Better to do it now than put it off. She knew Joseph wouldn't leave her alone until this was done. She took his hands as the room faded, and Esther felt herself being drawn inward.

As her mind cleared, disorientation washed over her. The expected lush greenery of the garden was nowhere to be seen. Instead, she stood in a dusty layby at the side of a steep roadside.

A shiver ran down Esther's spine. This place, this exact spot, was etched into Esther's memory. To her right, cars sped past up a steep incline; on her left, a layby on the M4. Panic gripped as she whirled around to face Joseph, her heart hammering against her ribs. Before she could speak, a deafening screech of tyres tore through the air. Forcing herself to turn, she watched as a car skidded to a stop, kicking up a cloud of dust and gravel. The passenger door flew open, and a man burst out, his face flushed and voice thick as he shouted over his shoulder.

'Move it, Fatboy! I need a piss!' Ray bellowed, scaling the crash barrier and stumbling towards trees at the back of the layby. A small man, his belly pushing out against his shirt, lumbered out of the back seat and followed him, swaying dangerously as he tried to keep up. Esther saw herself hunched over in the driver's seat, the engine ticking quietly, waiting. Seconds ticked by until the air exploded as a scream filled the air.

A cold dread gripped Esther's heart, and her stomach twisted into a knot as she watched herself scrambling out of the driver's seat, running towards the back of the parking area. Her words, sharp with urgency, reverberated through the trees.

'Ray! Ray, can you hear me? Where are you?' What's happened? Ray, Kevin! Where are you? A tense silence. The only sound was the tyres of the cars speeding past.

Laboured breathing and the occasional sob broke the silence as Kevin stumbled back into the layby. His arms were a mess of scratches, thin rivulets of blood trickled down to his fingertips. His face was ashen, eyes wide with shock as he gasped out words between ragged breaths.

'Fuck, Esther, fuck,' he panted, his voice barely above a whisper. 'He's fallen right down. Get help. Get help now.' His words grew more frantic, the pitch rising. 'Oh God, Esther, there's a sheer drop. He's gone, Esther. I can't see him. Get help!' With that last plea, Kevin's legs gave out, and he collapsed onto the gravel. His massive frame shook as he sobbed. His fingers clawing at the ground as if trying to anchor himself to reality.

Esther watched herself turn back to the car. With her hands trembling slightly, she tried to flag down passing cars. When that failed, she dialled 999. Then she ran to the edge of the tree line, calling out for Ray, as Kevin, on his hands and knees retched violently onto the gravel.

As the scene played out before her, Esther experienced a series of emotions. Grief, guilt, and relief.

She turned to Joseph, her eyes pleading for the reason he was forcing her to relive this memory.

He turned, and taking her hand, led her through a doorway which appeared behind them. Esther breathed a sigh of relief. They were back in the garden. As she sat with Joseph on the bench, she noted the doorway did not disappear. It did not become an arch. Esther turned her head to look at Joseph.

As if sensing her confusion, he said. 'Esther, that was a painful memory, but there are further details we need to discuss before we can fully resolve it. Can you tell me about the accident?' He had turned to face her. A shiver went down her spine. He knew. It was a secret she had buried deep, but in that moment, she could feel it unravelling.

Esther looked down at her hands and began speaking. Her voice was barely a whisper.

'Ray supported Woking Football Club and he wanted to go to an away match in Yeovil with his friend Kevin. They could have gone on the train, but Ray said I would drive them. When Ray decided something, that's what happened. We were on our way back when Ray told me to stop, saying he needed to pee. I didn't want to stop because it would be so embarrassing. Everyone would see him. There wasn't much cover. I knew of a place a couple of miles on, so I told him I'd stop there. He started shouting in my face, but I kept going and stopped where there was tree cover. And that's when it happened.' She glanced up at Joseph, who was still staring at her.

'It's alright Esther. You need to say this.'

'I stopped there because I knew there was a steep drop on the other side of the barrier.' Esther let out the breath she had been holding. As she exhaled, a weight lifted off her chest. Joseph put his arm around her. 'Well done. I know you blame yourself for Ray's death, but I think there was sufficient provocation for you to absolve yourself of the guilt you carry.'

As Esther looked around, the doorway was still there. She sat up straight.

'Joseph, I can't see him,' her voice filled with alarm.

'Ray is not here, but in another place. If you join me, I can show you why Ray is beyond saving.' Joseph stood there, his hand outstretched, waiting for her response.

Chapter 30

Joseph stood in the doorway they had just come through, giving Esther time.

'I can't avoid seeing him again, can I?' she mumbled under her breath, her voice, thin and feeble as she spoke.

'He was much younger than me. We met when the electricity supply needed upgrading to cope with some new high-tech equipment on the Surgical Unit. Ray was around the unit for several weeks. During that time, he charmed me. To please him, I changed my clothes and hair. I even developed an interest in football.' Esther gave a high laugh. 'I was so worried he'd lose interest, but he was keen and before I knew what was happening, he'd moved in with me and Kate.' She sighed and looked over at Joseph, who nodded his encouragement.

'Until that point, I was independent and level-headed, not easily swayed by others' influence.

At first, the attention was intoxicating, but I soon realised his obsession was unhealthy. The extreme mood swings, the suffocating displays of love intertwined with outbursts of anger. The middle-of-the-night rants and incessant phone calls when I wasn't with him became overwhelming. When the chance to get rid of him presented itself, I took it.'

Joseph came over and sat beside her.

'Esther, I need you to come with me and see what happens to people like Ray. Not everyone has the courage or conviction to face their shadows. You are exceptional in your choice to do this in order to free yourself. Come with me and see what happens when someone has no awareness of themselves or the impact they have on others.' Standing, he held out his hand to her.

'We must go to a lower place to find Ray, Esther. You need to see what became of him.' Joseph's words hung in the air, a warning of the grim journey ahead. Esther's hand trembled as Joseph took it, and he guided her back through the doorway.

A deserted street lay before them. The light was a dim, sickly glow that seemed to drain all the energy. There was no colour, only a wasteland of greys. Dilapidated houses lined the street, their facades crumbling. Most of the shops stood with windows either boarded up or shattered. It reminded Esther of photographs she had seen of London's East End after of the Blitz.

As they moved along the forsaken street, a flickering movement caught Esther's eye. From the shadows, a child appeared. She couldn't tell if it was a boy or a girl. The child was so dirty. The eyes were wide with a mixture of fear and determination as they went to stand by a shop. With a sudden movement, the child disappeared inside, to emerge moments later, arms laden with pilfered sweets and crisps.

The shopkeeper came charging out of the doorway, a giant of a man waving his enormous arms as he gave chase. His roar of anger echoed off the decrepit buildings, but the child was too quick, weaved through the legs of passersby, before vanishing into the gloom.

Joseph's hand tightened around Esther's and drew her towards a building on the corner. Esther looked up at the sign above the door as it creaked in the breeze. 'The Jolly Hangman.' The pub's name was perfect in this desolate place.

As they went in, the stench of stale beer hit Esther. As her eyes adjusted to the dimness, they locked onto a figure at the bar - Ray. The sight of him, perched on a stool with a pint clutched in his hand, sent a wave of revulsion through her.

Ray was holding court, his voice bellowing in the dingy space. A few cheered him on with drunken enthusiasm, while others remained motionless at the bar, unconscious, drowning in cheap booze.

'The only way to let a woman know who's boss is to give her a good slap,' Ray proclaimed, to a chorus of cheers and grunts of approval.

'Bloody right, Ray!' came a shout from the crowd.

Ray continued, his words slurring. 'I kept my missus in check, and that ugly brat of a daughter. Had a face like a slapped arse. Needed keeping in line, that little tart.'

Bile rose in Esther's throat as Ray, clearly relishing the attention, leant into the man next to him. 'I'd teach her a lesson when she came home from school when her mother was at work!' He got down from his stool and thrust his pelvis backwards and forwards. That drew raucous laughter from those still conscious.

A scream tore from Esther's lips before she could stifle it. Her hand flying to her mouth in fear and disgust. But there was no reaction from Ray or the others. It was as if she and Joseph were ghosts, unseen and unheard in this realm of the damned.

Turning to Joseph, confusion and horror on her face, Esther saw only understanding in his eyes.

'He cannot see or hear you.' Joseph's voice was soft, and sorrowful. 'His mind cannot fathom the wrong he has done. He continues in this perpetual cycle day after day, reliving his sins without comprehension or remorse.'

The full weight of what she was witnessing crashed over Esther like a tidal wave. It wasn't just Ray's fate that horrified her. What had he done to Kate? The pain of not knowing was physical. Esther's voice was barely a whisper, choked with emotion. 'Will he ever change?'

'If he ever shows any sign of remorse, we will encourage him to face the consequences of his actions. But until that time, no, he will continue to relive his life.' Joseph gently took Esther's arm and guided her away. Esther wondered who the 'we,' were, but her mind was too cluttered to take in anymore.

They left Ray behind, but the horror of what she had seen would stay with her forever. Everything around them felt ominous and intense. Each face they passed, each crumbling building and discarded piece of trash, spoke of choices made and consequences reaped. As they walked back through the door, she staggered forward as if every ounce of energy had seeped from her body.

Esther practically collapsed onto the bench, her mind full of unbidden images, her insides knotting. No wonder her daughter hated her. Not only did Kate not understand the circumstances of her father's death, but Esther had exposed her to that monster. Why had Kate never told her? She realised Joseph was sitting quietly beside her. As she straightened up, he gently took her hand.

'Esther, not all of Ray's boasts are true.'

'What do you mean?' her voice was harsh but as she looked at him. How could Joseph possibly know that?

'The point of taking you there was to make you understand you cannot help everyone. If people like Ray refuse to take responsibility, they remain in a perpetual cycle of denial. Unless Ray can realise the effect his actions have on others, he will remain locked in that cycle. There is nothing you or anyone else can do to help him. He must find his own way out.'

'But that doesn't change the fact that I engineered his death.'

'Did you, Esther? Did you know he would rush headlong into those trees? Did you know he would fall and fatally injured himself? You might have willed it to happen, but you are not responsible for Ray's actions that day. He made his own choice and sometimes the world has had enough, and that person's time is at an end.'

It was clear now that Ray made his own choices, despite what Esther wanted to happen. 'But did I will his death, Joseph? It seems too much of a coincidence, his accident.'

'Who knows?' Joseph looked upwards with a smile. 'It released you from his grip, but not completely.' Esther turned to look Joseph directly in the eye. 'What do you mean?'

'What about Lily, Esther?'

Chapter 31

Kate was sitting squashed in the boxroom, which served as her home office, but also as a junk room for all the boys' rubbish. Her morning had been spent in a dreary monthly team meeting on Zoom. When she retrieved her phone, there was a missed call from Grace. Kate hesitated. The call she was expecting was from Richard. She didn't want to talk to Grace after letting her guard down during their previous conversation. She didn't want Grace's sympathy, and felt a prickle of irritation at the thought of having to speak to her again. Taking a deep breath, she pressed redial.

'Thank you for getting back to me, Kate.' There was no hesitation in Grace's voice, only the direct, no-nonsense tone of someone used to getting things done. 'Richard has found a phone number for this, Joseph. We have passed it to the police.'

'Why the hell didn't you contact me?' Kate's voice barked.

'We felt it was a vital piece of information. I am telling you now.' Before Kate could react, Grace continued. 'Richard also found a purple notebook which we have not given to the police. It contains information which we think you should read and decide what action to take.'

'Go on.'

'The notebook is full of your mother's hand-writing. In it she describes how she has visited a place she calls the garden. It involves a child called George. Kate, I must ask you a hard question.' Kate waited. 'Do you think your mother ever killed anyone?'

'What. Why would you ask that?'

'Well, for one, you told me she caused your father's death. In this journal, she alludes to the fact that she was also involved in the death of this child named George.'

'What?'

Grace continued, 'Do you remember when she was ill? She called out for George. I don't know if she was complicit in his death, but it might explain why she was so fixated on him.' Kate was silenced. Changing tack, Grace continued.

'The journal also discusses Joseph and several visits he made to your mother's house. One section refers to Joseph living in Wales.' Kate's mind was racing. Could her mother be involved in the death of a child? The thought scared her. It took her a moment to realise what Grace was saying.

'So, we have proof that Joseph exists and that if my mother is with him, she could be in Wales.'

'Exactly.'

'Do you have this journal now?'

'Yes, I can either courier the whole thing to you or scan the relevant pages.'

'Could you do both? Kate's mind was a muddle, she couldn't get it straight in her mind. Was her mother a murderer? Who was her mother? Suddenly, she felt she didn't know her at all

Grace's tone brought her mood crashing down. 'Once you have read the journal, you must decide what to do with the information. I must tell you I have personal problems to deal with, and both Richard and I feel we can no longer be involved with what's going on. I must ask you to deal with this from now on.' In the pause that followed, Kate's face screwed up and her spare fist balled in her lap. She wanted to say many things to Grace in those few moments, but took a deep breath and said.

'Fine. If you could send over the information, I would be grateful. Thank you for your help.' She said through gritted teeth before disconnecting the call.

DC Braithwaite answered on the second ring.

'This is Kate Cooper. I understand that Grace Carmichael, my mother's neighbour, has contacted you with a phone number for Joseph.'

'We've tried that number, but it's disconnected.'

Of course, what did she expect? She continued.

'A journal has been found which suggests that this Joseph lives in Wales.'

'I see, and do you have this journal?'

'It's being sent to me.'

'I see. And what makes you think this information is correct?'

'I'm sorry, this is a lead. To find my mother. Who is a vulnerable person.'

'It would be useful if you could provide evidence of this information so we can pursue our enquiries in that direction. Does this journal contain any further information we should know about?'

'I haven't read the contents yet.' Kate froze. This was the moment she must decide. The entries about George couldn't rule out the possibility her mother was involved in his death.

'There is some information about her mental health.'

'Would you care to elaborate?'

'She appears to have been having hallucinations where she is reliving experiences.'

'I see. Are these relevant to our enquiry?'

'They may be,' Kate said cautiously, 'but I think the key priority is for you to find my mother.'

'I think I will decide the relevance of the information once I have scrutinised it, Mrs Cooper, so if you could ensure we have it as soon as possible, that would be most helpful.' There was a long pause before he continued, 'Whilst I have you on the phone, I will give you a brief update on our findings.'

Kate was silent, as the weight of her actions and their consequences settled over her. Could she implicate her own mother in the death of a child? 'Are you there?' Kate's attention was drawn back to what the DC was saying. She murmured a response.

'We have revisited the hospital to find out if anyone had knowledge of the individual called Joseph. Whilst there are eyewitness reports that your mother was seen with a man, but no one can give us a description.'

Kate's attention was refocused on what the DCI was saying. 'That's strange. What, no-one can tell you what he looks like?'

'No. We have identified the white Range Rover from CCTV footage at the hospital. The car is a lease car, and it's registered in your mother's name.'

'What? No way could she afford a car like that. There must be some mistake. How could she even drive with her leg in the state it's in? This is ridiculous.'

DI Braithwaite coughed, 'We can only proceed with the information we receive, Mrs Cooper. It is our intention to widen the net and have traffic searching for the car on CCTV. We will chase up the Wales connection as soon as possible and will be in touch as soon as we have anything further. The journal please, Mrs Cooper, as soon as you can.' Kate disconnected the call as an icy dread spread through her as the implications of what she might do settled within her.

The net was closing in. What would happen when the police read the journal? What would happen when her mother was found? Had she unwittingly made her mother an accessory to murder?

Chapter 32

With the salty air filling their lungs, Esther and Joseph strolled along the beach, the last rays of the early spring sun warming their faces. A pink glow spread across the sand and sea as the sun dipped, its warmth fading into a calm evening. As the sun began to set, the sky glowed, the light dancing on the surface of the waves lapping on the shore as the seagulls called. It felt perfect.

There was a lightness in Esther's step, even though her progress was slow. Her leg was still adjusting to not being surrounded by metal. The weightlessness of her foot was odd after months of carrying the heavy cage around. As she stopped and turned to look back along the beach, her body cast a long shadow. She glanced towards Joseph, who was walking a few yards in front of her. There was something odd about him. What was it? His body glowed with the light of the evening, but he cast no shadow.

Esther shivered despite the warmth of the evening.

Who the hell was he and what the hell was she doing here? The whole thing was surreal. She knew if she ever told anyone about this, they would think her mad. She wanted to turn and run away, go back home and forget this ever happened. Go back to being normal, back to a mundane life of fetes, cream teas and village gossip. She turned to walk back towards the cottage. Perhaps she could call for a taxi to take her to Aberystwyth. From there, she could get a train home.

'Esther, what's wrong?' Joseph startled her, appearing alongside.

'I want to go back home.' She said emphatically.

'What has bought this on?' His voice was gentle.

Esther stopped and turned towards him. 'I don't know what you are or who you are, but I don't feel safe here anymore.' Joseph stood, looking puzzled. 'You have no shadow,' Esther blurted out. The words hung in the air.

Joseph laughed then, a light musical sound. 'Esther, I have told you, I have been here to help you. You are no longer chained to painful memories.

Memories you created in your mind. You poisoned yourself with your misinterpretation of memories, but you have freed yourself. We have come so far, Esther. If you feel it is finished, you are free to leave at any time. If you wish to return home, I will take you in the morning and then leave you to your life.'

'Tell me who you are.'

'Who do you think I am, Esther?' Esther walked on, trying to think what she wanted to say. He was supernatural, not of this world. Was it ridiculous to imagine such a person existed? 'I think you are here for me.'

Joseph smiled down at her. 'Yes Esther, I am, and I always will be.'

Time seemed to slow as the dusk gave way to evening. There was little conversation. Esther was suddenly uncomfortable with Joseph's company. His presence unsettled her. She knew there were still issues she needed to face and deal with, but she could do that on her own. There was no need for all this supernatural stuff. She was clear now. Kate was her priority. She needed to know the truth about Ozzy. She had to find Lily. All she wanted was to return to a normal life without doorways, memories and ethereal beings. Tomorrow she was going back to her life. Esther went to bed after a silent supper, leaving Joseph to gaze at the dying embers.

Her dreams were of the garden and Esther woke disorientated as bright sunlight filtered through the patterned curtains. The sound of waves gently lapping through the small open window brought her mind back into focus. She was at Joseph's. The memory of the previous evening made her pulse quicken. Why had she allowed herself to be drawn into his strange world? The hallucinations; the re-visiting her uncomfortable past. She sighed, lifting her arms above her head. Despite the uncertainty, a wave of self-assurance washed over her. All the blame she carried for the deaths of her mother, George, and Ray, no longer caused pain deep within her. Her sleep may no longer be haunted. So, this was the end. She could restart her life. She jumped out of bed, feeling renewed, but then remembered her foot as her ankle ached.

Joseph was in the kitchen as she made her way gingerly down the narrow wooden staircase. He poured coffee from a cafeteria as soon as he saw her. As she took the mug from him, she looked him directly in the eye.

'I am going home, Joseph.' He stood looking at her and, as she looked at him, Esther noticed a change in his demeanour. He looked smaller, older, and worn out, like the light had gone out of him. Regret washed over her in a hot flush, as guilt immediately set in. Her decisions had a physical effect on him. A well of emotion surged within her. She wanted to cry.

'Joseph, are you alright?' He dropped his gaze and moved towards the stove. 'Why do you look so sad?' Esther asked him.

'I thought we would have more time. Although you have erased the ghosts of the three deaths, there are still other shadows. I was hoping to help you deal with those so you could be totally free. Take a seat. Your breakfast is almost ready.' He whispered.

'Oh, Joseph,' she breathed, relief washing over her, 'I'm so grateful for your help in showing me I was wrong, but I want to go back to a normal life. I have had enough of soul searching. My mind is clear now and I feel able to move forward on my own, whatever else surfaces.'

He came towards her and placed scrambled eggs and toast in front of her. Just as she liked them, not too soft but not overcooked. 'As you wish, but you will not see me again. I cannot again take human form, but I will be with you always, Esther.' He paused before changing the subject. 'The cottage is available for you to use until the end of the month, so please stay and recuperate properly. I will leave the car for you.'

His words hit Esther like a physical blow. She would not see him again. The implications shook her to her core as she realised how much she would miss him. 'So, I won't go back to the garden?'

'One day you may go back as you transition to the world beyond, but I sincerely hope it is a distant day.'

Esther pushed her plate away, untouched, as an enormous need ran through her. Before she went back to her normal life, she needed to see it one more time. 'Can I go to the garden one more time, please?' Joseph smiled, his mood lightening. 'Of course.'

He came towards her and as he took her hands, the familiar blurring of this reality signalled the journey back to her garden. As her vision cleared, Esther laughed. Before her stood Joseph, holding an enormous bunch of flowers.

'Well done, Esther.' He said, coming towards her and holding out the flowers, which now had a large green ribbon around them.

She took them, smiling at him.

'Look around at all you have achieved.' The garden was in full bloom, almost every inch of space in the circle within the three arches, bursting with colour and fragrance. The exception was the far corner, where there was a patch of bare earth to the side of the archways which stretched several feet into the perfusion of flowers. Esther did not ask about it, but sat down on the bench and breathed deeply. Joseph came to sit beside her and gently took her hand. 'I know there are other episodes in your life that you are not proud of, but you have cleared the deepest shadows.' Joseph sat beside her. 'What have you learnt, Esther?'

'I have learnt we construct stories in our minds. Over time, those stories become our reality. My stories lodged in my brain until I convinced myself they were true. But those stories were not true. I feel almost foolish for squandering so many years on self-pity when I could have been happy. I made poor decisions which affected those I love and it's time to put that right.' As she turned to look at Joseph, she saw he was glowing with pride. His whole being was radiant. 'It is time for you to go back, Esther. I am sorry we couldn't finish our work together, but I hope your earthly life is as full and fulfilling as it can be.'

'Aren't you coming with me?' She gazed into eyes that had seen centuries.

'No. Not this time.' his voice carried the weight of ancient wisdom. 'It is time for you to go forward alone.'

A sharp pain pierced Esther's chest, as if her heart were truly breaking. Was she making the right decision? Yes, she needed to leave Joseph behind. What he represented was not something she could continue with. If she was ever going to make a go of her life, she needed to be free from delusions or hallucinations, however helpful they had been. She needed to be grounded in the reality of the world.

As they got to their feet, Esther reached up and placed her hand over Joseph's heart before reaching up and kissing him lightly on the cheek.

'Thank you,' she said simply.

'You are most welcome, Esther Morgan. Keep up the good work now you know how to free yourself. Goodbye.' Feeling a mixture of relief and apprehension of a life without Joseph, Esther took one last, deep breath to fully appreciate her garden's fragrance, silently wishing herself well for the rest of her life.

As she looked for the last time at his beautiful face, she saw a tear fall silently down his cheek as the garden faded.

Chapter 33

The next day, Esther woke in a room she didn't recognise. She heard the ocean lapping on the shore as the early morning sun cast pale light across the room. She breathed deeply. Wriggling her toes and luxuriating in the soft warm bed, she felt good, alive, exuberant, but where was she?

As she got up from the floral-covered bed, she stretched. The memory of someone was on the edge of her mind, but she couldn't pin it down. Wherever she was, it was peaceful. Moving towards the small, low window, she looked out and laughed in delight. The beach below her was bathed in soft rosy light. Opening the window, Esther breathed in the fresh air, beginning to warm as the sun rose higher. She had always dreamed of living by the sea. Smiling to herself, she shuffled into her slippers, but as she did so she winced as pain shot up her leg.

'That's sore.'

Bending to examine her ankle, she noticed it was red around one of the pin sights. I hope I'm not getting an infection, she thought, not after everything I've been through. Having the metal frame removed was such as relief and coming here to recuperate seemed such a good idea. '

'But it seems miles from anywhere. I don't know where I am. I must look it up on Google maps,' she resolved as she swallowed some pain killers with water on her bedside table. Making her way onto the small landing, she checked the other bedroom for signs of someone else being here but finding nothing.

'Funny, I was sure there had been someone else here.'

As she made her way down a narrow wooden staircase into the room below, it opened out into a kitchen, dining and sitting room. She thought how quaint this little place was.

There was food laid out for her and the smell of fresh coffee. Someone else must be here. Whoever had left her breakfast would be back at some point. Perhaps it was the person who owned the cottage. It was reassuring to know someone was around. She would check her phone and see if there were some contact details. Esther also had a strong desire to ring Kate. There were things she needed to say, but where was her phone? First though, she was going to enjoy her breakfast. The rest could wait.

Sitting at the small table eating a warm croissant, Esther felt a memory of a garden. A beautiful garden, and she sighed. Somewhere within her, this felt like the first day of her life. As she finished her breakfast and drank her coffee, she tried to remember how she had got here. She remembered the fall and having her leg in a metal brace. The brace had been removed. Her sole purpose in coming to this place was to regain her health and well-being, nothing more. She was here to get over having the metal frame removed from her foot. Although the soreness in her ankle was irritating, the painkillers were easing the discomfort. I'll have a relaxing day to regain my strength in this peaceful place. How long could she stay? What day was it, and where exactly was she? Although she didn't know, she didn't feel alarmed. She was calm and happy. After eating, she took her coffee upstairs.

Back in her room, she smiled as she looked out at the view. Turning, she opened the drawers of an old, battered oak chest and discovered her clothes. Hobbling to the small bathroom, she showered using the toiletries provided. The jasmine and rose shower gel smelt wonderful. She rinsed her thick hair, which was longer than she remembered, and after drying herself, she looked in the mirror. The face, looking back, surprised her. She looked so well, if a little flushed. Her skin was clear, her black hair shone hanging like a smooth curtain around her face. Her eyes sparkled. She laughed. This place has done wonders for me.

After dressing, she looked in the drawers for the anti-depressants she knew she took every morning. After finding them, she sat on the bed. No, I won't take them. I don't need them anymore. Putting them aside, she noticed some notebooks stacked neatly further back. Taking them out, she recognised her own handwriting. Strange, she didn't remember writing anything. Had this place also stimulated her long-held dream of being a writer? What had she written in these pages?

Going back downstairs, she made another coffee before going out into the morning. The sun was warm as she sat on a bench in the small garden at the back of the cottage, overlooking the sea. Propping her foot on another chair with a cushion, she opened the notebook at the top of the pile and began reading. After each notebook, she sat back and thought through what the writing was telling her. It was certainly a tale. It was her tale of all the shadows that haunted her dreams.

The story was of a mysterious stranger who helped her to forgive herself for all the wrongs she thought she'd done. It was wonderful to think it was true, and I do feel so much better. When at last she finished, it was well into the afternoon.

What a wonderful story I've written, but it's too personal? I would never let other people read it. They would recognise themselves.

By writing a story about a garden and an imaginary being called Joseph, she had faced shadows that plagued her for years. The pages provided an alternative explanation for the deaths she always blamed herself for. Her mother and Ray, but there must be more journals as the story was not complete. The journals, surprisingly, contained no mention of George, a fact that struck her as odd. Perhaps there were other journals. George had been the major cause of her distress, so she must have addressed it somehow, otherwise she wouldn't be feeling so calm and peaceful.

Esther was disturbed by what she had written about Ray and his relationship with Kate. She needed to know if any of that was true. She remembered the urge to ring her daughter. Where was her phone? Getting up to go back into the cottage, she gasped as the pain in her ankle took her breath away. She was going to have to call a doctor if it didn't improve. More concerned about finding her phone, she searched the lounge. There behind a cushion was her battered cloth handbag, but no luck. Perhaps it was upstairs. She'd look when she went up, but not now, she was tired and wanted to enjoy the warm weather.

'I'm not hungry, even though I haven't eaten since breakfast.' The person who owned the cottage hadn't returned, but she knew there was food in the fridge if she had wanted it.

Making herself a cup of tea, she went into the garden and sat feeling the warmth of the afternoon sun on her face. With a thoughtful expression, she carefully considered the significance and implications of the different entries she'd found in the journal pages.

There was also no mention of Lily. Deep in the pit of her stomach, a stark, nervous sensation began, a cold jolt that sent a shiver through her. Shaking herself to stop that train of thought, she breathed deeply, concentrating on the sound of gulls circling high in the pale blue sky.

The absence of Ozzy from her writing was also strange and unexpected, given their close relationship. Esther thought about her strained relationship with Kate, questioning why she hadn't directly confronted the underlying issue that was at the root of their difficulties. She'd compose a letter to Kate.

After a while, Esther went back into the cottage and, finding some paper, wrote what she was thinking. When she finished, she folded the piece of paper and stacked the notebooks neatly in a pile, placing the letter on the top.

Sitting back in the chair, the urge to call Kate made her get up and make her way carefully back upstairs. She needed to talk to her about Ray. What were these nagging doubts about Kate and Ray?

After searching, she found her phone in the pocket of her dressing gown hanging on the back of the bedroom door, but the battery was dead. She was hot, so she took off her jumper to cool down.

With a sigh of relief, Esther plugged her phone into the charger next to the bed before, overwhelmed by tiredness, she collapsed into the soft comfort of her bed.

'I'll have rest, then call Kate. By the time I wake up, the phone will be fully charged and ready to make a call.' The moment her head hit the pillow, she immediately fell into a deep, dreamless sleep, completely unconscious and unaware of her surroundings.

Sometime later, her mind pulled her back to being awake as she realised someone was banging on the door downstairs. She could hear them calling her name and through blurred vision, Esther could make out blue lights flashing against a dark sky. How strange, she thought as her eyes slowly closed once more.

Chapter 34

Her mother's hand was icy. The rhythmic whoosh of the breathing machine was hypnotic. Kate had arrived just after midnight to find her mother already hooked up to a ventilator with an array of drips and syringe drivers around the bed. There was a nurse in constant attendance, checking observations on the large monitor. Even the bed itself was moving as its mattress inflated and deflated to prevent Esther's body staying in the same position for too long.

It was early morning now and the seven am handover was taking place. Kate tried to listen to the nurse's exchange of information, but they might as well have been talking in a foreign language for all she understood. The nurse taking over came gently over to her.

'Hello, I'm Nurse Dimond. I shall be looking after your mum for the next twelve hours. Do you have questions?'

'Yes, can you tell me what's going on, please?' The catch in her voice embarrassed Kate.

The nurse knelt beside Kate.

'Is it alright if I call you Kate?' she nodded. 'Your mum has sepsis caused by an infected wound on her ankle. Thanks to the police finding her, we began treatment straight away, so we hope she will recover.'

'What do you mean, hope she recovers?' Panic rose in Kate's throat. This was sudden. This was unexpected.

'Let's just take each hour at a time, shall we? She's stable now and we're monitoring her closely. If there's any change, we'll detect it straight away. Now what about you? Have you had anything to eat or drink since you arrived?'

'I've had lots of tea,' Kate grimaced.

'But nothing to eat?'

'No.'

'I want you to go down to the canteen which is in the basement and get yourself some food,' Nurse Dimond raised a hand as Kate shook her head. 'You must try to eat even if you don't feel like it.'

'Can you tell me anything about when she came in?'

'One moment.' The nurse went back to the head of the bed and scrolled through the notes on her iPad.

'They admitted your mum via A&E at 10.30 pm. The police found her unconscious at an address near Borth. They had gone to the address to try to locate her. As I understand, she had been missing?' Kate nodded.

The nurse explained that the police called the ambulance.

'Thank you, that's helpful. Could you tell me the address where she was found? What sort of place was it?'

'The paramedics said it was a holiday cottage.' Kate was surprised by this. She'd assumed her mother had been with this Joseph. At his house. What was her mother doing at a holiday cottage? There was little point in asking the nurse who would only have limited information.

'The police will be here later this morning so you can ask them for further information then.' The nurse smiled in a kind manner. 'Why don't you go to the canteen and whilst you're there, we can see

260

to your mum.' Kate got painfully to her feet. Sitting for so long had given her cramp in her leg.

After eating some overcooked bacon and solid scrambled eggs, she felt better. She sat, trying to get her head round what was happening. Her mother, once again, was intent on adding more stress to her already stressful life. But seeing her in that bed made something stir within Kate. She was her mother, after all, and Kate was her closest family. But now, with this power of attorney, she was responsible for her mother. That was a burden she didn't want to carry.

Why couldn't her mother have been normal? Helping her instead of the other way around? She didn't need this. She really didn't. But what if she died? Would it be a relief, or would she feel guilty for not being a better daughter?

Sitting back against the hard plastic chair in this stark hospital canteen with too bright lights and constant noise, Kate thought about what kind of mother she had been. Leaving her poor father to die, then subjecting her to a life with that bastard Ray. No, it was hard to feel any sympathy for a woman who had made such as a mess of her own life, and as a result, Kate's as well.

When she returned to the unit, washing her hands and donning an apron as she entered, she saw a young police officer standing at the central nurses' station. He was joking with the nurse sitting at the desk, but straightened up and composed his features when he saw Kate approaching her mother's bed.

'Mrs Cooper.'

'Yes.'

'I am PC Williams. Could I have a few words?'

He picked up his helmet and pointed to a side room off the main unit which said relative's room on the door.

'Please take a seat.' Kate sat awkwardly on the low couch, which she presumed acted as a bed. The young, fair-haired police officer opened his notebook.

'Just to clarify from the information we have,' he looked at his notes, 'your mother disappeared from the hospital five days ago and you think she went with a man known as Joseph?' Kate nodded, 'The Worcester police had been looking for her and traced her to an address in Borth.' Again, she nodded. 'When they arrived, they found your mother in a state of collapse and called an ambulance.'

'That is what I have been told.'

'Could you tell me anymore about this man called Joseph?'

'He appears to have been visiting my mother at home. He took her to hospital appointments, but neither her neighbours nor myself have ever seen him.'

'I see. And this concerns you because?'

Kate signed, 'My mother's had mental health issues in the past and experienced hallucinations.' PC Williams consulted his notes.

'Now can I move on to this journal that has been found in your mother's home? Can you confirm the journal was written by your mother?' Kate nodded, feeling the heat rising within her.

'The journal entries you sent to the Worcester police referred to someone called George. Is that correct?' Kate nodded as an icy shiver ran down her spine. 'The Worcester police are following up on that information, so we will let you know if they come up with anything.'

'What do you mean?'

'I cannot say more other than we are pursuing our enquires into the death of a child named George.' Kate's head went down. What had she done? But this was not her fault. It was more about what her mother had done. Kate had read the journal. The story of the death of a child from COVID. Was it her mother's fault? Had she given too much of that drug? The rambling, frantic scribbling in the journal of some hallucination her mother experienced seemed to exonerate her. Was that her own imagination trying to justify what she had done? Was her mother responsible for the death of a child?

Was her mother a murderer?

'Is there anything else you would like to add at this stage, Mrs Cooper?' His gaze was penetrating, which Kate found unnerving in such a young man. Kate shook her head. It would be unwise to say anything more.

'Very well. I'll inform the investigating officer that the information we have is correct and we'll go from there. We're actively searching for this gentleman, Joseph, as a person of interest. Is there anything else you would like to ask me?' Kate gathered herself.

'The place where she was staying. Where was it? I'd like to collect some of her things if possible. If it's a holiday let, they'll want her belongings removed, won't they?' The PC wrote an address and contact phone number on a piece of paper from his notebook and passed it to her.

'The property is owned by a Mrs Bennett, so if you wish to visit the cottage, I advise ringing her first.' Kate nodded as the PC got up to leave. She followed him back to the unit and went to sit at her mother's bedside. Her mind was in turmoil. She didn't know what to think. Her mother looked like a rejected doll, lying so still in the bed. What the hell had been going on? Kate wanted to cry. This was all too much.

By lunchtime, her head kept dropping to her chest. Nurse Dimond suggested she go outside for some fresh air and to give herself a break.

'Is there anywhere you could go for a few hours to have some rest?' Kate told her about the cottage. 'I think it would be a good idea to go there if you feel up to driving. It's not far, about twenty minutes from here. We have your contact details and I'll let you know if there's any change. Take your time. Your mother's condition is stable for now.'

Getting up, Kate gathered her things, grateful for the opportunity to get out of the unit. As if remembering, she turned to her mother and, taking her cool hand, told her she would be back soon. She didn't know if her mother could hear her, but the nurse had encouraged her to communicate with the lifeless body in the bed.

The entrance hall of the hospital was like an amphitheatre as Kate stopped to get her bearings. High glass ceilings were supported by enormous metal struts, giving the place a space age feel. No wonder the NHS is broke, she thought. This place was more like a posh hotel. Kate retrieved her phone from her bag and began texting the boys before going outside. Finding a seat far from the main entrance, she could still smell the acrid smoke of the cigarettes from the people gathered there. It truly irritated her. How come the hospital permitted them to do that? Taking the piece of paper, the PC had given her, she called the number.

'Hello,' the voice with a Welsh lilt answered.

'Hello, I am Kate Cooper. Esther Morgan is my mother.' There was a pause.

'Oh yes. I know who you are. So sorry to hear about your mother. How is she?'

'She's very ill, but they say she's stable at the moment. Would it be alright if I collected her things from the cottage?'

'Of course, anything you need, but there's no hurry, my love. She's got it booked till the end of the month. You can stay there if you like. It's not many minutes from the hospital in Aber.'

'Did you say she booked it?'

'Yes, you know how it is these days - it was all booked online. Didn't you know?' Kate decided not to answer this. Instead, she said.

'Do you know if there was anyone staying with her?'

'Not to my knowledge. The cleaner doesn't go in if there are guests, so she would have seen to herself. I sent all the instructions about the place and gave her my contact details. She replied and said everything was fine, so I left her to it.'

'I see. Thank you.' Kate's mind was whirring at a million thoughts per second that she almost forgot to ask, 'Where might I get the key?'

'I'll text you the key safe number. The police should have put it back after the ambulance took your mum. If there's any problem, just give me a ring and I'll come straight over.'

'That's very kind.'

'Anything I can do to help, you just let me know, bach.'

Kate ended the call as a lump appeared in her throat. What was the matter with her? She decided she would go to the cottage and see if she could find any trace of Joseph that the police might have missed.

As she went to find her car in the packed car park, she couldn't understand what her mother had been doing. Why was the cottage in her mother's name? First the car and now the cottage. She needed to find out what the hell this Joseph had been doing with her mother and she also needed to get the police to check her bank accounts. Or was Joseph another figment of her mother's imagination? What the hell had been going on?

Chapter 35

As light filtered through Esther's eyelids, confusion washed over her like a gentle tide. The warmth of sunlight touched her skin, a stark contrast to the cold, sterile touch of medical equipment she last remembered. A soft breeze carried the scent of flowers, tickling her nostrils. Where was she? Her last memory was lying in an ambulance, the wail of sirens piercing her ears as she was rushed to the hospital. Was her life going full circle? A mixture of fear and curiosity swirled in her mind as she struggled to understand what was happening.

Carefully, she opened her eyes, squinting against the sudden brightness. As her vision adjusted, she found herself in a garden which took her breath away. Cascading flowers in every colour covered the ground as three arches stood on the perimeter, covered with elegant rose blooms of every colour.

A wave of recognition washed over her, filling her with a mixture of emotion. This was her garden. Relief mingled with apprehension. The voice inside her head was trying to make sense of what was happening.

Why am I here? I released myself from the shadows; the deaths of three people. Why am I back here? Esther rolled over on the soft green carpet that cushioned her body as her thoughts ran on.

The three deaths were not my responsibility. If it's one thing I have learnt, it's that people create their own destiny. Mum allowed herself to be manipulated by Frank, just as I allowed myself to be controlled by Ray. Ray ran headlong off that cliff. I must forgive myself for choosing to stop at that layby. And George, poor little George. He was a victim of a deadly virus. Whatever I did, George was going to die. There was nothing anyone could do to save him. But why am I back here? Why am I not free to live my new life, free from guilt?

Esther turned, the soft grass yielding beneath her. A figure was walking across the gently sloping land that stretched endlessly behind the archways. Her heart leapt in recognition, a mix of comfort and uneasiness as she sat waiting.

Joseph smiled, and she saw he was back to full, glowing health. With his vibrant and flawless complexion, his golden hair stood out even more, making him truly captivating. As he walked, his white tunic and trousers swayed gracefully, the thin material catching the light. As he approached her, Esther noticed that despite his springy step, there was a slight frown on his beautiful face. She stood as he came towards her, holding out his arms. Esther moved towards him, walking easily, her ankle no longer painful.

'Esther, what a surprise.' His tone was disconcerting. As he enveloped her in his arms, she could feel the warmth radiating from him penetrate through her. But she didn't understand.

'Joseph. Why am I back here?'

Joseph held her at arm's length.

'I am not sure. Could you tell me what has happened since we last saw each other?'

'You mean you don't know?' Joseph surprised her even more by shaking his head. 'Something must have brought you back.'

Esther turned and, seeing the familiar bench, walked towards it and sat on the edge as Joseph came to sit beside her. She explained to Joseph she had woken at the cottage but had forgotten all about him and their journey together. Joseph nodded as if he understood. 'It wouldn't have stayed in your memory after our connection was broken.'

'I felt unwell. My ankle was red and swollen. I went to lie down and was woken by someone banging on the door. The next thing I remember was being in an ambulance and arriving at the hospital. After that, nothing until I woke and found myself here.'

Joseph was nodding slowly, gazing out across the landscape beyond the archways. 'We need to assess the situation, I think, before we can do anything further.' He stood and held out his hand to her. 'Let me show you what is happening.'

They walked together towards the back of the garden. Esther was surprised to see a window, its glass sparkling in the sunlight, but when she looked through it, there was nothing but space. Joseph motioned to Esther to look closely, and as she did, her eyes widened in astonishment. An image appeared within the window. Esther recognised it as a critical care ward in a hospital.

A body strikingly resembling her lay in the bed before her. The person was attached to a mass of drips and wires. The sound of the ventilator filled the room with a gentle sigh, accompanied by the hushed voices of two people. One was sitting next

to the bed and the other, a nurse, was whispering. As the nurse turned to take the hand of the
woman on the bed, Esther realised the visitor was
Kate.

Esther turned to Joseph. 'What is going on now,
Joseph?' She was shaking. 'I don't think I can go
through anymore of this.'

The nurse was talking to Kate in hushed tones.

'Your mother's body has a severe infection.
Sepsis.' Esther saw Kate's face grow pale.

Esther turned to Joseph. 'Oh no. Why didn't you
stop this? Aren't you supposed to look after me?'

'Something is happening which is beyond my
comprehension. I need to seek guidance, but I
think this may be something only you can solve.'

'What do you mean?'

'Once again, you have deviated from your life
plan. You are back here for a reason. Your subconscious is seeking resolution of other matters.
Perhaps it is the other areas of your life that you
still need to deal with?'

'What do you mean?'

'I am unsure, Esther. It is your inner consciousness driving this.' Esther didn't know what he
meant.

'You need to let your intuition guide you. Come Esther, let us sit. You can use the window to check on yourself in the physical world.'

She turned to find two comfortable chairs had appeared behind them. Joseph gestured and Esther dropped into the soft pillowy cushions.

Even after all she had been through, there was more to consider. It must be to do with Ozzy, but she had left the letter for Kate. Surely, that would provide Kate with the information she needed. Lily was the other person who she needed to help.

Esther let out a long, anguished sigh. Even with all these flights of fantasy, she'd still let people down, particularly her own daughter. It would be best not to return. But if she didn't go back, she could never make amends to Kate. She looked at Joseph for help. The evidence of her disastrous efforts was everywhere. A trail of destruction.

'Why do you feel that you have wasted your life?'

'Well, what good have I done? All I seem to do is discover another wrong decision. I feel as if everything I have done has let people down.'

Joseph laughed then, a huge belly laugh, which caught Esther completely off guard.

'Oh Esther.' Joseph stood and held out his hand. 'Come with me.'

Chapter 36

As soon as Kate turned off the main road, she could see the distant cottage in the fading light. The road was a narrow, bumpy track which was full of pot-holes. The bottom of her car hit rock several times. Kate hoped it hadn't damaged the undercarriage. The cottage looked like it was on the beach. When she arrived, she realised it was some way back, with a garden separating it from the sand dunes. There were no other houses visible, giving the place a remote feel.

Kate's hands clenched the wheel as she saw a white Range Rover parked outside. Was Joseph here? There were no lights on as the sun dipped below the horizon, a red sky promising a fine day tomorrow. Before the light went completely, Kate marshalled herself and, accessing the key, let herself in through the front door.

'Hello, anyone here?' Silence.

As she flipped on the light, she saw the cottage was open plan with a living, kitchen and dining area which felt very warm and cosy. The thick stone must hold the heat. Standing in the middle of the cottage, she wasn't sure what to do. She quickly made her way round the downstairs before going upstairs to check the bedrooms to check if anyone else was there.

The first, with floral wallpaper and a small window looking out over the beach, showed evidence of her mother. The wardrobe and drawers were filled with clothes. A suitcase was balanced on top of the wardrobe. Kate would have to pack up these things to take to the hospital.

Next, she found the bathroom and her mother's toiletries. The orange Sanctuary wash bag, a gift from Kate years ago, felt soft and familiar in her hands. Kate's heart ached, knowing her mother still used it. Beside the washbasin, her toothbrush was in a mug. The room had a sloping roof but somehow the designer had fitted a large shower. Kate realised she hadn't showered and wondered if she might use it later.

The second bedroom was spotlessly clean, with not a single item to show anyone had used it. No sign of Joseph.

Going back downstairs, she found tea and coffee as well as milk in the fridge, so made herself a hot drink before doing anything else. Sitting at the small dining room table, she cradled the cup. What the hell was her mother doing here? Where was Joseph? Had there ever been a Joseph or had her mother imagined the whole thing? Was he real or not? Given the most recent turn of events, Kate thought not, but did that make her mother so mentally ill that she had created another imaginary friend? Kate put her head in her hands.

She let out an exasperated sigh and looked towards the lounge. On the table was a pile of what looked like exercise books. A white envelope was balanced on the top. Getting up, she went to look. The envelope was addressed to her. Her hands shook as she carefully opened it. It was a long letter written in her mother's handwriting. Kate lowered herself onto the settee as she read.

My darling girl, I love you and I always will. In this letter, I want to tell you what happened with your father and apologise for my horrendous decision to embark on a relationship with Ray.

I loved your father. I was sixteen when Ozzy and I met, and after I was cast out by Frank. You know we met at college when he was doing music and design.

He was popular, funny and a couple of years older than me. As you also know, he was a talented musician and even then it was clear he would do well. I was studying health and social care, but wasn't at college every day. I had to work to make enough to pay for my room, so it was some time before he noticed me, but I'd noticed him. Your dad, being your dad, spotted me sitting on my own in the canteen and scooped me up. He introduced me to loads of people and at last I felt part of something.

I remember being so nervous the first time I went to your dad's house, but your grandparents welcomed me into their family. They knew about Frank throwing me out, and they were kind enough to take me in. Despite being mixed race, I was always accepted and made to feel like I belonged. I saw what family life could be like - laughing together, having family meals. Sarah told me once I was the daughter she'd never had. When I got pregnant with you, it was a surprise, but Sarah and Joe accepted it, saying they would support us both.

As you know, they set us up in a small flat in Kingston after you were born. Your dad looked after you during the day when I worked in a care home. He would go gigging at night. Everything was good until he got the roadie job. Then he was away. He was away all the time. Your grandma was wonderful, looking after you so I could work, but in the end, I didn't need to. Your dad was making good money. We moved into our house in Cheam after a couple of years and I concentrated on bringing you up. I became a proper mum. It was a good life, Kate, till the drugs took hold.

Your Dad started acting weird. I couldn't work out what was going on. It seemed like he didn't care anymore. He had lost himself in a world of his own. You were too young to notice, and I worked hard to keep it from you. He'd sit for hours in his studio strumming his guitar. I was so upset. I couldn't understand what we'd done, but then the truth came out. The rehab, recovery, relapse cycle began. You know the rest except for the end, Kate. The reason I left.

I couldn't deal with the consequences of his addiction. He was so thin and malnourished. The drugs were eating him alive. His arms were covered in sores from injecting himself, his mind was clouded, he didn't eat, and he reeked. He was spiralling out of control, on a path of self-destruction. He'd lost touch with reality and wasn't working properly anymore. Your dad owed money to people I didn't want anywhere near an eight-year-old. Evil men, Kate. We weren't safe. Then they started coming after me for the money. So, to protect you, the two of us just disappeared. I sold the house and paid off as much as I could, but there was still more owing. Oh Kate, it felt so wrong abandoning him, but I had to keep you safe so we cut all ties. Grandma and grandpa said they would look after your dad. I was riddled with guilt, but my only motive was to save you. I know you don't see it that way. After Ozzy died, the guilt made me ill, but I kept going for you, my love.

Do you remember our room in that huge Victorian house in Croydon? The room was cold, damp, and had a shared bathroom. It was all I could afford on the money I made. An eight-year-old shouldn't have been there. I know you hated me for making you change schools and that we had to live in that hellhole. Once I'd qualified and was earning a proper salary, we moved to our little house in Willow Crescent. You were doing well at school and it felt like a fresh start ... until I met Ray.

My self-esteem was at an all-time low, so I was easy game. Just as my mother was taken in by Frank, I was taken in my Ray. I fell for his lies. It wasn't until he'd established himself in our lives, moved himself in, that I saw him for what he was. The way he twisted my words. I thought everything was my fault. He made me less of a person and somehow it was easier to go along with everything. So I put up with his mood swings, to keep the peace, to protect you. It was such a relief when he died. Oh, my love. If only I could turn back the clock and change our past. I, the one person who should have been there for you, let you down.

Kate, I need to know what Ray did to you. I need to know the truth. I also need to tell you something, something that happened after you left, after Ray died. Please contact me so we can talk. When you read this letter, I hope you will forgive me. I did what I thought was best to protect you, but I failed and I have continued to fail you.

Now I have faced those demons that have plagued my life. I feel I have been given a fresh start. A new start where I want to be part of your life, to be the mother you deserve. The mother I should always have been.

I love you, my darling daughter.

Mum.

Tears streamed down Kate's face, leaving it damp and glistening. With an angry swipe, she brushed them aside, her frustration visceral. Why was she crying? Was she convinced by her mother's story? Was her mum's decision to leave her dad to die driven by a desire to save hers? And what did she mean about Ray?

She needed a drink to help her calm down and process all this new information. Kate scoured the cupboards and found a bottle of red wine. Getting a glass, she placed the bottle on the table. What if the hospital called? She'd said she would be back this evening, but the idea of sitting by her mother's bedside, overwhelmed with unanswerable questions, made her want to scream. Kate rang the hospital to say she was staying at the cottage. The nurse said her mother was stable and they would ring if there was any change.

Damn the woman. Why was she trying to screw with Kate's brain after all these years? I don't want to forgive her for what she's done; she screamed at the ceiling. But the letter …

Reaching for the bottle, she filled the glass. As she took a large gulp, Kate reached for the first notebook on the pile and began to read. What other secrets was she going to discover?

Chapter 37

In the garden, Esther didn't know what Joseph was planning. Why was he laughing at her assertion that her life had been pointless? All she had achieved through her interactions with him was to forgive herself for the deaths of her mother, George, and Ray. The fundamental lack of a relationship with her daughter and the guilt about the daughter she abandoned still laid heavily on her mind. What was Joseph so keen to show her?

As Joseph took her hand, the surrounding air began to vibrate. Esther was confused. Where was he taking her? Her feet lifted off the ground and she could feel the wind on her face as she rose into the air. Her heart leapt as she was filled with pure exuberance. This differed from any other experience. There was no door, no sense of panic, just pure exhilaration.

As soon as the sensation began, it was over. They were standing on a hill overlooking a valley. There was an immense sycamore tree in the middle of the valley and beneath it a dais. Wildflowers of every colour filled the valley floor, and a gentle breeze filled the air with the smell of cornflowers, sunflowers, foxgloves and camomile. Esther wanted to rush down the hill and bury her face in their fragrance. A path snaked its way up through the flowers towards the dais, which was draped with soft silken fabric which moved gently in the breeze.

The sky above was overcast, but a soft light filtered through the clouds, casting a glow on a long line of people moving steadily along the path. On the dais was a single photograph of the person they were here to honour. Someone who had touched each of their lives.

The crowd was filled with people of all ages, races, and walks of life. Mostly older adults, walking carefully, with faces lined with experience. They moved slowly, but with purpose. Some of the older women wore headscarves or shawls wrapped snugly around their shoulders. Some of the men leant on canes, dressed in well-worn suits.

There were some children, small and bright-eyed, who were quiet as if they sensed the importance of this day. They might not fully understand what was going on, but they understood they were part of something larger and greater than themselves. A collective expression of thanks for a life that had made a difference to theirs. Esther was reminded of the scenes at Gandhi's funeral. Who were all these people and who were they honouring?

Some turned and talked to each other in quiet conversation, but mostly the people walked in peaceful silence. Some carried flowers which they laid at the foot of the dais. Others clutched small tokens, a letter, a photograph, or a carefully folded note of thanks.

When they finally reached the dais, each person took their turn. Some paused only briefly, bowing their heads or closing their eyes in a silent thank you. Others knelt or raised a hand in acknowledgment.

Esther felt tears welling up as she surveyed the scene before her. The sheer number of people gathered, the overwhelming atmosphere of love and thankfulness made it very moving. This person must have been someone important.

'This person must have been someone remarkable, like Mother Teresa, to draw such a crowd of admirers,' Esther said, turning to Joseph beside her.

Joseph's face broke into a wide smile, so broad that Esther thought he was laughing at her. Feeling a flicker of irritation, she looked away, wondering what could be so funny.

Gently taking her hands in his, Joseph said, 'Look at me, Esther. These people aren't here to honour Mother Teresa. They have come to honour you.' Esther gasped, her eyes widening in disbelief. 'That can't be true. Who are all these people? I don't know them.'

'You might not remember them, but they certainly remember you,' Joseph replied softly. 'Come, let's find out what they're thanking you for, shall we?'

Faces in the crowd came into focus. Many now seemed familiar to Esther. They appeared unaware of her presence, their attention fixed on a large, framed photograph on top of the dais. The image showed a smiling woman with cinnamon skin and unruly black hair poking out from under a cap, wearing a nurse's uniform. With a jolt, Esther recognised herself, from many years ago. The photo was taken on the older adults' care unit where she'd worked. Memories flooded back. How she had loved that job, seeing not just old people, but a rich tapestry of life stories, resilience, and wisdom.

As they drew nearer to the dais, snippets of conversation drifted to her ears as people filed past.

'Thank you, Esther, for giving me money for groceries when I lost my purse.'

'Thank you for offering me your seat on the bus.'

'Thank you for helping me when I collapsed at the shopping centre.'

A well-dressed business executive whispered, 'Thank you for the £20 you gave me at McDonald's on New Year's Eve. It gave me the courage to get off the streets and start over.' Esther's breath caught as she recalled the dejected homeless man she'd met that night.

'Thank you for staying with me through the night as I passed away. It meant everything,' man with steel grey hair said, placing his hand on the photo.

Her dear friend Sara's voice rose above the others: 'My dearest friend, thank you for supporting me through Steve's affair. I wouldn't have survived that terrible time without you.' Esther's hand flew to her chest, her heart pounding. She turned to Joseph, overwhelmed.

There was her mother, young, slim and filled with such radiance that Esther wanted to run and enfold her in her arms. With her was another figure she recognised, but again, not the shrivelled, sunken frame. Ozzy was back to his strong, vibrant self. The man she had met and fallen in love with. Her mother stepped forward and touched her photo with such tenderness, Esther's tears flowed freely down her face. 'I am so proud of you, my darling girl. Thank you for setting me free.' She stood aside to let Ozzy move forward.

'I failed you completely, Esther. I am so sorry. I love you and always will.' Ozzy gently picked up the photo, his fingers tracing the outline of her face before softly kissing the image.

'You thought you were insignificant, that you had failed to achieve anything meaningful,' Joseph whispered. 'But look, Esther. Look at all the lives you've touched.'

A small boy who had been hidden by Ozzy came forward. George smiled up at her image, his presence making her heart skip a beat. She wanted to kneel and wrap her arms around him.

'Thank you for trying to save me,' he said, 'but it was my time to come home.'

As she watched him skip away, in that moment she understood the profound impact of minor acts of kindness, and the ripples they had created throughout countless lives. She was humbled by the steady stream of people who continued to pass by her photograph. Warmth spread through her chest. The weight of self-doubt and perceived inadequacy she had carried for so long lifted. She turned to Joseph, her eyes shining with a new light of understanding.

'I never knew,' she whispered, her voice trembling with emotion. 'All these years, I thought I was a nobody.'

Joseph squeezed her hand gently. 'Every act of kindness, no matter how small, has the power to change lives. You've been a beacon of hope and kindness, Esther, even when you didn't realise it.'

As they stood there, surrounded by the outpouring of gratitude. The realisation hit her. The true beauty of her life wasn't in material things, but in the countless smiles and grateful hearts she'd touched with her kindness and care.

Chapter 38

Kate groaned as she opened her eyes the following morning. She was lying in the pretty bedroom at the top of the stairs that her mother had occupied not so many nights before. Sunlight streamed through the window as Kate grabbed her phone to check the time. It was only seven thirty. She sank back against the pillows with a sigh of relief. Her mind was reeling from the shock of what she had read in her mother's journals.

After she'd got used to the writing, it was easy to flick through the pages of the five journals. The earlier ones described Esther's recovery after she left work, the pages filled with unfocused ramblings about the mistakes she had made. The writing in the first notebook became more coherent toward the end. Esther had written about her relationship with Ozzy and the information matched the content of the letter her mother had written her. Reading those words again made Kate realise that her mother had been in an impossible situation. What would she have done if the same had happened with Shaun? Her primary motivation would be to protect her boys. And she would protect them, even if it meant sacrificing herself. A wave of understanding washed over Kate. Her mother was trying to save her. The understanding was accompanied by guilt. How could she have been so immovable in her ideas? The story she'd constructed differed from the reality. But I still can't forgive her, her inner voice said.

As for the story of her grandmother's death ... that was horrific. Kate knew nothing about Frank and his feeding obsession. The descriptions of the doctor's decision to aid her death were frightening. Was her mother somehow complicit in the death of her own mother?

The confession in the latest notebook about Ray. Had her mother engineered his death, too? If she had, I would applaud her, Kate told herself. She rid the earth of a vile creature. These stories implicated her mother in the deaths of three people. What was she supposed to do with the information? She needed her mother to wake up. She needed answers.

Sitting up again, she dialled the number for the critical care unit. The phone rang out until eventually it was answered by a doctor. Kate explained who she was and there was a pause at the other end as a muffled conversation took place.

'Good morning Mrs Cooper. Are you coming in today? There is something the consultant would like to discuss with you?'

'Yes, yes. Is everything alright?' Kate sat up straighter.

'You mother is stable but her condition is not responding as well as we would expect to the treatment she is receiving. We can discuss this more fully when you arrive.'

'I'll be there within the hour,' Kate replied, getting up quickly and heading for the bathroom. She needed a change of clothes, so rummaged through the bag she had hastily packed looking for clean underwear. It was surprisingly cool in the cottage, so after a shower she pulled on one of her mother's jumpers. As the familiar scent washed over her, tears pricked her eyes. What did they want to discuss with her?

Kate didn't know why her mother had come to the middle of Wales to finish writing these confessional stories. What did she think would happen? What had she planned to do with them?

There was mention of the mysterious Joseph being with her in the stories, but there was no evidence of him at the cottage. The car and cottage were booked in her mother's name, leading Kate to conclude he was a figment of her mother's imagination.

But that would all have to wait. She needed to get to the hospital and find out what was going on. Grabbing her coat and bag and checking she had the keys, Kate made her way out into the cool morning air.

When she arrived on the unit, having taken off her coat, washed her hands and donned the obligatory plastic apron, she made her way to her mother's bedside. There was a huddle of doctors around the bed looking at the monitors and the file of notes. As Kate approached, a nurse detached herself from the throng and came towards her.

'Mrs Cooper, thank you for coming so promptly. Could I ask you to wait in the visitors' room for a few minutes? Dr Cunningham, will come and have a word with you.' Seeing the look on Kate's face, the nurse continued as she steered her away. 'Try not to worry until you have spoken to the doctor.'

Kate sat nervously on the lumpy sofa, rocking from side to side. Her stomach churned. What were they going to say? Her throat was tight, and she was having difficulty fighting back the tears. What was the matter with her? Yes, it was possible her mother was going to die. Yes, that would be tragic, but after all she'd put Kate through, why was she feeling so upset? Reading her mother's journals made it clear. Some things are better left unsaid, their shadows better left deeply buried.

She crumpled forward, her arms hugging herself. Whatever had happened between them, Esther was still her mother. Kate thought back to the letter where her mother tried to explain why they had left her father to die. A shiver went down Kate's spine and glanced around, half expecting to see someone else in the room. What if she'd got it wrong all this time?

The comments about the unscrupulous men her father owed money to. What if her mother had done what she thought was best? What if her mum had been trying to protect her? Her train of thought was interrupted by the door opening. A large ruddy faced man with thinning grey hair dressed in scrubs with a stethoscope around his neck came in holding out his hand. Behind him was the nurse who had spoken to Kate earlier.

'Mrs Cooper?'

Kate went to get up, but he waved his hand, showing her to stay seated. She sank back and put out her hand to shake his.

'May I?' he asked, pointing to the seat opposite her. She nodded. The nurse stayed standing by the door.

'My name is Dr Cunningham and I am the consultant anaesthetist in charge of the unit. We've been having a chat about your mother's condition.' He paused, looking up to gauge her reaction. Kate sat on the edge of the sofa, rubbing her hands.

'I know this is difficult for you, but we are trying our best to save your mother's life.' The implications of his words slammed into Kate, a physical blow to her chest that stole her breath. Continuing, the doctor provided more information. 'The infection in her leg, which is the root cause of the sepsis, isn't responding to the antibiotic therapy. To stop the infection worsening, I'm afraid the only option is to amputate her leg.' Kate's hand flew to her mouth. After all her mother had been through with that cursed frame and those months of immobility, it didn't seem fair.

'Is there anyone here with you?' Dr Cummingham sounded concerned. Kate shook her head as the nurse came to sit beside her.

The doctor continued. 'We must ask you as her next of kin to consider if this is something your mother would consent to. Do you know if your mother put a power of attorney in place?'

'Yes, I am the attorney'

'Good, good.' Getting to his feet, he said, 'I'm going to leave you with Staff Nurse Mohammed, who will talk you through what would be required. Do you have questions?'

'What will happen if you don't do,' Kate paused, 'the operation?'

Dr Cunningham took a breath. 'We could not control the infection which would continue to ravage your mother's body and would ultimately lead to her death.'

Kate looked at her hands as she fiddled with the tissue the nurse had passed her.

'I see. Thank you for being honest.' Kate said as the consultant nodded to the nurse and left the room.

'Can I get you a hot drink?' Nurse Mohammad asked. Kate shook her head. They sat in silence for a couple of minutes before the nurse continued.

'I know this is a shock and it's a lot to take in, but I have to ask if you have the power of attorney documents available.' Kate looked confused. 'In order to decide on behalf of your mother, it is important for us to have a sight of the original power of attorney paperwork.'

'Why?' Kate was bemused. The nurse paused, trying to phrase her next sentence correctly.

'We know that your mother suffered some mental health issues. As she has appointed you her executor, you are acting on her behalf. Say if you decided that your mother would not want an operation, the doctor would take that into consideration. This important decision requires us to ensure you have a power of attorney and can act on your mother's behalf.'

'Can't you get that information online?'

'Unfortunately, no. We must see the original documents.'

'I see.' Kate's mind was racing. The documents were at her mother's in the folder. She'd have to drive all the way to World's End to collect them. That would delay things.

'How quickly does Mum have to have the operation?'

'Within the next twenty-four hours.'

Richard, Kate thought. Richard could help.

'I need to call someone. They should be able to bring the documents.'

'The signal isn't good in here. Would you like to come to the office and you can use our phone to call?

Kate got up, her legs shaking, and followed the nurse back out into the unit. She glanced over at her mother lying so forlorn in the bed. She seemed so small and vulnerable. 'Don't worry Mum, we're going to save you.' Kate said silently as she followed the nurse into the office.

Chapter 39

Sitting at his desk trying to complete a design for a client, Richard's mind was elsewhere, thinking about Esther. As he looked out of his office window, he remembered the white Range Rover and the shadow in the garden.

Since the conversation with Kate and the subsequent feedback from Grace, he was feeling uncomfortable. He didn't know what was going on - a situation he detested. Kate's relationship with her mother was an enigma. Even after Grace's revelation about Kate blaming her mother for the death of her father, Richard still thought the level of her hostility was unjustified.

His mother had always been supportive, even when he came out at seventeen. His early years as a gay man were wild. Her door was always open when he needed shelter to sleep off a hangover or recover from a broken heart. Colin's story was very different. Public school, prestigious university, good career in publishing, marriage, children. The whole thing was a lie, of course. He perpetuated it out of fear of recrimination. But Richard smiled as he remembered how he proved to be Colin's downfall.

They'd met in a gay bar in Vauxhall and were instantly attracted to each other. Colin was insatiable. He would go away 'on business' so he could meet Richard and fulfil his suppressed desires. Even Richard, who was active sexually, was overwhelmed by Colin's appetite. Phone sex kept Colin happy when his 'normal' life kept him away, but proved his ruin when his wife found and read their text messages.

When she threw Colin out, he moved into Richard's tiny flat in Pimlico. His career didn't suffer and when all the fuss died down, the divorce happened. The division of assets left enough for them to move to a bigger flat in Chelsea. That was ten years ago, but Colin became tired of London life hence the move to World's End for a quieter life. They felt content being together with their friends in the Cotswolds, and their regular dinner-parties.

Richard invited the neighbours to their legendary Christmas drinks party and Esther fitted right in.

Her stories about her nursing career were grand entertainment. But then came the breakdown and Kate's abandonment, leaving Richard to mop up the mess.

Richard's guts twisted as he remembered how he looked after Esther when her own daughter wouldn't. That sullied their relationship, but still he felt responsible for Esther and worried about what had happened. As if the gods heard him, his phone rang.

It was Kate. She sounded tearful as she told Richard that Esther was in hospital. An emergency admission. Not again, thought Richard. What now? Kate asked if he would go to the house and find a green folder with Esther's important documents in. She needed it urgently. Without asking why, Richard grabbed his jacket against the keen March wind and helped himself to the key from the key safe. The house smelt musty and damp. Richard wondered if he should put the heating on for a bit, but decided against it. It was spring now, so the weather should be warm enough to prevent any damp. It just need-ed a good airing.

He found the folder easily. As he pulled it out of the drawer, a long white envelope fluttered to the ground. Richard could feel the hairs on the back of his neck bristle as he carefully opened the envelope and extracted a single white sheet. What he saw made his heart race. He had to tell Grace, but wait, he couldn't. She would tell him off for snooping. Well, he'd make damn sure Kate knew about it. Getting up, Richard turned. He had the feeling he was being watched again. He could almost feel someone's breath on the back of his neck. He hurried home to ring Kate back.

His call was answered by a ward clerk and when he explained who he was, she handed the phone to Kate.

'Richard, I need the power of attorney documents. Can you check in the folder that they're there? They want Mum to have surgery and she can't consent. They won't let me decide on her behalf without seeing the documents. Richard, if she doesn't have the operation within the next twenty-four hours, she could die.' A choked sob escaped her lips as her voice quivered.

'What are they going to do?' Richard clutched his throat, horrified but still wanting details.

Kate's voice broke. 'They want to amputate her foot.' Richard gasped.

'Oh my God, Kate, I'm so sorry.' He paused, considering what to do. 'Listen, I'll drive up now. I'll be there just after lunch.'

'You don't need to do that. Couldn't you courier them?'

'No Kate, I'm coming. I've found something else you need to see. I'll tell you when I see you. Now, do you need anything else?'

'No.' Richard could hear the tears in her voice. 'Thank you. I appreciate everything you've done for Mum.'

'It'll be alright, Kate. See you later.'

Richard rang Colin to tell him what was happening. 'I've got to drive up to Aberystwyth.' Richard told him about Esther's readmission to the hospital with sepsis and Kate needing the power of attorney documents.

'That's not good, is it?' Colin's tone was sombre. 'I don't like to say this, Rich, but you said you weren't getting involved in Esther's business again.'

'I know, but what can I do? Kate needs the documents.'

'Well, send them by courier.' Colin sounded exasperated.

'I have to see Kate.'

'Why, are you besties suddenly?'

'I found something else she needs to have.'

'What?' Richard didn't answer. 'Should you be poking your nose in? What's the big secret?'

'I can't tell you.' Changing the subject, he said. 'Do you want me to leave you some dinner?'

'No. I'm sure I can manage if you're not back. See you later. Love you.' The way he said it irritated Richard. He knew Colin thought he was getting involved in things which were none of his business.

As he prepared to leave, he thought again about how complex Esther's life was. Who'd have thought such an ordinary woman would have such a chequered past? As her life hung in the balance, would the contents of the white envelope ever be explained?

Chapter 40

Esther sat on the armchair in the garden, watching the drama of her illness unfold before her. Kate was sitting by her bedside, holding her hand. Something serious was happening. She looked for Joseph, but he wasn't there. Esther shivered. Despite the warmth and beauty of her garden, her breath quickened. She was vulnerable here without him. Not because she was here in the picturesque surroundings, but because part of her lay unconscious in a hospital bed. As if sensing her discomfort, she turned to see him entering through one archway. Esther's breath eased, and she sat back, looking back at the window.

Joseph came and sat beside her and took her hand.

'Something's happening Joseph,' she turned to him, her expression fearful.

'Your earthly body is not responding to the treatment. Kate is deciding for you as you wished her to do. This could be happening for her benefit rather than yours, Esther.'

'What do you mean?'

'The walls Kate has erected and the defences she has built are crumbling. The letter you wrote has opened her eyes to the possibility of another version of events surrounding her father's death. She is realising why you took the actions you did and that is challenging for her.'

Esther sighed deeply. Having witnessed so many people coming to pay their respects to her, her once insignificant life overflowed with their gratitude. All those people whose lives she had touched.

Joseph answered her unspoken thoughts. 'Many of the actions you took to help others were spontaneous and came from a place of love and compassion. That is what you hold deep within you, Esther, a pure and loving soul.'

'Why have I made such a mess of things, then?'

'Esther, you have not. Having revisited the situations that caused you pain, what have you learnt?'

'That I was not responsible.'

'You constructed stories in your mind that convinced you of a sense of responsibility. You still need to let go of this feeling of failure. Can you not see what a truly wonderful person you are?' Esther's eyes filled with tears. The biggest problem Esther faced was her inability to forgive herself. Although issues remained unresolved, he was right. She was the architect of her own unhappiness and it was time to stop blaming herself and start being grateful. She squared her shoulders and looked towards the monitor.

As they sat watching the scene, Kate suddenly turned to see Richard striding down the unit towards her. Kate rose to meet him and they embraced before speaking to the nurse, who led them away from the bedside.

'Why can't I hear what they are saying?' Esther asked.

'Do you wish to hear Esther?'

'Yes.'

When she looked back, Kate and Richard were sitting in a bland room on an uncomfortable-looking sofa. Esther started. She could suddenly hear what they were saying. It was like watching her life in a film. She leaned forward, desperately wanting to know what was going on.

The nurse was asking if they would like a drink.

'Oh yes, I'm dying for a coffee,' Richard said without thinking, then put his hand to his mouth, 'Sorry that came out wrong.' Kate smiled for the first time in days.

'Thank you for coming all this way Richard.'

'There is an ulterior motive, but first things first - here's the folder.'

Kate sat on the lumpy sofa and drew out the documents. The power of attorney document was on the top. Kate leafed through to make sure the Health and Welfare document was there. Checking the signatures were all in place, Kate stood.

'I need to give this to the staff straight away. Are you alright here for a minute?'

Richard nodded as she swept out of the room. He wriggled as he sat on the uncomfortable sofa. He wondered why there wasn't more comfort in a room where people full of grief came for a rest. Richard didn't use the NHS, Colin had private health insurance.

The nurse came in with two plastic cups filled with a brown liquid which did not resemble coffee on any level when Richard took a sip. But he thanked her before putting it down on the worn coffee table. Looking around, he noted the attempts to make the space more homely. There were prints of dogs and kittens and one of a garden in full of flowers with arches surrounded by blooms. His attention was drawn to the folder lying open on the sofa beside him. He thought about the envelope inside. How was he going to broach the subject with Kate? Just as he was contemplating how to start the conversation, she walked back in.

'What are you looking so guilty about?' she asked.

Richard shifted on the lumpy sofa. 'I was just thinking about how much better private healthcare was. Did you get everything sorted out?'

Kate collapsed onto the sofa next to him with a sigh.

'Yes, the consultant has seen the documents, which they will copy for her records. They've put her on the list for the operation this afternoon.' Suddenly full of tears she said 'Oh God, Richard. Am I doing the right thing? Mum said she didn't want to be alive if she wasn't independent,' she whispered, her tone tinged with fear.

Richard automatically reached and folded her into a hug. 'Come on, love, you're doing the right thing. If the doctors are saying this will give her a fighting chance, you must do it. Even if you refused, I expect they would insist.'

'What do you mean?' Kate pulled back.

'I have a feeling the doctors could overrule you if they thought it was in your mum's best interests.'

'How the hell would you know that?'

'Suppose I've watched too many real-life A&E programmes? So, by you agreeing with what they are recommending, it is the best thing you can do. You are giving her a fighting chance.'

Kate's face crumpled as Richard hugged her again. Whatever he thought of Kate and her past behaviour towards her mother, she was stepping up now and that was all that mattered. What a terrible decision to make. He was glad it wasn't him.

Kate sat up and blew her nose on a tissue from the box on the table. She picked up her cup of plastic coffee, taking a large sip. She was quiet for a few minutes before she turned to Richard.

'The whole situation is so strange. I went to the cottage where she'd been staying. There was no sign of Joseph. The owner of the cottage said it was booked in Mum's name. The police said that the Range Rover, which was still parked outside, was registered in her name. She paid to hire it for three months.'

'What the hell? Why would she do that? I saw someone driving that Range Rover, honey, and it wasn't your mother. I'm convinced Joseph is a real person. Grace went to your mother's and there had been someone else there. Whatever is going on, we need to be wary of this man called Joseph.' Kate's head went down.

'I don't know. It's all such a mess. I found a stack of other journals at the cottage. Some of the stuff she had written ….' Turning to look at Richard, Kate decided now was not the time to tell him her mother could be implicated in the deaths of three people. 'Not being able to speak to her makes it worse. It's a mystery we might never solve.' Her voice caught as she turned to Richard.

'Kate, talking of mysteries.' She turned to face him, knowing that tone showed he knew something more. 'Do you have a sister?'

'What, what the hell are you talking about, Richard?' Kate looked at him with a quizzical expression.

'Have a look at the envelope in the folder.' Giving him another questioning look, she reached for the folder and extracted a long, white envelope. She slowly withdrew the single sheet of yellowing paper and gasped when she read the contents.

'Oh my God, I have a sister.' Turning to Richard, there was confusion etched into every line of her face. 'A sister called Lily.'

Chapter 41

Esther's hand flew to her mouth, and she moaned as Kate extracted the envelope from the green folder she had opened on her lap.

'This is a birth certificate, Richard. For a baby girl called Lily born the year Ray died. The year after I left.' Kate let out an enormous sigh. She looked back at the certificate. 'Mum is listed as her mother and Ray as her father.' Kate stared at the piece of paper in her hands. 'But she was born after Ray died. What does this mean, Richard? What the hell does this mean?' Kate's eyes were wild, as if she couldn't take anymore. Richard wished he hadn't started this. It could be too difficult for Kate.

'Why wouldn't she tell me she'd had another child? This is madness.' She was on her feet, pacing up and down. Richard sat helplessly watching her, trying desperately to think of something useful to say.

'To be fair, you didn't really see Esther after Ray died, did you?'

'No, no, but that's not the point. When I got back in touch, why didn't she say anything? Richard sat thinking.

'She was ill when you reconnected, wasn't she? During COVID?' He didn't want to discuss the whole, 'you didn't come and look after your mother's scenario.' That wouldn't be helpful. Kate sat back down on the sofa.

As Esther watched the scene unfold, a hollow ache spread through her chest. When she glanced up at Joseph, he was gazing at her with concern.

'Why haven't I had to relive how I abandoned Lily?' she whispered.

'Lily lives, Esther. She remains your daughter whatever the circumstances. I know that you have tried to reach her, but you have been blocked by Ray's parents. There is a future for both Lily and Kate. Whatever happens, this will work itself out.' Esther looked at Joseph, her face full of doubt. 'Do you want to talk about Lily?'

Esther turned back towards to watch as Richard held Kate's hand. She'd never told Kate. Why would she admit to another failure? Lily was a deeply held secret. Esther's failure weighed heavily on her as she thought about another person she had let down badly. But at least Kate knew of her existence now.

'Tell me about Lily, Esther,' Joseph said gently as he sat beside her.

'Why? What good would it do?'

'Understand you are back here so you can dispel all your shadows. Lily is one of those shadows. Until you admit the truth of what happened to yourself, you will not be free.'

Esther shuddered, knowing this was going to be difficult to talk about. All the emotions surrounding this situation were painful.

Joseph took her hand.

'Try to put it into words, Esther.'

'Kate had left a long time before. It was a mercy.' Esther paused as if gathering the strength to go on. 'Ray's behaviour got worse after Kate left. He went to the pub after work every night. I would never know what mood he would be in when he walked through the door. He expected his dinner to be on the table, but I never knew when he was coming home. I would be on tenterhooks, my heart pounding, waiting for him. This one night he came home with a face like thunder. I knew there would be trouble. I placed his meal in front of him and he stared at it. 'What the fuck is this mess?' He sneered at me. 'I could get better food in a pigsty.' He threw the plate across the room. It smashed against the kitchen units.'

'He stood up and came towards me until I was backed into the corner of the kitchen. He wasn't a large man, but he was strong from all the lifting he did at work. He grabbed me round the arms and spun me round. Grabbing my hair, he pushed me down onto the counter and clawed at my leggings. I heard him unzip his flies. It hurt so much I cried out so he thrusted even harder. 'I'll teach you to respect me, you filthy whore,' he whispered in my ear before grunting and pulling out of me. I slid to the ground in a daze as he walked away. That was the night Lily was conceived.'

Joseph waited for the tears to abate as he rubbed Esther's hand.

'Well done Esther. Well done. That wasn't the first time he'd done that, was it?'

'No, it happened every few weeks, but that night he was more brutal than he'd ever been previously. I wished him dead as I had so many times before. And within days he was.'

'It was weeks before I realised I was pregnant. Ray was dead, and I was sick with guilt, thinking I was responsible for his death.' Esther stopped and looked at Joseph, a shadow of a smile on her lips. 'I now know that's not true, thanks to you, my dear friend.' They sat in companionable silence before Esther continued.

'I didn't eat or sleep for weeks afterwards. My mind was filled with the horror of all that had happened. I was angry with myself for not leaving. For being so weak. I put the sickness down to the stress I was feeling. Eventually, I went back to work and tried to contact Kate, but she didn't want to know. She'd come to the funeral and said it was the best day of her life. I didn't see her again for years after that.

When the doctor advised me to take a pregnancy test. I was shocked when the result came back positive. I didn't want his baby, but by the time I realised I was pregnant, I was sixteen weeks. The thought of aborting a foetus so well developed filled me with horror. I decided the child could be adopted when she was born, but that was before Ray's mother found out.'

Esther paused again and getting up paced up and down.

'You don't need to carry on if this is too much. We can revisit it another time,' Joseph whispered.

'No, best get it all out in the open,' Esther said, taking a deep, shaky breath, her hands clenched as she continued her restless pacing. 'Lily was born early, at thirty-six weeks, with a low birth weight. Ray's mother was at the birth. She was a constant visitor in the first few weeks, checking up on me. She couldn't understand why I couldn't bond with Lily. 'What's the matter with you?' She'd say. 'Look at the state of this place.. I can't believe you've been a mother before. Are you feeding her properly? She looks underweight to me. You need to get a grip of yourself, my girl, or I'll be reporting you to the social'. I was on maternity leave but went back to work after six months. Tina, Ray's mother, took care of the baby. As time went on, Lily spent more time with her grandmother. In the end, they took control of Lily's life from me. 'Better off with us,' Tina would say. 'You're not fit to be her mother.'

'And it was a relief, if I'm honest. I didn't want Lily and was glad to be rid of her, but as the years passed, I realised the mistake I had made. Lily was my daughter. It wasn't her fault that she was conceived in such a violent way. I tried to get her back, but the whole family formed a barrier around Lily and I couldn't get to her.

'On the rare occasions I saw her at the school gates, she would run screaming to her grandmother, who would shout obscenities at me. They completely turned Lily against me. I know the main reason they keep her is to claim benefits. She's nothing more than a meal ticket to them. I worry for her. I worry about her future. That estate where they live is full of gangs and drugs. It's not a safe place for a child.' Esther's hands trembled as she reached out, as though she could gently touch Kate's ashen, stricken face. It was clear that feeling the weight of this latest devastating news had hit Kate like a physical blow.

'Esther, sometimes things happen for reasons we cannot fathom.' Joseph was murmuring.

'What are you talking about, Joseph?' Esther turned, a hint of anger in her voice.

'Lily is alive for a reason, Esther. A life never happens by chance.'

Chapter 42

As Richard's footsteps faded away, Kate's head dropped forward feeling more alone than ever. When the nurse came to find her, Kate's weary eyes met hers with a mixture of hope and exhaustion. Her gentle words told Kate it was time for Esther to go down to the theatre.

The nurses suggested she took a break. It felt like a reprieve from the hours of worry. The unit's calm hum of machines and whispered voices did nothing to quell her anxiety, guilt, and confusion. She nodded, unsure if she should seek the sanctuary of the cottage. She asked how long Esther would be in surgery. It would be several hours, Nurse Mohammad told her. Kate said she might go back to the cottage. The nurse nodded her agreement.

As she gathered her things, she noticed her hands trembling almost imperceptibly. Kate longed to be home with the boys, desperate to escape this nightmare which consumed her every waking moment.

Arriving mid-afternoon, Kate let herself into the cottage and immediately felt the presence of someone else having visited. She dumped her bag on the sofa and kicked off her shoes, walking barefoot into the kitchen. On the counter there was a plate with scones, jam and cream waiting for her. Kate was struck by the kindness of the owner. What a lovely thought. She must remember to thank her.

Taking her tea and scone out onto the decking, she settled into a comfortable recliner and took a deep breath. This was just what she needed. There was so much going on in her head she was exhausted. The one good thing to come out of this was Shaun stepping up to look after their sons. This morning, when she phoned the boys, they were talking about all the things their dad had done. When Shaun had taken the phone, she thanked him with genuine appreciation.

'No problem, babe, you concentrate on getting your mother sorted. I'll stay here until you get back. Mum is going to pick Jack up from school when I'm working and Ben has offered to cook. That's got to be a first.' As she disconnected the call, she smiled and her heart softened towards her husband. It was in times of trial when you found out who your supporters were.

The weather was mild, and as the light softened, Kate relaxed. As she sat looking out at the beach, the gentle ebb and flow of the tide whispering against the shingle, Kate allowed herself to think of the sister she'd never known. Was she still alive? As Kate sat, the awful possibility that she may never have known the truth if her mother had died, hit her with full force. A cold shudder, ran down her spine, making her breath catch in her throat. A profound sense of loss, a gaping hole in her understanding of her mother's past. Getting to her feet, she went in search of the notebooks, hoping to find some clues.

As she reread the entries, she realised her mother went through hell thinking she was responsible for the death of her mother, Ozzy, and Ray. With the information about the child George from the purple journal, Kate experienced a moment of clarity.

Kate realised her mother's breakdown had been a direct result of her accumulated guilt. Kate's stomach turned when she remembered her behaviour. The stories in the journals exonerated her of any blame, but was that right? Sitting back, she methodically thought about each of the deaths. Her grandmother had been given an injection by the doctor, not her mother. Even though she had agreed, she was not culpable. Now she thought about her father. Ozzy was the engineer of his own death. She saw that now. As for Ray. He got what he deserved. The only question was the child, George. The detailed account in the journal, with its compelling evidence, completely cleared her mother's name. George, like thousands of others, succumbed to the relentless grip of COVID, his life cut short by the invisible enemy. Nothing more. Guilt washed over Kate, how she had been so unhelpful, judgemental and unkind. All these hidden secrets. She didn't know her mother at all. What more was there to learn about her?

What did her mother mean about Ray? What did she think Ray had done to her? Kate's relationship with Ray was bad. She had never accepted him as being anything to do with her. Ray tried to dominate her as he dominated her mother, but Kate stood up to him. The situation deteriorated, but at least he never resorted to violence.

To control her, he made her do housework and grounded her, stopping her from going out with friends. He changed the TV channel to annoy her. When she left with Shaun on New Year's Eve, she hadn't given her mother a second thought. But what happened after she'd left? Why had her mother had another child, with him? What happened in the time between her leaving home and finding her mother curled in a ball during COVID? There was so much she didn't know. If only she could talk to her mum, what other secrets would she uncover? Now her mother was lying on an operating table, her life in the hands of the surgeons. Kate resolved to find out the truth once Esther had recovered.

Kate jumped as the doorbell rang. She was momentarily disorientated. She visibly shook herself awake, then stood and carefully smoothed the familiar, slightly itchy texture of her mother's jumper. She ran a hand through her short hair, realising she must look a mess. Who the hell this could be, she wondered, as she made her way to the front door.

She was met by a cheerful woman, small and round, with a cloud of grey curls framing a kind face. The worn corduroy trousers, knitted cardigan, and gilet offered little protection against the late afternoon chill, but her smile was warm and inviting.

'Mrs Bennett,' she said, holding out her hand. 'You must be Kate. I just wanted to come round and make sure everything was alright.' Her accent was lilting and suited her comforting nature.

'Yes, thank you. Would you like to come in?'

'Just for a moment bach.'

'I'm about to have a cup of tea. Would you like one?'

'That would be lovely. Milk and two sugars, please.' Mrs Bennett took off her gilet and hung on the pegs by the front door before pulling down her hand-knitted cardigan.

'Would you like one of these delicious scones you left?'

'That would be lovely too bach, but I didn't leave you anything. Oh, those are nice and fresh. Cream and jam as well. Now tell me how your mother is?' A shiver ran down Kate's spine as she felt a prickling sensation. She spent an hour talking to Mrs Bennett about her mother, which was comforting, as the older lady just sat and listened.

'Your mother is lucky to have such a caring daughter,' she said as she got up to leave. If only she knew, thought Kate.

After she had left, Kate cleared the tea tray. She wondered about the mystery of the scones. There was one explanation she didn't want to consider, as it was too bizarre. She settled comfortably on the sofa, planning to rest for a few minutes, and woke two hours later at the shrill sound of her phone ringing. It was the hospital.

'Could you come in please, Mrs Cooper?' The voice at the other end sounded worried.

'What's happened?'

'Your mother's operation went well, but unfortunately, her postoperative recovery is not going as expected.'

Kate struggled to push herself out of the armchair, her mind instantly on high alert. But all the strength had left her body. Her mind was numb as she rushed around the cottage, trying to find her car keys, bag, and coat. Where the hell had she put the keys? She was almost sobbing with frustration. Here they were, in her bag all the time. The drive to the hospital was interminably long. Every slow car caused Kate to swear. Several cars tooted her as she overtook them in a dangerous manoeuvre.

'Slow down Kate.' A voice said. She looked round, expecting to see someone sitting in the back, but there was no-one. 'Take a deep breath,' the voice said again. It was not her own voice talking to her, it was a man's. She took a deep breath and slowed the car. Within minutes, she screeched into the hospital car park and miraculously there was a space right by the entrance. Grabbing her bag, she ran into the foyer and turned left towards the critical care unit. She rang the bell repeatedly, trying to get someone to open the door. Her heart pounded as she almost screamed with frustration. After only minutes, which seemed like hours to Kate, a staff nurse wearing a mask, came to let her in. She shoved her bag and coat on the bench by the door instead of hanging it up neatly like she usually did. She washed her hands so quickly the nurse had to ask her to do them again. Grabbing the plastic apron, she followed the nurse through the swing doors into the unit.

There was frantic activity around her mother's bedside. Doctors were barking orders at a nurse handing them equipment. Another nurse was drawing up drugs into syringes as another ran through a bag of blood. A nurse came towards her with open arms, telling her she needed to go to the relatives' room, but Kate stood frozen to the spot. What was this? Was this it? Was this the end?

Chapter 43

Esther sat on the edge of the chair watching the scene before her with horror. She had no sense of herself in her physical body. Her consciousness was here in the garden, with Joseph by her side. Pulling her gaze from watching Kate in the waiting room and the doctors intently working at her bedside, Esther forced herself to focus.

'What is going to happen?' Esther was shocked when he gave a bemused shake of his head. He was quiet for several minutes whilst she waited anxiously for him to respond.

'Your situation is unique and not something I have encountered before. When we met, you had been given two choices, if you remember. Lying in that ditch, you could have lived or died. You called out for help and I was sent as your guardian, in human form, to help you. Against all odds, and to everyone's astonishment, you lived. To make that mean something, I was asked to help you dispel the shadows that haunted you. To help you kick-start a new beginning.' He sat pondering again as if waiting for answers to come, his face turned towards the endless sky.

Turning, he gestured to where the barren ground had been.

'The current events seem to be closely linked to your subconscious, based on my understanding.'

'How do you feel about yourself now?' Joseph asked.

'This is hard to do right now, Joseph.'

'I know, but it is important to acknowledge all you have achieved. It will help you make the right decision.'

'What decision?' But seeing Joseph would not elaborate, she continued.

'All those people I've helped made me realise my light shines brighter than I ever knew. Small acts of kindness make the difference. I've got to stop absorbing other people's sadness. Feeling all that pain has worn me out.' Taking a deep breath, she said, 'I have forgiven myself. I'm proud of myself, not disappointed as I have been for most of my life. I can hold my head up high. I am in control of my destiny.'

When Esther glanced over at Joseph, he was beaming, glowing brightly.

'I am so proud of you,' he said.

Esther wanted to know. 'Does everyone have a Joseph?'

'The answer is yes. Every human being has a guide or guardian who travels with them. But most people are not aware of their guides. They may hear whispers, or receive signs or experience coincidences. But most people do not acknowledge their guides. There are individual guides, guides for families and guides for communities. When a person realises, they have a guide, they can ask for and receive help with their life journey.

'So, you have always been there?'

'Yes Esther, I have tried to guide you on many occasions, but your mind got in the way. But now you know. I am always with you. Even if you do not see me, you can ask for my help.'

Esther looked across to where the barren land had been transformed. A carpet of wildflowers nodding their heads in the slight breeze. 'How have I resolved things?'

'Kate knows the truth about Ozzy. You saw at the dais that Ozzy accepts responsibility for his death and for the way he let you down. But that doesn't mean he doesn't love you still. He lost his way but recognises his wrong turns.'

'Unlike Ray.' Esther mused. Joseph nodded.

'You have revealed the secret of Lily to Kate so your garden is now complete.' But Esther's smile turned to horror as she saw two doorways veiled in mist.

'What are those?' her voice filled with panic

Joseph's bemusement returned, his eyes unfocused, a quiet hum escaping his lips. Eventually he spoke.

'They are your way out of the garden. The time is coming when you are going to have to choose again, Esther. You must go through one of the doors or you will be trapped here forever.'

Esther stared at him in consternation. 'What do you mean, trapped?'

'Your work in the garden is finished, Esther. It is time to move forward. You must decide whether you wish to return to the physical realm or move onward.'

'Forward to where.'

'The spiritual realm.' Esther nodded for him to continue.

'You will be at peace to examine your life's journey.'

'But if I go back to my life, I can make peace with Kate and reclaim Lily. If I go back, Joseph, will you be with me?'

'No. As I said before, I cannot take physical form again. I am unsure whether you will remember any of this.'

'So, if I go back to my life now, I won't remember the garden, or you?'

'I do not know.' Joseph looked down, almost embarrassed.

Esther leaned back, releasing a massive sigh. 'Joseph, I'm at a complete loss and don't know what to do. All this talk about purpose, energy, life plans, learning. You have put me in an impossible situation, Joseph.'

'I do not think it is I who has put you in this position. You are being given another chance to decide your destiny. And that is a decision only you can make.'

Esther went back to the armchair. As she looked at the window again, Joseph took her hand as they watched events in the physical world.

'The time is running out Esther. You need to decide.'

Chapter 44

Doctors and nurses clustered around Esther's bedside. The doctors continued to give orders as the staff moved quietly, efficiently and with purpose. After what seemed like an eternity, the consultant in charge stepped back.

'Okay. We've done as much as we can.' His voice was low, and he looked exhausted. 'I'll speak to the daughter.' A nurse followed him.

Esther watched him walk slowly, almost dragging his feet. As he entered the room, Kate leapt to her feet, her arms reaching towards them.

'Is she?'

'Take a seat please, Mrs Cooper.' The nurse whispered.

The consultant sat as the nurse stood next to him.

'We have done all we can for now. I am sorry to say that your mother's condition has deteriorated despite the operation. The infection has spread.

Your mother has responded to the therapy we have instigated, but I am not sure for how long. We can only wait and see what happens now.'

Kate stared at him, feeling a heavy silence settle between them, knowing he meant every word.

'But what about the operation? Wasn't that supposed to save her?'

'That was our intention. Although the operation was successful, the consequences were not. Staff Nurse Copeland will take you to sit with your mother.'

The consultant got to his feet, signalling the discussion was over. Kate marvelled at his attitude. How could he be so matter a fact when he was talking about her mother's life?

Kate stood as if in a daze and followed the nurse to where Esther's body lay. The monitor continued to bleep as Kate leant over and stroked her mother's thick profusion of black hair away from her face.

'Can she feel anything?' Kate asked, taking her mother's hand.

To her surprise, Esther was aware of her physical body. Aware of Kate's touch. Part of her consciousness was back in her body. She tried to squeeze Kate's hand, but nothing happened.

'We are lightening the sedation, so she may have some sense of where she is. She may regain consciousness to some extent, so it is important that you talk to her and let her know you are here.' The words were fragments of conversation to Esther as her consciousness drifted between worlds. For the first time, she was aware of the tube. The intrusive, alien presence forcing air into her lungs which felt heavy and then weightless. It wasn't painful, just profoundly uncomfortable, and she longed to pull it out.

Sounds were muffled and distorted. The hiss of the ventilator was the only constant amongst the distant voices, which sounded like they were underwater. Conversations giving gentle instructions. Esther's consciousness was drawn back to Kate.

'Why hasn't the treatment worked?' Kate stared tearfully up at the nurse.

'The drugs are in her system. All we can do is wait.'

'How long has she got?' Kate whispered, as if she was protecting Esther from hearing the truth.

'Only Esther knows that.' The nurse said gently, putting an arm around Kate's shoulders. Kate leaned forward and took her mother's hand again.

Moving her chair closer to her mother, she spoke, her voice faltering, 'Mum, thank you for writing the letter. I'm sorry I've given you such a hard time over Dad's death. I think it was the way he died that upset me more than anything.'

'But I suppose he wasn't aware of what happened to his body. It just seemed so sad, so pathetic for him to be sitting there alone with no one realising he was dead.' Kate shifted in her chair. 'I believe you when you say you were trying to save me. I didn't know he owed money to the wrong people. I didn't know we had to get away before they came after us.' The silence which followed, held a sense of forgiveness before Kate spoke again.

'Mum. In the letter, you asked me about Ray, but he never touched me. He tried to bully me, but I stood up to him and he left me alone. He tried to control me. Making me do housework and limiting my time out with my friends. But he never touched me Mum. I'm not sure why you thought he did. If he'd tried, I'd have thumped him.' Esther heard the defiance in Kate's voice and smiled to herself, inwardly sighing with relief. It had been an empty boast. Joseph was right, not everything Ray had said was true. Kate was speaking again.

'Mum, I have read the journals and I understand now. I understand all the horrible guilt you've been feeling about Grandma, Dad, Ray and the child,

George. Your journals say you have found peace within yourself. I'm glad for you,' Again Kate paused.

'Who *is* Lily, Mum? I found the birth certificate. You mention her in the journals as well, but I don't know who she is. Why didn't you tell me I had a sister?' Esther recognised the sharpness in her voice. Another pause before she continued with a sigh. 'I am going to find her Mum and whatever happens, I'll make sure she's alright. It's alright Mum. I'm here.' she stifled a sob. 'I know this isn't want you wanted. I can't do anything about it. It's up to you now, Mum. I'm sorry I wasn't a better daughter. I love you Mum. I'm so sorry I didn't tell you enough.'

The nurse moved towards Kate. 'Mrs Cooper, the consultant, would like to speak to you again.'

Dr Cunningham came to stand by the bedside. He spoke. 'Your mother's condition is unusual,' he said, using his words carefully. 'This infection is creating an extraordinary battle within her body. The most recent blood results show something we haven't seen before.'

Kate straightened in the chair. 'What does that mean?'

'It means,' he said slowly, 'that your mother's own resistance is creating a medical anomaly. Her white blood cell count is fluctuating in a way which suggests her body is trying to decide, whether to fight.'

Esther's consciousness shifted away from the warmth of Kate's touch, away from her physical body with the sensations of pain and discomfort.

Back in the ethereal space of the garden, Esther now stood beside the two doorways.

'The time has come for you to choose,' Joseph said quietly.

The golden doorway to the right now whispered the promise of rest and release. The green doorway to the left pulsed with connections yet to be made. As Kate watched helplessly, Esther's internal struggle matched the rise and fall of her chest as she fought an invisible battle.

'Choose quickly,' Joseph's voice was urgent, 'to live and make amends or rest knowing that you have no more shadows. Choose before the chance is taken from you.'

Kate stood as her mother's fingers twitched, and her eyelids flickered.

The choice was here. The choice was Esther's.

Chapter 45

Six months later

Kate parked her car several streets away. She didn't want to risk being too close. The estate loomed ahead, its tower blocks dark against the gloomy sky. She had been here before when Ray insisted they visit his parents, but those visits were mercifully rare.

Kate remained shocked by the discovery of the birth certificate hidden in the file. A sister, born just after she'd left. Her mother never said a word. A secret kept from her, but now, after months of searching and researching, she was here to see for herself.

Kate had not seen Ray or his parents in the years following Kate's rapid exit from the house that fateful New Year's Eve.

He was the reason she left. Left home at sixteen when he attacked Shaun. All they wanted was to go out and celebrate New Year's Eve. Shaun said to Ray, 'We'll be back about one after the fireworks.' Ray had said he wanted me back by ten. Shaun said no, we would stay out. I went to get my coat. Ray hurled himself at Shaun and knocked him to the floor. He kicked him so badly, he could hardly stand. She had left and never gone back. The only time she saw her mother was at Ray's funeral. That was the last time she had seen Tina and Mick, Ray's parents.

Kate was surprised they'd taken Lily. They had a poor opinion of Esther, that at least she knew. They couldn't understand why their son had taken up with an older black woman with a child. In their eyes, he could have had anyone. They held Esther responsible for Ray's death. She became the scape-goat. They blamed her completely, wearing their grief like a badge of honour.

Lily must be about eight years old. A girl who never knew her father. Kate knew her mother spi-ralled into a deep depression after she left with Shaun. Would Esther have been incapable of raising a baby? It seemed Tina and Mick had taken their granddaughter in to live with them. Now Kate was standing at the foot of the tower block where they lived, bracing herself for the confrontation she was dreading.

The block looked as grim as she remembered. Concrete walls covered in grime and graffiti. The wind whipped around her as she approached the entrance. The broken intercom buzzed under her finger as she pressed the button for Flat 19.

After a few moments of silence, a harsh, crackling voice came through the intercom. 'Who is it?'

'My name is Kate Cooper. I'm Esther Morgan's daughter.' Her voice was tight.

There was silence. The response was slow.

'What the hell do you want?'

'I want to see my sister, Lily. I have some news for her.'

Another pause stretched on long enough to make Kate think they wouldn't let her in. Finally, there was a sharp buzz as the door unlocked and she pushed her way inside. The stairwell was dim, the walls peeling and stained. The stale smell of cigarettes and damp filled the air. When she reached the door to Flat 19, it opened before she could knock. Standing in the doorway was a woman she barely recognised. A gaunt woman with thinning hair and yellowing skin. Age had not been kind to Tina Belcher. Her eyes looked Kate up and down before she stepped aside to let her in.

The flat was cluttered, the air stale. The smell of old cigarette smoke was here too, together with the stench of fried food. Ray's father sat in a sagging armchair, his gaze fixed on the large TV which took up most of the space on the living room wall.

'What do you want?' Tina barked.

'I told you I want to meet Lily. I have some news about our mother.'

'Why now, after all this time?' Tina crossed her arms across her chest.

'I'm her sister,' Kate said firmly, 'I only found out about her recently. I didn't know she existed until then.'

'We look after her. Put a roof over her head and kept her fed after your mother disowned her. Don't think you can come in here now with your good intentions.'

Kate glanced round the dingy flat, taking in the neglect. The cigarette butts crushed into the carpet, the plates of half-eaten food on the coffee table. It was hard to see how they'd looked after Lily. As if reading her mind, Tina snapped, 'She has what she needs. We're registered with the social, get our benefits. We've done our bit,' Tina continued. 'We've done more for her than your mother ever did. That girl's lucky she didn't end up in care.'

Kate's blood ran cold. Her sister was nothing more than a meal ticket for them. They didn't care about her.

'Can I see her?' Kate asked, forcing herself to stay calm, though the tremble in her voice gave her away.

'Don't go filling her head with any nonsense, missy.'

Kate didn't wait for another word. She made her way down the narrow hallway, her hearting thumping. At the end, a door stood ajar. She could see the glow of a lamp, even though it was still morning. Kate gently knocked before going in.

As Kate's eyes adjusted to the gloom caused by windows covered with newspaper, she saw a figure on a child's bed. Lily was sitting crossed legged clutching a dirty worn stuffed rabbit. Her brown eyes looked frightened. She was small, too small for her age, her raven black hair matted as it fell in lank strands down her shoulders.

'Hello Lily. I'm your sister.' Kate stayed in the doorway, not to alarm the child.

'My sister?' Lily clutched the rabbit tighter.

Kate nodded and went to kneel so she was at eye level with the girl. 'I didn't know about you until now.

But I'm here and I want to get to know you, if that's alright?'

Lily didn't smile, but there was a flicker of hope in her eyes. At that moment, Kate knew she had to do whatever it took to get her sister away from here. From the neglect and indifference.

'Lily, do you go to school?'

The girl looked suspicious and backed away from Kate.

'You from the social?'

Kate sat back on her heels, aware of the sticky, torn vinyl flooring. She smiled reassuringly.

'No. No, nothing like that.'

'I go sometimes, but I don't like it.'

Kate nodded.

'I hated school. There was this girl, Bonnie Taylor. She made my life hell. Is there someone like that at your school?' Lily nodded.

'Sarah Jenkins says I smell and no-one will sit by me,' Lily mumbled softly into her stuffed rabbit. She looked puzzled, then said, 'How come you're my sister? You're old.'

Kate chuckled. 'We have the same mum, but I have a different dad.'

'My dad's dead. Is yours?' Kate nodded sombrely. 'Yes, I'm afraid so.'

'I never met my dad. He was dead when I was born.' The words escaped from the small mouth as if she had been wanted to talk for so long.

'What do you remember about our mum?'

'She didn't want me. I had to come here.' Lily mumbled, shuffled her feet on the worn blanket. The bed had no sheets, and the pillow was worn and discoloured.

Kate leant forward and took the child's hand. 'Lily, I have come to see you to talk about our mother.' Kate fell silent as the sound of footsteps on the bare floorboards made Kate turn to the doorway.

'What you talking to the kid about?' It was Ray's father, Mick. 'Best you get off now.' He said, folding his arms firmly across his thin chest. Kate wondered where Ray had got his good looks from. It certainly wasn't this weedy, balding, bucktoothed slob.

As Kate went to get up, Lily put her small hand on Kate's arm. She smiled reassuringly at the sad face before her.

'What were you going to tell me?' Her voice was urgent.

'It can wait until next time when we see each other again,' she said, patting the little hand.

'Who says they'll be a next time?' Mick sneered.

Lily's head went down as Kate moved forward and whispered. 'I will see you soon. I promise.'

Chapter 46

As Kate drove away, a heavy sadness settled in her chest. How different that little girl's life could have been? Why had Esther abandoned her? From what she'd heard, it sounded like Mick and Tina didn't give her a choice. They took Lily from her.

Her phone rang as she manoeuvred through the traffic from Peckham back to Raynes Park. She stared at the caller ID, deciding whether to answer it.

'Hi Richard,' she said with little enthusiasm.

'Hi Kate. How are you?' He was trying to sound upbeat.

'As well as expected, Richard. What can I do for you?'

'I wondered if you were coming up this way to sort things out at the house?'

Kate sighed. She needed to get Esther's house cleaned up. Ensure everything was in its proper place, neat and tidy. There was a stack of paperwork and documents she needed to collect.

'I'll have to talk to Shaun and see if he's free to have the boys, but I'll try to make it this weekend.'

'You can stay at ours if you like.'

'No. It's fine. The house will need airing and it would be good to give it a clean.'

'I'll make up a bed for you, shall I?'

'Thanks, that would be good.'

'Come for supper with Colin and me. There's something we want to talk about with you.'

'That all sounds mysterious. Any clues.'

'Just let me know when you're arriving and how long you're staying, okay?'

Kate agreed to message Richard when she'd firmed up her plans.

When she arrived home, Shaun was waiting for her. Both boys were out at friends.

'How did it go?'

'Oh Shaun, it's awful. That poor little girl.' He came to her and wrapped his arms around her.

'Tell me all about it," he said, guiding her to the sofa by the patio doors that looked out over the tiny garden. Kate pulled the thin voile curtain across against the bright sunshine. Shaun handed her a cup of coffee and sat beside her as she told him the entire story of her visit to Lily. They talked about what options she had and how she could help the child.

'You need to think this through, Kate. If you involve social services, they will look for someone to take responsibility for Lily. You need to think about who that might be and how it would fit in with your life now.'

'I know you're right and yes, I will think about it and talk it through before I do anything.'

'I'll make us a sandwich, shall I?' he asked. He was about to get up when Kate put a hand on his arm. He sat back down.

'Shaun. I want to say sorry,' she paused as if marshalling some inner strength. 'Not all our problems are down to you.'

'Thanks very much,' he said, laughing as he brushed his hand through his dark hair. She liked the way he always wore it longer at the front. It made him look like an Italian. She also knew this gesture signalled his discomfort at this expression of emotion. He wasn't used to Kate being nice.

'I've been so consumed with the past. So angry with Mum for the stuff she put me through, I never really gave us a chance. We met when I was trying to escape the hell that was Ray. It wasn't the right reason, but then I got so comfortable around you and your mum and dad. You gave me a glimpse of what life could be like.'

'And now?' He spoke with a hopeful tone in his voice.

'After we got married and had the boys, I wished for a life that didn't exist. I wished you to be some-one you're not. All this business with Mum has made me think. I couldn't have managed without you these last few months.' She paused again. 'I've realised that I had what I wanted all along. It's been such an emotional journey. Finding Lily has added another layer to the story. I just feel exhausted and wrung out.' She flopped back against the sofa, let-ting out an enormous sigh on the verge of tears.

Shaun sat looking at her with such intensity, she had to look away.

'Kate. I love you. I always have, but I'm not good at words. But I'm here for you and the boys. I also realise I've been a crap husband. The thought of losing all of you now isn't something I ever want to consider again.'

Kate leant forward and kissed him gently, her hand on his cheek. Then she kissed him again, feel-ing the familiar stirrings of passion, something she hadn't felt in months. Shaun knelt in front of her and kissed the side of the neck. His embrace was so familiar, so comforting. Before long, they were undressing each other with such fervour that it took them both by surprise.

'What about the boys?' Kate moaned as Shaun's hand travelled up her thigh.

They won't be back for hours,' he mumbled into her hair.

Afterwards, Kate lay in Shaun's arms in contented silence. She gazed into his face and reached to kiss his cheek.

'Is it time for you to come home?' He looked down at her and nodded.

Richard shuffled Esther's notebooks absentmindedly on his desk, while wondering if Kate would agree to their plan.

She'd handed the notebooks back to him at the hospital saying they should remain in Esther's house for now. The police hadn't asked whether any more existed, so they only had the purple one Kate had handed to them. He'd put them back, but after months, niggling curiosity got the better of him. He couldn't resist having a quick scan, so he retrieved them from the bureau.

This led to a massive row with Colin, who could be such an idiot. He was one for sticking to the rules and respecting others' privacy. He told Richard he had breached the boundaries of friendship by reading the journals, and they hadn't spoken properly since.

A life of profound guilt was laid bare in the pages of the journals, but interwoven with confessions of wrongdoing were also tales of redemption, a gradual shedding of the guilt's suffocating grip. Esther had punished herself for crimes she did not commit. When he finished reading, Richard was more convinced than ever that something good needed to come out of Esther's life.

He left the notebooks on the kitchen table and noticed someone had moved them when he sat down with his brunch the next day. Colin came home for dinner that evening and spoke for the first time since the row.

'I owe you an apology,' he said, placing a glass of red wine by the side of the range where Richard was stir frying. Richard didn't respond. Colin came up behind him, stroked the back of his neck.

'Don't think you'll get away with a quick shag by way of an apology,' Richard retorted.

Colin laughed. 'Oh, stop being such a diva. Look Richard, you were right, okay, you were right.'

Richard spun round, almost dropping the two bamboo spatulas he was holding.

'Right about what?' he probed. He intended to get every ounce of contrition out of Colin.

Sighing, Colin folded his long legs onto one stool, leaning forward on the kitchen peninsula. 'There is definitely a story in there and a bloody good one at that. I think I can do something with it.'

'Kate's coming at the weekend. Do you think we could pitch it to her?'

'Yes, I do, but I don't know how she'll react.' We need to double check we won't implicate Esther. What's happened to the notebook the police got hold of?

'I don't know. We'll have to ask Kate. Who's going to write it?'

'Well, that what we're going to have to discuss, isn't it?' Colin replied.

Chapter 47

Kate arrived the following afternoon, just after lunch. She'd grabbed a stale sandwich and a frothy coffee at Oxford Services. The house smelt dry, drained of any moisture. Dried out during the hot days of summer. She flung open the kitchen windows, and finding the key, opened the back door. Going upstairs, she opened the bedroom windows to get a through draft from the light warm breeze. The house seemed to sigh in gratitude. Someone, she presumed Richard, had moved the bed from the downstairs back to the small spare at the rear of the house. He had a knack for helping others, even when they didn't ask for it.

Although the kitchen was clean, there was a thin layer of dust everywhere else. So, after making herself a mug of tea, Kate set to work dusting, hoovering and cleaning. She was frenetic, not giving herself time to think. It was an invasion of Esther's privacy. This was her house, not Kate's.

Feeling tired after a long afternoon, Kate flopped down on the sofa, not wanting to go to Richard's for dinner. If she didn't go, she'd have to go to the shops to get something to eat. That prospect was equally unpleasant. Pulling a comb through her short, cropped brown hair, she found a cardigan in case it got cold later and locked the door.

Richard opened the door before she used the Ring doorbell. He was wearing an expressive Ralph Lauren pink shirt open at the collar. Kate wished she'd changed and conscious of her dirty and unkept appearance next to him.

'Come on in Kate.' He opened the door wide to let her in, taking her cardigan and hanging on a peg by the door. Everyone came to the back door at Richard's, which led through a utility into a vast open plan kitchen and dining area.

'Red or white,' he asked as soon as she was through the door.

'White, I think.'

'Good choice. We're having fish. Is that alright? You can have bubbles is you prefer.'

'Not much to celebrate is there.'

Richard's face paled. 'No, I suppose not. Colin's on his way, so let's go out into the garden while we wait for him. How's your day been?'

'I've given the house a good clean. Thanks for taking the bed back upstairs.'

'I didn't,' Richard said. 'I noticed it had been moved when I made up your bed.'

Kate screwed up her face, trying to think who else could have done it. An unbidden thought popped into her head, but she dismissed it immediately. 'It must have been Grace, or someone she knew. Thinking about Grace, how is she?'

'Good, good. All the business with her ex is sorted. He's been locked up in Thailand for the foreseeable future so she's back to her usual organised self. She said to tell you if you need any help with anything, to just ring her.'

'If I have time, I'll pop and see her, shall I?'

'Yes, that would be good, but no pressure. She understands this is a difficult time for you.'

Kate waited for him to probe, but as if sensing this, he said,

'You know we're here if there is anything ...' his voice trailed off. Kate smiled weakly and, patting his hand said, 'Thank you, Richard, I appreciate it.'

A moment later, Colin arrived home from work. 'I'll change, then I'll be with you, he said, looking at Richard, who gave an indiscernible shake of his head.

'After dinner.' Colin said, his gaze locked with Richard's, conveying a silent message.

'What are you two up to?' Kate smiled.

Dinner was excellent, as she knew it would be. Pear, walnut and Rochefort cheese as a starter followed by sea bream with asparagus and minted new potatoes. Kate had no clue how the chocolate frothy mousse she had for dessert had been concocted. There was a different wine with each course. Kate wondered if they ate like this every night, but couldn't believe it was so. Why were they buttering her up she wondered?

'Let's have coffee and brandy in the garden, shall we? Make the most of the early autumn evening.'

Richard bustled in the kitchen as Colin fiddled with their fancy coffee machine. Once everyone was settled, Colin began.

'Kate, you know the notebooks you found at the cottage and the one from the house?'

'Yes,' Kate said slowly.

'Have you read any of them?'

'I have. The one the police had access to linked mum to the death of a child. That incident led to the breakdown Mum during COVID. I never knew she thought she'd killed a child. No wonder she went mad.' Kate saw Colin's eyebrow raised and defensively said. 'She didn't kill anyone. The police scrutinised the contents of the journal and found the medical notes. George, like so many other died from COVID.'

'What about the rest of it?'

Kate paused. She took a swig of her brandy to steady herself. 'What do you mean?'

'The stories about your grandmother, your father, Ray?'

Kate looked up, trying to get her thoughts in order. Then, looking Colin directly in the eye, she said,

'After reading the journals, it's clear my mother wasn't responsible for their deaths. My grandmother was given an injection by her doctor, my dad died alone from addiction and Ray's death was an accident.'

'I wasn't accusing her of anything.' There was an edge to Colin's voice, as he changed the subject. 'What about the garden and releasing her shadows?'

'And this character, Joseph?' Richard added.

Kate sat back against the soft cushions of the garden chair, letting the warmth of the brandy soothe her.

'Joseph,' she paused, considering if she should say anything but emboldened by the wine, she said, 'There were indications someone had been at the cottage after my mum was hospitalised.' She decided not to discuss the voice in the car as she'd rushed back to her mother's bedside.

'I've had a feeling in her house a couple of time.' Richard agreed. 'It was if someone was watching me.'

Kate let out a sigh of relief. 'It's so hard to tell what's real and what isn't. I think through the process of writing, she found peace with the situation. These visits to the garden seem to be a catalyst. I suspect they were probably hallucinations but, 'she sighed, 'we may never know.'

Richard leant over and patted her hand.

'Sorry Kate. We didn't want to drag up painful memories.'

Kate sat up straight. 'Why are you so interested in all this, anyway?' She had reached her limit of this conversation.

Richard looked at Colin, showing he should take the lead.

'Regardless of whether the stories are true, they make fascinating reading.'

'So?' Kate sensed there was more.

'I think this would make a fantastic novel, Kate.'

'What?' Kate looked at him in disbelief. 'You want to take my mother's private thoughts and turn them into a book?'

'I know how it sounds, but not to acknowledge what Esther has written would be such a waste.'

'Who the hell would write it?' Kate felt hot as a surge of indignation at the thought of her mother's journals being poured over by other people.

Colin sat back and put his arms behind his head with an air of exasperation.

'I'm sorry, Kate. I think you're missing the point. It would not present as your mother's actual words. The writer would include the stories in a work of fiction. Do you know what a ghost writer is?'

Kate shook her head.

'Ghost writers take the ideas and inspiration of others and write them into a story. The owner of the original ideas keeps all rights.'

Kate took a deep breath. This was going to need some thought. Kate knew Colin was the director of a prestigious writing house. He was obviously serious about this project. The idea of crafting her mother's ramblings in children's notebooks into a novel seemed bizarre.

'I don't know what to say, Colin. I'm absolutely flabbergasted at the suggestions that my mother's confused fantasies could create a novel. I need to give this some thought and discuss it a little more.'

'Of course, Kate. Just let me know if you want to take it further.' Colin raised his brandy glass. 'A toast to Esther,' he said, as the others raised their glasses.

Chapter 48

As consciousness slowly seeped back, Esther noticed her surroundings. She lay on a soft bed, her head cradled by a feather pillow. The air was sweet as a light breeze brushed her cheek. Her eyelids were weighted down by a deep sleep. As her vision cleared, she found herself in a world of colour and scent. She stretched and yawned as she looked around.

Her garden was resplendent with colour and scent. Each archway was barely visible beneath cascading curtains of flowers. Roses in shades of pink and gold were intertwined with jasmine and honeysuckle. Confusion raged through her. Where was she? Was this the spiritual realm? It looked exactly like her garden. But as the realisation slowly dawned, panic gripped her like a steel claw. She cried out in fear. Dread seeped into her consciousness. This was her garden. Why was she still here?

Her garden, once a haven, now felt like a suffocating prison.

Her eyes stung with unshed tears as her throat constricted. The grief and sadness of the truth hit her. Anger, hot and fierce, surged through her veins. It built in her chest until it erupted in an agonising scream, which shattered the peace and tranquillity of the garden. Her voice echoed in the vastness as she collapsed back onto the bed. Sobs wracked her as she buried her face into the pillow. What had she failed to do? Why was she trapped here?

Time seemed to lose meaning as Esther wept. Eventually, the grief-stricken tears calmed, leaving her empty. She sat up, wiping her red eyes, looking around her. Perhaps there was still a way out. Getting up from the bed, she circled the garden's perimeter, her eyes scanning the dense foliage for any sign of a doorway. She stepped carefully onto the flower beds, brushing away petals that fell at her touch. She searched for the outline of a door.

'Esther,' a voice called from behind, startling her. She whirled round, nearly losing her balance. Joseph had materialised out of nowhere.

'What the hell am I doing here, Joseph?' she demanded, her voice trembling with fury. 'What have you done?' She raised her arms, her fist clenched, wanting to strike him. But as quickly as it came, the fight drained out of her. Turning away from him, she made her way back to the centre of the garden and the bench. Taking a seat, Joseph came to stand silently by her.

'What happened Joseph?' Esther whispered.

'Esther, you never left the garden.' Joseph said carefully.

She looked at him as if he'd gone mad. 'What are you talking about?'

'You didn't go through a doorway in time.' She raised her head to look at him with an expression of horror.

'So, what are you saying?' She held her breath, already knowing what he was going to say. 'I'm trapped here, aren't I?' Joseph sighed a deep sigh before nodding his head.

'Does this happen to other people?' Esther demanded.

Joseph took a deep breath. 'Yes, people get trapped in this intermediate space if they cannot let go of their earthly life. Until they let go, they cannot move forward. They do not have the choice to go back.'

'So why did I have the choice?'

'The option to go back to your earthly life was so you could put your learning into practice. I wanted you to benefit from it by living a life of fulfilment and happiness. It was your choice which one you took, but you took neither.' Joseph paused again to let this sink in.

'Do I still have that choice?'

Joseph shook his head sadly. Anger flared once again within Esther. 'So, this is all your fault? Am I dead?' Esther demanded, walking right up to him and staring directly into his troubled face.

'No, your mortal body is also trapped between worlds, just as you are.'

'You are not making sense.'

'Go to the window and ask it to show you.'

'This is your fault' Esther reached up and poked him in the chest. Joseph stepped back, over-whelmed by her reaction. 'If there had only been one door, I wouldn't have hesitated and would now be free. By offering me a choice, a choice I couldn't make, you have condemned me to an existence trapped in this garden.

'A choice was offered to you, but you chose not to take it.' Esther had never heard Joseph shout before. His voice, loud and harsh, startled her.

"I'm going to leave you now," he whispered, as his eyes filled with tears, 'but I will return. I must get you out of here, before it's too late. I need guidance.' Before Esther could answer. Joseph seemed to dissolve into the air, leaving only a faint shimmer in the air.

Esther turned away and looked for the window to find out where her physical body was. As she sat in one armchair, still in position in front of the window, she whispered in a small voice.

'Please show me.'

The image slowly appeared, its blurry edges sharpening and gaining definition with each passing moment. The room was filled with her belongings - photographs, some of her treasured souvenirs from home, and flowers. She could almost smell the bulbs of hyacinths in bowls and the vases of roses. Going closer to the window, she stared at the body in the bed. It was her, but she lay still as stone with no movement at all save the rising and falling of her chest. There was no ventilator or drips attached. She just lay there, seemingly asleep. Where was she?

Left alone in the garden once more, Esther felt the weight of her situation descend on her as the cold grip of fear took hold again. What had she done?

No, what had she failed to do? The sudden realisation hit her, the fear was replaced by an icy wave washing over her. This wasn't Joseph's fault. It was entirely her own, a consequence of her own inability to decide. In that moment of grief, suspended between life and death, past and future, Esther faced the consequences of her indecision.

The garden, once her paradise, was now a prison holding her because of choices unmade. Returning to the armchair, she almost collapsed into it, completely consumed by a sense of failure. What had she done? What new hell had she created for herself? Waiting seemed her only option. As she sat watching the window, Esther wondered if Joseph could save her again or if this was all there was.

But somewhere, deep in her subconscious, a small voice whispered that this was not the end of her story. There was still the possibility of a way out. As she watched her lifeless body in the bed, Esther was jolted by the door opening. She cried out when she saw who entered the room.

Chapter 49

Two months later

It was a beautifully warm autumn day with skies the brightest blue. Lily watched a flock of white birds flying high. She wondered if the birds were going away for the winter. Despite the purpose of the journey, she was enjoying this rare outing. They were going to see her mummy. She had little memory of her. Only blurred images from before her grandmother took her away. She remembered a woman with thick black hair, like hers and she smelt like a rose from the school garden.

'The Willows.' Lily read the sign as they pulled off a suburban street near to where Kate lived.

'What is this place?' She asked, turning to Kate.

'This is a nursing home that looks after people like mummy.'

'Has mummy always been here?'

'No, she was in a hospital in Wales for a long time.'

'Did you go to see her?'

'When I could. But mummy has two good friends called Richard and Grace. They would go to see her regularly. That was kind of them, wasn't it?' Lily nodded, wishing she had good friends. She smoothed the fabric of the new skirt that Kate had bought her.

There was a car park at the back and as she jumped down from Kate's big blue car, she had butterflies in her tummy. What was her mother going to look like? Would she look like a dead person? Lily had seen dead people on the TV. They were grey and mottled. She shivered. She hoped her mummy wouldn't look like that. What would she smell like? She reached for Kate's hand as they made their way round to the front entrance. There was a buzzer that Kate pressed. As they waited for someone to come and open the door, Kate smiled down at her reassuringly. A woman in a pale-yellow uniform came and greeted Kate as if she knew her.

The nursing home room was hushed, with thick carpets that led right and left from a central entrance hall where there was a desk. Kate wrote something in a book and then, taking Lily's hand again, led her down the right-hand corridor. They stopped at number 8 and Kate opened the door.

The room was still and quiet except for Esther's shallow breathing. Pale summer sunlight filtered through the half-drawn blinds, casting striped shadows across the motionless figure in the hospital bed.

Kate drew up two chairs for them to sit on and let Lily take in the scene in front of her.

'Lily, this is our mum, Esther Morgan.' Sitting back, she let Lily get used to the strangeness.

'Why won't she wake up?'

'Mum is in a coma. She's asleep and doesn't wake up.'

'Why?' Lily asked.

'She was very ill, and everyone, the doctors, nurses and me, thought she was going to die, but she didn't.' Kate was telling her in adult words, which she liked. Her grandma said her mummy was a cabbage, which Lily didn't understand at all.

'So, she's alive, but asleep.'

'That's exactly it.' Kate had smiled proudly at her, and Lily had a warm feeling inside.

'When will she wake up?'

"We don't know. No-one knows.'

'Why isn't she in the hospital?'

Kate paused for a moment. 'She's not ill. Just asleep, so she doesn't need to be in the hospital now. The nursing home where she lives looks after Mummy and other people like her.'

Kate stood and guided Lily closer to their mother's bedside. Lily's small hand gripped her sister's fingers tightly, her dark eyes wide and uncertain.

She pulled a chair closer for Lily, then sat on the bed's edge. 'She looks peaceful, doesn't she?'

Lily nodded, her gaze travelling over Esther's brown face.

'Will she ever wake up?' Lily's voice was a whisper with hope.

Kate took a deep breath. 'I'm trying to help her wake up, but she's sleeping soundly. I talk to her and tell her everything that's going on. She knows I have found you. Sometimes I play her music from when I was little. This song is from my favourite Disney film. We used to sing this together. Do you know it?'

A song played which Lily recognised and, as Kate sang in a trembling voice, Lily joined in, too. She only knew one bit but sang, 'It's the circle of life, and it moves us all.' She hummed along to the rest but was impressed that Kate knew all the words.

As Kate sang, Lily glanced round the room and saw family. Images of a small girl who wasn't her.

'Is that you?' she asked, when the song finished, pointing to the photo of a little girl playing on the beach.' Kate nodded.

'Why don't I look like you?'

'My dad had fair hair with freckles. I look like him. Your dad had dark hair like mum so you look like them.' More music was playing as Kate hummed along. Lily looked back at the woman lying in the bed. She did look like her. They had the same skin colour and hair. Lily reached to touch the woman's hair. It was soft and wavy like hers. Her skin smelt like the flowers in the school garden. Her small hand reached out, hesitantly touching Esther's pale, motionless fingers.

Turning to Kate, she said, 'Tell me about her, will you please?'

'What do you want to know?'

'Has she got any brothers and sisters?'

'No, she was an only child.'

'Why is our skin dark?'

Kate took a deep breath, as if deciding what to tell Lily.

'Her father was from the Caribbean. Do you know where that is?' Lily shook her head.

'Where is he now?'

'He had to leave before our mum was born.'

'Did he die like my daddy?'

'I don't know. He wasn't allowed to stay in this country and had to go home.'

'Why did Mummy never go to find him?'

Kate laughed. 'I don't know Lily.'

'Do I have a grandma?'

'No, she also died when I was a little girl.'

Lily huffed with disappointment. Hoping to escape her small, dirty, and foodless room, she longed for another grandmother to live with.

'Lily.'

She turned to see Kate holding out her arms. She went to her and buried her face in Kate's shoulder. It felt nice to be hugged.

'Grandma says my mummy didn't love my daddy.' She felt Kate take a sharp intake of breath. Standing back, she looked into Kate's face.

'Didn't you like my daddy?'

'It's a long story.' Kate had a sad face.

'Grandma says he was a great bloke. She says it was mummy's fault he died.'

Kate sat back and looked at her mother before glancing back at Lily.

'When something happens, people sometimes see things differently. When we lived with Ray, your dad, Mum and I had a bad time. Bit like you have living with Grandma.' She screwed up her face, like Lily did when she'd said something she shouldn't have. 'Your grandma thought your daddy was wonderful. Me and Mum didn't. It's just the way it is sometimes. There's a saying, 'there are two sides to every story. Do you understand?'

'I think so,' Lily said, biting her bottom lip with concentration.

'You didn't like Daddy but Grandma did?'

'That's right.' Kate said, looking relieved.

'Can I live with Mummy when she wakes up?' Lily asked, swinging from side to side.

Kate pulled Lily to her again and whispered into her hair. 'Of course you can, but would you like to come and live with me for now?'

Lily jumped back.' Whoa, yes, please. Do you mean it? Do you really, really mean it?'

'It might take a little while, but I am going to make sure you do.'

Lily's face dropped. 'They'll never let you. They'd lose the money.' Lily turned away again, back to her mother.

Kate said, turning Lily back to face her. 'I might have a fight on my hands, but I'm going to make sure you get away from them, I promise.'

Lily nodded, turning back to the bedside and, taking hold of Esther's hand, she gently raised it to her lips.

'Please wake up Mummy, then we can all be together again.'

Chapter 50

Tears streamed down Esther's face as she watched the scene before her. Getting up, she went towards the image in the window and touched the little figure by the bedside. What had she done? Her indecision cost her the possibility of a life with the daughter who she had abandoned. As she stepped back, she felt a swell of pride in her chest for Kate. She had found Lily and was offering her a home.

How Kate had changed in such a short space of time. Since Esther was readmitted to the hospital and Kate read the letter, she seemed to have softened, mellowed. And now she was prepared to do the job Esther should be doing, should have done. She slumped back against the back of the chair, feeling overwhelmed with hopelessness and despair. Exhaustion overtook her as the image in the window faded. Was this her fate to be condemned to stay in this garden of her own making for eternity?

The garden mirrored her mood as the flowers dropped their petals, and vibrant colours faded.

Getting up, she wandered listlessly around the perimeter, gazing through the archways. Where did they lead? Perhaps she should go through and see what happened. At least she would be away from this entrapment. Moving toward the archway where she had last seen George, she put out her hand to test if there was anything stopping her. It hit an invisible barrier. Esther frantically felt around the doorway with both hands, but there was no way through. She stepped away towards the archway where she had been with her mother, but again. The barrier was there. She was afraid to attempt the archway leading to Ray's world. Esther did not want to get sucked into his version of hell. Tentatively she reached out, but again there was a barrier blocking her way.

'There is no way-out Esther.' The sudden, deep voice behind her made her jump, a jolt of fear shooting through her. Spinning round, she saw Joseph standing in the middle of the garden. She rushed towards him.

'What is happening? Can I get out?'

'Come and sit down, Esther.' He steered her towards the bench.

She sat down quickly and leaned towards him, eager to hear what he had to say.

Joseph took a deep breath.

'What?'

'I have been before the council who are reviewing your case.'

'What council? What are you talking about?'

'As I said before,' Joseph continued in a measured tone, 'your case is unprecedented and the council are considering what course of action to take. You see, you have been given two opportunities to choose. Your ability to heal yourself in this life must have been strong as the first time in the ditch, you lived. I came to your aid. This was unexpected, but allowed. It was an opportunity for you to rid yourself of your shadows. You ended our relationship before you finished that work. Because of this, your subconscious created a situation that gave you the opportunity to explore the remaining shadows.'

Esther interrupted him. 'So that I could see the good I'd done and talk about Ozzy and Lily?' Joseph nodded.

'Once you completed that work, once again you were free to choose. To return to your physical life or to move forward into the spiritual realm. The problem arose when you failed to make that choice.'

Esther sat back, exasperated. 'You are not telling me anything new here, Joseph.'

'The reason you are trapped, Esther, is you acted randomly. On both occasions, your behaviour was unpredicted, disturbing the timeline.'

Joseph paused, letting that information sink in before continuing. Esther's heartbeat quickly. What was he saying? That this was all her fault? Who the hell were the council? What gave them the right to decide her fate.

'The council act on behalf of the source.' He was reading her thoughts again.

'What is the source?'

'It is the living force that connects us all. The source is around us and within us and every living thing. We are all connected by the source. Joseph paused as something within Esther stirred as if a hidden part of her was responding to what he was saying.

'Do you feel it Esther?' Her mind expanded as she realised this wasn't just about her. She was a small part of something so much bigger than herself. Joseph continued,

'I have been speaking to the council on your be-half for a long time, but there is no progress. They are still in session and until a decision is made, there is nothing more I can do.'

Esther stared at him, trying to understand what he was telling her. A wave of grief rose as she sobbed. Joseph put his arm around her and held her to his chest. That moment of indecision. What had made her hesitate? That lack of making the choice must have shattered some delicate balance, broken some fundamental rule.

'I am so sorry, Joseph,' she cried. 'I have been so ungrateful. So disrespectful. I know this is my fault, and I've brought this on myself. You have shown me nothing but kindness, and I am so thankful to have dispelled the shadows that haunted me for so long. But I feel I have freed myself from one self-imposed prison to another. All I want is to make amends to my daughters, the people I have hurt the most. But I also want to be free. I want peace, to rest in the arms of peace, Joseph.'

'I understand, Esther, but until a decision is made, you must stay here. The council is exploring several possibilities.'

Esther sat up and wiped her eyes. 'Can you ex-plain what that means?'

Joseph stood motionless. His gaze pierced through the gathering dusk, looking not at the horizon but somehow beyond it, as if listening to whispers carried on winds invisible to human perception. As Esther watched him, the silence between them was thick, weighted with anticipation.

When Joseph finally spoke, his voice was low and measured, each word carefully selected. The council is exploring a rarely used, and somewhat controversial, solution.

She straightened, her breath catching. 'Tell me.' His eyes met hers.

'They are considering reversing the timeline.'

Esther's world tilted. 'Reversing?' The word escaped her like a gunshot. 'You mean undoing everything?'

'Not undoing. Realigning. This might be the only way out of the garden. The original timeline,' Joseph continued, his voice carrying the inevitability of distant thunder, 'needs restoring.'

'You cannot simply erase what I've accomplished,' Esther's voice was razor-edged and trembling. That earlier version of herself was afraid and unaware. That version was consumed by guilt. It was more than a reversal it would erase her personal transformation. The council's potential decision wasn't just about timelines, it would be a destruction of her entire journey.

Her hands, clenched with anger. 'I have been through too much to go back,' she told Joseph, her voice filled with an unmistakable warning, 'to be reduced to who I was before.'

Joseph's eyes lost focus, as though receiving transmission from somewhere beyond the visible world. Minutes passed until a subtle shimmer seemed to recede from around him.

'There might be a way,' he whispered, turning to Esther, 'where you do not lose yourself entirely.

'I might keep the memories of all I have achieved?' Her voice wavered. Joseph's eyes held a glimmer of hope. 'That is what I am hoping, Esther, but there is no guarantee.' To lose all she had gained would be to lose to herself all over again.

'So, when the timeline is reversed, I will go back to my life, but with all the knowledge I have gained?'

'Not exactly, Esther. When you go back, you will revert to the original timeline.'

'What happened in the original timeline, Joseph?'

Chapter 51

As the immediate impact of the fall faded, a creeping dread, cold and clammy, replaced the initial shock. Feeling the cold, damp earth against her cheek, fear gripped her tightly. The damp, penetrating cold seeped into her clothes and bones, the chill of the ditch clinging to her like a shroud. The air was thick and heavy, a cloying sweetness mingling with the musty smell of damp earth and rotting leaves, almost suffocating in its intensity. Stark terror, washed over Esther as she realised where she was.

Was this the original timeline.

She cried out for help, but her voice was only a whisper. Why was she back here, in this ditch? Twigs and leaves clung to her skin and hair. She could hear the rustle of unseen creatures and the drip, drip of water from the ferns which blocked light from the narrow strip of sky above. As the shadows lengthened, she felt her mortality as the dense woodland hid her from sight. A tremendous wave of self-pity engulfed her as she realised the loss of all she had gained.

But what was going to happen now? Was she going to relive all of it again? What would be the purpose? If she could not relive this last year, then what? If this was the original timeline. What was she supposed to choose?

But all she had experienced was not lost. Esther could remember it all. The garden, the doorways, releasing herself from the shadows. The stress she held in her body was gone. She knew now the three deaths were not her fault. Esther was no longer held within their prison. She was free from the ties that had bound her. She was free. With this realisation a lightness grew within her.

The walls of the ditch loomed steep and slick with mud, making the climb back to the path difficult. Should she try to get out? Should she try to use her phone like before? No, she would wait for Joseph. He would be here soon.

A sharp pain in her foot reminded her of the shattered ankle, but there was something else now. Esther was having difficulty breathing the damp, heavy air. Each inhalation caused a sharp pain in the right side of her chest. She didn't remember this from before. The weight of her predicament settled heavily on her, crushing her with a suffocating fear that left her trembling. No-one knew she was here. She was alone, cut off from the world. Where was Joseph?

Esther lay struggling to keep track of time. How long had she been here? The pain she felt subsided, replaced with a numbness that spread gradually through her frozen limbs. Her mind wandered.

What about her darling girls? Esther lay back, looking at the darkening sky, wishing she could see Kate and tell her how much she loved her. Tell her how sorry she was for all the pain she put her through. And Lily? What about Lily? That poor child would never know why she had given her up to that awful life. How had Esther thought she would be happier with Tina and Mick? But by the time she was back on her feet, it all seemed too late. Too late to wrench the child away from all she knew. 'She won't want me in her life now,' Esther had convinced herself. She should have tried harder.

If only she had gone to find her, she would have realised what awful conditions she was living under. Esther would have saved her, saved her own child. Sadness overwhelmed her as she realised she might never make amends. Thank God for Kate. But would she still save her? If the world had turned backwards, Kate wouldn't know about Lily. A wail of despair escaped her lips.

She might never see her girls again. Never get the chance to save Lily. This was so unfair. But wait, Joseph, he would come and rescue her, like he did before. She just had to be patient and wait for him to come.

Time became fluid as memories of her past played in her head. Her mother holding her tiny hand as she splashed in the shallow waves at the beach. Her first kiss was from the boy who always caught the same bus as her. The smile of the patient, silently thanking her as their life slipped away. Was she dying? This wasn't right. This didn't happen before. Esther tried to cry out into the darkness, but no sound came. The light was growing dim, and she could feel herself slipping away. Where was Joseph?

'Esther.' She could have cried with relief. He was standing before her, glowing with a golden light. Esther was disorientated, confused. This was not how he appeared before. Why was he so different, so beautiful?

'Have you come to carry me down the mountain?'
'No Esther, I have come to take you home.'

'But I don't understand?' she cried.

Joseph lay down beside her in the cold damp ditch and cradled her in his arms.

'Esther, my love. This was the only way to leave the garden. You cannot go back to the life you had. The timeline is being reset. You should have died in this ditch, Esther, all those months ago.' Esther gasped, but knew the truth in what he was saying.

'When you cried out to live, you were given a reprieve to release yourself from your shadows, but now it is time to come home. Look back with gratitude to all your achievements. You have been through so much, and you have freed yourself. The lessons you were sent to learn have been learnt, and it is now time to come home.' Esther could feel the warmth, comfort and sincerity of Joseph, but she was still troubled.

'But what about my girls?' Esther asked in a voice barely audible.

'They will be fine. Kate will find out about Lily. She will take care and love Lily as you would have done. Not only have you saved yourself, Esther, but you have also stripped away the anger and disappointment from Kate. You have freed her to live a life filled with love for her husband, her children, and her sister. You have left a legacy through your writing that will touch the hearts of millions. All is well, Esther Morgan. Come now, it is time for us to go where no shadows fall.'

Joseph stood, holding out his hand. A lightness filled Esther as she rose to meet him. Taking his hand, she turned to look down at the body she was leaving behind. There was no sadness now, only peace.

Joseph and Esther rose out of the ditch as a doorway appeared before them. Esther smiled up at Joseph as the door opened. 'Thank you for saving me,' she said as they stepped into the light together.

Epilogue

The sleek black car pulled up to the curb. Its glossy exterior reflecting the lights framing the entrance to the hotel which was hosting the awards ceremony.

Kate looked beautiful in a long silk green dress that hugged her slim figure. Her hair was sleek and smooth as it framed her face and her sparkling earrings caught the light.

By her side, Lily wriggled with excitement. She glowed with health and happiness and looked so pretty in her cream fairy-tale dress. The bodice was embroidered with small intricate flowers and the short, puffed sleeve hid her painfully thin arms. Lily's black thick hair was swept back into a high ponytail which swished around her as she reached for Kate's hand.

A valet opened the door, and Kate stepped out, adjusting her dress as the cameras clicked. They stood self-consciously for a moment, poised on the edge of the red carpet. The cameras flickered in the distance as they moved forward hand in hand.

The grand hall bustled with excitement as Kate and Lily were shown to their seats near the front. 'That's a good sign,' Richard said as he rose to meet them. Kate looked puzzled.

'So, you can get to the stage easily.' Kate laughed, not daring to think for a moment the book had won. Shaun stood. 'You look so beautiful,' he said, kissing her carefully on the cheek, afraid of spoiling her impeccable make up. She giggled, reaching for the boys to envelop them all in an enormous family hug. Noticing Lily standing slightly apart. Shaun drew her in to join them.

Colin and Grace arrived with a bottle of champagne.

'That's premature, isn't it?' Kate said to Colin.

'Not at all, he winked,' settling himself beside Richard. The evening began. Category after category was announced and Kate clapped politely, but her heart was beating faster with each passing minute. Lily was fidgeting, bored by the long evening. Richard tried to distract her by making paper aeroplanes with the napkins but it didn't work as they were linen.

The last category of the night was the Best New-comer. When the announcement finally came, a wave of nervous energy surged through Kate. She clasped Shaun's hand as Colin gave her a reassuring nod as the nominations were read out.

The award was to be presented by Lisa Jewell, an author who Kate admired. She had read all her books and was nervous at the thought of meeting her.

Lisa opened the envelope and slowly pulled out the card inside before looking up and saying,

'And the award for Best Newcomer goes to ...' As she paused for dramatic effect, Kate thought she would faint.

'Esther Morgan for Dispelling Shadows. The award will be collected posthumously by her daughter, Kate Cooper.'

The room was silent before erupting into ap-plause. For a split-second, Kate sat frozen, her breath catching in her throat. Then the realisation hit her. Her mother's book had won. Everyone on the table rose to their feet, Richard was whooping with joy as Colin ushered Kate towards the stage. Her heart raced as she stood in front of the large audience. She shuffled the pages in front of her, and taking a deep breath, spoke.

'I would like to accept this award on behalf of my beloved mother. If she was standing here today, she would have been overawed that her stories had become a best-selling novel. This novel came about by chance. I found notebooks full of stories after my mother, Esther Morgan, died alone on a Welsh hillside.' Kate paused, as her grief threatened to engulf her. Trying to anchor herself, she looked down at the table below her. There were the smiling faces of Richard, Colin, and Grace, and giving her the thumbs up, Lily.

'This story would not have come about without the help of Colin Forsyth and Iconic Publishing. Thank you so much for making this book such an amazing success. Thanks also to all you wonderful people out there who have read this book. Without you, I wouldn't be receiving this award on behalf of my mother today. She would be thrilled to receive this award as Best Newcomer.' Kate held the trophy aloft to loud cheers and applause. As the applause died down, she placed the trophy carefully back on the podium and picked up a copy of the novel entitled, Dispelling Shadows.'

When the audience had quietened, she continued. 'This book tells a story. The story of a woman who showed courage in adversity, cared when no-one could and gave so much to others she often had no love left for herself. Her life was not an easy one. Sometimes the burdens she carried became too heavy. But she found the courage to face her shadows, to free herself from those shadows and emerge victorious. Whether you believe the story within these pages doesn't matter. It bears testament to a life full of struggle, but shows us all that we are here to learn from our experiences. The story within these pages has healed my relationship with my mother, and reunited our family in our love and gratitude for my mother Esther Morgan. So let us learn from this story, face our shadows and support and love each other. Together we can make a better world for everyone. Thank you so much.'

The audience erupted as Kate held the trophy aloft again as Lily bounded up onto the stage to stand beside her big sister. Together, they moved to the front of the stage and bowed together before Kate sank to one knee and hugged her little sister close to her.

'Mum would have loved this,' Kate said, hiding her tears in Lily's hair.

'Yes, she would.'

As Kate looked out into the crowd, she noticed, right at the back, standing apart from the crowd, a figure dressed in white. The woman's cinnamon skin and thick black hair shimmered faintly, iridescent under the lights. Her smile was wide, full of warmth and quiet joy. Kate's breath caught in her throat as she lifted a hand in recognition. The woman smiled back, her eyes shimmered with tears of love and gratitude.

'I love you Mum,' Kate whispered as the figure faded and was gone.

Acknowledgements

This book draws from many real-life experiences, shared generously by those who trusted me with their stories. I'm grateful to Sue Williams for her patient editing, Dan Smith at Aspect Designs for creating another wonderful book cover, and Sam Godber for the website design. To my beta readers, Lucy Smith and Victoria Lyndon - thank you. Finally, thank you, dear reader, for choosing to spend time with these pages.

About the author

For over three decades, Helen Idris Jones worked as a nurse and nurse educator before embracing a new career as an author weaving together stories gathered from her rich life experiences. While her debut novel, "Missing Ella," tackles serious themes and celebrates resilience, her second book, "Where No Shadows Fall," explores the fascinating inter-play between light and shadow in human nature, inspired by Jung's psychology. Helen writes from her cottage in Worcestershire, where she lives with her two cats, Willow and Charlie (who are convinced they run the household).

Please leave your thoughts about her work by contacting her on Facebook, Instagram or Amazon, where you can purchase her books. Get in touch at: www.helenidris-jones.com or email: hbjonesauthor@gmail.com.

Printed in Great Britain
by Amazon